Disaster in the Desert

Disaster in the Desert

An Alternate History of El Alamein and Rommel's North Africa Campaign

Ken Delve

Foreword by
Major (Retd) Mike Noel-Smith

Greenhill Books

First published in Great Britain in 2019 by

Greenhill Books

c/o Pen & Sword Books Ltd, 47 Church Street, Barnsley,
South Yorkshire, S70 2AS, England
For more information on our books, please visit
www.greenhillbooks.com, email contact@greenhillbooks.com
or write to us at the above address.

Typeset in Janson by Concept, Huddersfield, West Yorkshire, HD4 5JL
Printed and bound in England by TJ International, Cornwall

Contents

Maps

List of Plates

Foreword

The battle for North Africa and its strategic control during World War Two has been well documented over the past seven decades. Campaigns over the deserts of Libya and Egypt between Allied and Axis forces were essentially a struggle for control of the Suez Canal and access to oil from the Middle East and raw materials from Asia. Generals such as Rommel, Montgomery, Patton and Arnim became household names as historians picked over the minute detail on decisions made and the greater impact that those decisions would eventually have on the outcome, not only in North Africa but that of World War Two itself.

However, what might have happened if certain key decisions and troop/equipment deployments had been different on the day? What if, instead of Operation Torch and the invasion of North Africa resulting ultimately in a joint Anglo-American victory, had the outcome gone the way of victory to the Axis forces? Or, what if the strategic island of Malta, 'the unsinkable aircraft carrier', had indeed not withstood the devastating attention of combined Italian and German naval and air forces and capitulated instead?

In this book, the author covers a very plausible and clever alternative, whereby in North Africa, Rommel's land forces are victorious leading to a completely different scenario of the outcome of the campaign. Small, but entirely realistic turns of fortune due to a misplaced field gun, a tanker intercepted in the night or poor timing in the arrival of combat ready aircraft lead us through the battlefields to a different picture – one that might so easily have actually happened ... an Axis victory!

Major (Retd) Mike Noel-Smith

Introduction

The North African campaign/Desert War was one of the most important of World War Two in terms of the development of land and air tactics, and lessons for major operations in other theatres of war, including D-Day. It also brought to public notice great commanders such as Rommel and Montgomery, as well as being the first theatre in which Anglo-American forces worked together – with mixed success. For the Axis forces it was a route to the all-important Middle East oil fields in Iraq and elsewhere, a key strategic objective for the Axis, as well as the political driver of destroying British influence in the area, and for Mussolini of growing his Italian Empire.

However, it was not a theatre in which the Germans were initially interested; they were dragged into the Mediterranean/Middle East by their Italian allies and only because of the abject failure of those Allies in 1940–1941. Once engaged, there was no way out, and the theatre became something of a logistics and combat unit challenge for the Germans, especially with the competing needs of other theatres, particularly Russia. As with all military operations, success or failure was frequently influenced by seemingly small changes – a decision, one combat action, luck – and the subsequent course of a battle or campaign, and ultimately the war, could have been different. This is the rationale behind 'alternative histories' such as this one; based on actual scenarios but with changes that then lead to new scenarios and outcomes. In this book we start with the actual history from early 1942 with the Allies in retreat, having in 1941 been close to winning the Desert War; from summer 1942 we start to change certain events – for example a tanker being sunk on its way to Malta rather than making it to port, a carrier being sunk earlier than it actually was, and thus fewer Spitfires making it to Malta. What if Malta had been invaded? What if Rommel did not suffer supply shortages? These events lead to other changes that in turn influence the overall conduct and progress of the Middle East campaigns, which, in our version, ends with Axis victory.

Some dates have been changed to aid the progress of events, and some quotes from actual accounts and reports have been used as illustrative of a mission, the quote being correct but when it occurred having been changed. Most of the units and commanders are as they were for real, but some changes have been made, based on the scenarios relevant to the new situation postulated by our account.

The final chapter then looks at the reality, a short review of the actual outcomes.

Ken Delve

Acknowledgements

This book stemmed from my work on the air side of the Desert and Mediterranean campaigns and it was during a conversation with Michael Leventhal and my comments of how easily the Axis could have won that he suggested I write this alternative history account. My thanks to Michael for the suggestion! Over my years of research, I have collected documents and stories from a wide range of organizations and individuals, and much of that material has helped inform this account, and my views and opinions on what "might have been". As always, my recognition and gratitude go to the Air Historical Branch, whose extensive archives and excellent cooperation always proved invaluable. As a source of primary documents and research papers, the Defence Technical Information Center is both easy to access and a mine of information. On an individual basis I much appreciate the time and military expertise of Mike Noel-Smith and Andrew Weavill, and Ben Delve in proof-reading and sense-checking the text, and to Mike for writing the Foreword.

Chapter One

CRUSADER to Gazala

After 18 months of war in North Africa, the Allies appeared to be on the verge of victory in 1941, having built-up and modernized forces, and developed new air-ground tactics. General Cunningham, commander of 8th Army, had framed his Operation CRUSADER with aims to destroy the enemy formations in Eastern Cyrenaica and relieve Tobruk, which had a garrison of a division plus two brigades. The assault was to be made by XIII Corps and XXX Corps, plus a sweep south by 29 Indian Brigade. The task for XIII Corps was to skirt the Halfaya Pass and then push via Sollum and Bardia to bring the Axis forces to battle, whilst XXX Corps skirted the Trigh el Abd and drove directly for Tobruk, spearheaded by 7th Armoured Division. The units moved into position from 12th November, shielded by poor weather that limited German air reconnaissance, and with strict signals procedures to minimize risk of the enemy picking up unit movements. Rommel was, however, aware that an offensive was coming, as it was clear the Allies had built-up strength and were under pressure to relieve Tobruk. He was convinced that his best chance for disrupting such an attack was a pre-emptive offensive, but there was the difficulty of finishing off Tobruk, and of convincing his notional Italian commander, Bastico, that the plan was workable. Rommel's intent was to begin his offensive around the 21st.

The Allied ground forces rolled forward on the morning of the 18th, heavily supported by air power: "Our fighters had no engagements in the air, but they shot up 18 EA on aerodromes in the back areas. Our bombers attacked enemy MT [Motor Transport] and advanced aerodromes, in particular Baheira, where later XIII Corps found damaged Henschels and Me.110s." The advance rolled on the following day, with increasing amounts of enemy armour being encountered, and the Luftwaffe making an appearance. "No.1 SA Brigade was heavily attacked by Stukas". The aircraft of 451 Squadron were flying TacR and one "gave timely warning of enemy tanks east of Sidi Omar to 4th Indian Division." (Report on Operation Crusader, Wg Cdr A. Geddes.)

The armoured spearhead had three prongs, 4 Brigade from Gabr Saleh, 7 Brigade in the centre to drive on Sidi Rezegh, and 22 Brigade from Bir El Gobi. Initial success meant that most of the day's objectives were reached, and 22 Brigade engaged and caused losses to the Italian Ariete Division's armour. Meanwhile, 15th and 21st Panzer were moving into positions from which to strike back; on the afternoon of the 19th, Battle Group Stephan from 21st Panzer struck the flanks of 4 Tank Brigade, and its tanks and 88mm gun line drove the British back over the Trigh el Abd. The British came on again but in the evening fighting lost 42 Stuarts, against a German loss of three tanks, and with the Germans in control of the battlefield they were able to recover vehicles. For XIII Corps the day had been one of minor engagements.

Both sides continued to manoeuvre on the 20th, with German armour moving towards the Deheua ridge, being engaged by artillery, whilst 4th Armoured Division was engaging 100-plus tanks near Gabr Taieb El Essem, a duel that meant they were out of ammunition by the end of the day and had to pull back. They were re-supplied that night by a Bombay aircraft. The division had also been the intended target of a Stuka attack, but the enemy, escorted by Me.109s, was intercepted by 250 Squadron, supported by Royal Navy fighters, and lost seven Stukas and two 109s. "Fleets of bombers with close fighter escorts and covering sweeps passed over XIII Corps all day to bomb and drop leaflets on MT at El Adem, Gambut and in the coastal wadis north of the escarpment. Beaufighters destroyed 14 Stukas and two Me.109s on the ground at Tmimi, and two Stukas and one CR.42 in a wadi north of Capuzzo, and a further six Me.110s were destroyed in air combat." One German report states that Luftwaffe activity was low in the first few days not only because of RAF air action but also because of a torrential storm on the 16th that flooded the German-Italian airfields: "Suddenly, high waves tore down the wadi and took everything along with them. Then tent camps in the wadis around Derna were flooded within a few minutes and several people drowned. This disaster caused by bad weather also damaged the airfields in the neighbourhood of Derna. The runway was partly flooded." (Report by Gen. Froehlich.) The battle was still confused, with action around Tobruk as the garrison pressured its besiegers, and various combats and manoeuvres all along the front, with neither side totally sure of where the enemy main strength was located. Rommel's two panzer divisions were now well-placed and en masse to play a decisive role, and 7th Armoured Division was soon being rolled up, forcing its commander to abandon any offensive moves and adopt an all-round defence, with both sides being exhausted as night fell.

Nevertheless, Rommel's forces were suffering fuel and ammunition supply issues and he ordered the Afrika Korps on the defensive until the supply situation was resolved. However, in the absence of determined Allied activity, and more clarity on enemy positions, he reversed this on the afternoon of 22nd and personally led 21st Panzer against Sidi Rezegh, where a major tank battle developed. The airfield was held by 7th Armoured Division Support Group and they were forced to retire south towards their parent formation; meanwhile, 22nd Armoured attempted a counter-stroke, only to be hit in the flank and to lose 45 out of 80 tanks before it too retired. The 15th Panzer were also causing chaos, having hit the rear eastern flank of 7th Armoured Division, destroying or disrupting a number of support units, as well as 35 tanks. So, on the evening of the 22nd, Rommel looked to be in a good position, his armour remained concentrated, had suffered few losses, and had destroyed almost 50% of 7th Armoured Division. "At nightfall the situation in rear of XIII Corps appeared confused with no news of XXX Corps except the report brought by General Cunningham on his visit at midday before his return to Battle HQ at Maddalena. Our bombers and fighters were turned on to attack the enemy as he approached the wire. Owing to lack of identification flags ... a certain amount of indiscriminate strafing from the air took place. Since Rommel was using a large proportion of captured British vehicles mistakes in identification were excusable. Nearly all columns both enemy and friendly in the so-called Matruh Stakes were moving in an easterly direction and it was singularly difficult for anyone either on the ground or in the air to pick out whether any particular cloud of dust was friend or foe." (Geddes.)

On the 23rd the 7th Armoured Division was surrounded when 15th Panzer linked up with Ariete Division; it was a weak encirclement and after further fighting the day ended with the Axis forces seemingly in control. However, they were a stretched and spent force, with heavy losses and lack of supplies. Most regiments had few tanks left as runners. Although XXX Corps had been mauled it was still in existence, and XIII Corps had suffered far less and was still advancing, albeit slowly. Likewise, the sweep by the Indian Brigade had made progress and had reached Gialo, and the Tobruk garrison had also had some success in seizing strongpoints from the Italian besiegers. Rommel seemed confident that he had broken the main Allied thrusts, and whilst Cunningham had failed to destroy the Axis forces, his second aim of relieving Tobruk was by no means ended. Operation CRUSADER was not yet dead.

Rommel's plan was a "dash to the wire" with his two panzer Divisions and with no thought of protecting flanks but rather carving his way forward and disrupting the overall Allied strategy; in part this was predicated on his belief that British commanders were indecisive and unable to react to the fast-pace of an armoured battle – and they had yet to learn the concept of concentration of armour. By the afternoon, German armour was at the Egyptian frontier, having caused chaos and confusion, but lack of supplies meant that no tanks accompanied the units that pressed on into Egypt. Whilst the Allies were confused, so were the Germans, as communications broke down and reliance was placed on recce patrols to try to maintain operational control between units. Rommel expected the British to pull back and this would enable him, from his flank position, to engage and destroy them as they moved back on Egypt. His orders for the 25th were for the destruction of British forces in the Sollum-Sidi Omar area, and to clear up the Sidi Rezegh battlefield area, with 21st Panzer positioned to intercept the retreat south of Halfaya. In the Sidi Omar area, British artillery and anti-tank guns proved effective in preventing 21st Panzer Division achieving its aim, albeit at heavy cost to the gunners. "The enemy in the defensive line opened a terrific fire. The regiment [5th Panzer] charged this line of guns and after hard fighting silenced two batteries and six anti-tank guns. More enemy batteries and anti-tank guns on the left flank of the regiment now entered the fight. The regiment then tried to bypass the enemy on the right ... but brought up anti-tank and field guns ... and extended his line. The regiment was now running short of ammunition and was forced to deploy to the right and move away south to break off the action. The regiment had been reduced to the strength of a reinforced company and had little petrol or ammunition." (Operational Summary, 5th Panzer Regiment.)

The 25th was also significant in that the encirclement of Tobruk was broken when the 2nd New Zealand Division made contact with the garrison. Rommel was unaware of this for some time, as his forward position was out of touch with Afrika Korps HQ for much of the time; he became aware when he realized that 21st Panzer was no longer where he expected it to be; it had been redirected by Afrika Korps HQ to strike the New Zealanders and restore the situation around Tobruk. Meanwhile, 8th Army's losses in tanks were being made good by the supply depots and its strength was rapidly building up, albeit with less experienced crews. However, in the next few days of fighting, as Rommel gradually developed a better tactical feel for the battle, the 2nd New Zealand Division virtually ceased to exist, with over 2,500 men taken prisoner. The new battle around Tobruk and towards Sollum was poised to disrupt or destroy the British XXX Corps and, according to a German account, they were saved by "well-planned flying mission by RAF units. The British flying units inflicted heavy losses on the Afrika Korps. Strong British flying units intervened during daylight hours almost without interval in the ground fighting. They controlled the Via Balbia all day, so that vehicles could use it only during darkness." Even more critical was the Allied domination of the Mediterranean logistic routes, which ensured Rommel was continually short of supplies.

After setting up the battlefield on the last few days of November, Rommel launched his decisive stroke on 1st December with 15th Panzer striking north from Sidi Rezegh, supported by 90th Light Division. Tobruk was cut-off once more and the Axis forces destroyed the isolated pockets of New Zealand resistance, taking over 2,000 prisoners. By the end of the day all sides were exhausted and had few combat units ready for action; CRUSADER effectively ended on the 2nd, the British having failed to achieve their aims, and both sides had suffered heavy losses, although in armoured vehicles the loss of around 260 German/Italian was far outweighed by the 800 or so lost by the British. It was without doubt a German tactical victory, but it was not a strategic victory, as it would have been had Rommel's push to the wire been a success. It could be argued that it was a British strategic victory, having drained Rommel's fighting capacity and seized territory. There was also the fact that the Allies were able to very quickly restore front-line strength thanks to their proximity to the supply depots in Egypt. Whilst both suffered heavy losses of armour, it was the British that came off worse, including the loss of many experienced tank commanders and crews. This was in large measure down to the piecemeal use of armour, starting with the initial three-pronged armoured assault, which after the first surprise was over, enabled the Germans to achieve local superiority whilst the Allied tank formations could not provide mutual support; also, the excellent use by the Germans of anti-tank gun lines proved highly destructive of Allied armour. This was also the first major battle in which Allied air power had been dominant. The Axis forces around Tobruk continued to retreat and the Allied air forces continued to make life difficult for the enemy ground forces. Another convoy was set upon on the 6th by 80 Squadron: "The target was a convoy of about 40 vehicles moving SW of El Adem. The vehicles were first scattered by accurate dive bombing after which the pilots went down and strafed at leisure. There was no opposition and the convoy, which had 2 staff cars with it, was wiped out, 11 lorries being left on fire and many casualties being caused. It was learnt later that the convoy contained an Italian Division HQ. There was no doubt that this type of target was eminently suitable for the Squadron to attack, the bigger convoys being left to Blenheims and Marylands." (80 Sqn ORB.)

The loss of landing areas started to have an impact: "No ALG [Advanced Landing Ground] could now be used, since Sidi Rezegh and Gasr El Arid were not suitable and it was not possible to construct an ALG near Advanced HQ XIII Corps in the time available due to the number of slit trenches and damaged vehicles along the Trigh." This did not stop the intensity of air action and bombers and fighters of both sides were constantly in action. Sometimes the effect of the bombing was discovered in a personal note, such as in the diary recovered from a soldier of the 361st Afrika Regiment: "During the bombing attack of last night the Afrika Corps stores went up in flames, with 9 million cigars and cigarettes, 7½ litres of beer per man and the Schnapps and wine that go with it. This was our Christmas present." (Geddes.)

The British attack was renewed on the 8th and as Rommel had insufficient force to hold his positions he ordered a withdrawal to the Gazala Line. Dominance in the air was an important aspect of Allied strategy, although the Axis air forces tried to counter. In his post-war study, Lt-Gen Felmy noted: "On 12 December German fighters shot down 23 British planes", but of more significance "Since the beginning of December, German-Italian air activities had been coordinated for the first time with the ground operations of the Panzer Group, whereupon the air operations started a noticeable influence on the course of the fighting. However, the air forces were too weak to stop the British pursuit altogether.'' (*The German Air Force in the Mediterranean Theatre of War*, Lt-Gen Helmuth Felmy.)

By mid-December the advance had reached a point 1,000 miles from Cairo. This offensive, like so many in the vast Western Desert theatre, was defeated by lack of supplies and support facilities; German forces were able to disengage from their pursuers and establish a defensive line. With his established defensive position from Marada to Mersa el Brega, Rommel was in a position to rebuild his exhausted units, and even though his supply position was still precarious, his overall strategy remained the same – offensive action to disrupt Allied offensive planning, the destruction of the 8th Army, and the capture of Cyrenaica prior to the final assault on the Suez Canal. He remained convinced of the weakness of British command and decision-making, but also concerned over the Allies' seemingly endless flow of supplies. It was not enough to destroy parts of the Allied army, he had to destroy it all and prevent reinforcements. To do that he would also have to ensure his own supplies kept pace with his advance.

By the end of the first week of January 1942 Rommel had consolidated his forces in the El Agheila area and was considering his options. The supply situation had markedly improved and many of his units had been brought up to strength in major equipment, including tanks. Luftwaffe reconnaissance showed that the Allies were not ready to move and that the German forces were not well placed to defend against a concerted attack. Westphal suggested it was better to attack whilst the Allies were not ready and before they could launch their own attack. After initial reluctance, Rommel agreed and moved his divisions into place, again planning a sweeping movement to outflank and cut-off the British. The orders were issued for an attack on 21st January by the newly-designated Panzer Army Africa. The planned punch initially failed because the Allied forces were weaker than expected and their immediate action when threatened was a rapid retreat.

"I had maintained secrecy over the Panzer Group's forthcoming attack eastwards from Mersa el Brega and informed neither the Italian nor the German High Command. We knew from experience that Italian Headquarters cannot keep things to themselves and that everything they wireless to Rome gets round to British ears. However, I had arranged with the Quartermaster for the Panzer Group's order to be posted up in every Cantoniera [Road Maintenance Depot] in Tripolitania on the 21st January – the day the attack was due to take place.

Excellency Bastico in Homs learnt of our intentions through this, of course, and was furious that he had not been told before. He reported to this effect to Rome and so I was not surprised when Cavallero turned up in person at Mersa el Brega a few days later." (*Rommel Papers.*)

Agedabia was taken on the 22nd and 21st Panzer and the Marcks Combat Group attempted to encircle the British forces centred on 1st Armoured Division. The unit had arrived in the Middle East the previous November and by January was under the command of Maj-Gen Frank Messervy, with 2 Armoured Brigade and 7 Motor Brigade as the main combat units, supported by various artillery and other units. As the panzers crashed forward, the Allies relied on air reconnaissance to build a picture of the fluid battle, and relied on air power to hold off the Luftwaffe and support land operations. 33 Sqn: 23rd January 1942: "Owing to the fluidity of the fighting area an advance party of two lorries left Msus for LG165. The remainder of the Squadron was at one-hour notice to move backwards. Sgt Genders and Sgt Wilson carried out a TacR of the area between Antelat and Agedabia. They reported considerable MT interspersed with tanks. Six aircraft took off to strafe the MT on the road between Antelat and Agedabia. One petrol bowser and two lorries were set on fire and 25 lorries were damaged. Plt Off Edy was shot down and crash landed about one mile away from the enemy MT. He was last seen running away from his aircraft in a northerly direction. The other aircraft returned safely to base. Four airmen of the rear party arrived at Msus having safely come through the battle area. Orders came through at 2000 hours that the Squadron was to move to Mechili at first light. Sgts Kelly and Crichton slept in the Bombay so as to be ready for an early morning take-off to Gazala." (32 Sqn ORB.)

It was only on the 23rd that the British truly became aware of the scale and intent of the German moves, the initial assessment having been that it was a 'reconnaissance in force' and perhaps some repositioning – but not a full-scale assault. Aerial reconnaissance discovered a large convoy off Misurata, which was duly attacked; whilst three supply ships and two warships were hit, the majority of supplies got through and the plan to hold a line from the coast at Beda Fomm, Antelat and Saunu looked less promising. Indeed, despite air attacks, on the 25th "The forces on this line were so roughly handled that they were in no condition to stop the enemy's advance, and it was decided to evacuate Benghazi." (*The Eighth Army*, HMSO.) Although the German attempt to encircle 1st Armoured was not a total success, a small corridor enabled some to escape; the battle had cost the division 117 tanks and armoured cars, as well as 33 guns and large numbers of other vehicles, as well as thousands of prisoners. Of equal significance was the capture of an intact depot at Msus, which netted Rommel nearly 900 vehicles and 127 artillery pieces. Most valuable were the supplies of POL (Petroleum, Oil, Lubricants), ammunition, rations and even mobile workshops. Meanwhile, Rommel was having his usual problems with his Italian allies, who considered they had not been consulted on or agreed to the offensive: "... Cavallero said make it no more than a raid and then come straight back. I was not standing for this and told him that I had made my mind to keep at the enemy as long as my troops and supplies would allow. I told him that nobody but the Führer could change my decision, as it was mainly German troops who would be engaged." (*Rommel Papers.*) On 25th January, Auchinleck had flown to see General Ritchie, the battlefield commander, to urge him to rescind the general retreat order and to launch a counter-offensive. He was accompanied by Tedder, who subsequently reported to London: "... as a result of last night, I hope that the Army will now launch a counterattack. The only way to stop this nonsense is to hit back. Our fighters under Gp Capt Cross are in a bad mood ... it seems that they are at this time the decisive and equalizing power."

For the last week of January, the Kittyhawks of 112 Squadron had flown at least one sweep a day to strafe enemy concentrations, and the 28th was recorded as "the last day before the next move backwards and the last show of the Fighter Wing's lone stand against Rommel." Four aircraft made an afternoon sweep along the Sceiledima Road and at Fort Sceiledima "A concentration of six vehicles and a tank were selected for attention and all were raked in turn by all pilots in a run each way. There were at least twelve tanks and several hundred vehicles dispersed around the fort, and the general direction of the enemy's advance was towards Soluch." The Army would no doubt have been unimpressed by the "lone stand" comment! Air attack was always viewed with dismay by ground troops, as it came unexpected and rapid, and for most ground troops there seemed little they could do to fight back – and the standard cry was "where is the RAF" (or Luftwaffe if the Germans were on the receiving end). The psychological impact was, at this stage of the campaign, often greater than the physical damage and casualties. The firepower of the tactical aircraft was still limited and tactics were not yet developed; both of these were issues that the DAF (Desert Air Force) was to rectify in 1942 which turned it into a truly effective air component of the ground campaign.

The next success came with the capture of Benghazi on the 29th, a port that the Allies had almost returned to usefulness – and would now start bombing again! The city yielded up yet another haul of supplies and vehicles to Rommel. This would shorten his supply lines but by no means solve his supply issues. Shortage of fuel meant that Rommel had to limit his pursuit of the retreating Allies, enough to keep them moving but not enough to be decisive. With Benghazi back in German hands the port facilities became a key target once more. If Rommel was able to get supplies unloaded at Benghazi, then much of his logistics problem would be resolved. Preventing this, by attacking convoys, ships in port and the port facilities, was therefore crucial. Rommel had recovered Cyrenaica and the Allies were falling back to the east.

"By the 14th he [Rommel] had gathered a striking force consisting of most of his Germans in this sector. But the air support on which he had counted was virtually destroyed the same day by a formation of Kittyhawks which wiped out 20 and probably 30 dive bombers and fighters in a single action." (*The Eighth Army*, HMSO.) Seldom did an Army account give such credit to the RAF, especially for a single day's activity. It was of course an oversimplification, but it does provide an indication of how important air cover and air support were to both sides. Rommel now halted his advance, and this also draws an end to Auchinleck's campaign that began in November with early success and promise but ended in his forces being pushed back – albeit the line had stabilized much further west that it had been before CRUSADER. The lull was to last some three months, to late May.

In the period between mid-November, the start of the Allied CRUSADER offensive, and mid-February (the stabilisation after the retreat), the Desert Air Forces had flown over 10,000 sorties and claimed over 500 enemy aircraft (air and ground). The salvage and repair organization had 'rescued' 1,035 damaged aircraft and returned 810 of those to the battle, an impressive and invaluable contribution. More importantly, the RAF operations had played a key role in preventing a fluid retreat from becoming a rout. Whilst the ground forces on both sides went into a period of quiet and rebuilding and resupply, the air forces kept the battle going. The DAF was also continuing to reorganize: "The fighter squadrons were now placed under separate operational control; this was organised on the 'leapfrog' principle with two identical operations rooms, one forward and one rear, which under fluid conditions could act in the same way as squadron forward and rear parties and so maintain continuity of operations in spite of frequent moves. Simultaneously the principles of air support were defined more clearly for the benefit of air and ground forces alike, and in order to overcome the vexed problem of identification of ground targets agreement was finally reached on the marking of all British vehicles with the RAF roundel. The maintenance and repair organisations were further developed and expanded while airfield construction was pushed ahead, and facilities improved." (*New Zealand Operations in RAF.*)

Although in terms of the overall campaign the period from February to May was quiet, air operations were still very much in evidence, and for the DAF this included further development in close air support tactics. "On 10th March there was a significant development. Sqn Ldr Caldwell made the first practice bombing dive, carrying an unfused 250-lb bomb, to see whether it could be dropped without carrying away the propeller. Since this might mean a crash it was done over the sea with the ASR [Air-Sea Rescue] organization laid on. This experiment was a success and it was repeated during the afternoon with a live bomb." The following day four pilots did some practice bombing and "At dusk the CO went off to have a go at the enemy at Martuba, but the bomb fell wide of the target." (112 Sqn ORB.) This development of increasingly turning the Kittyhawks into Kittybombers – with a more 'useful' bomb load – was one of the most significant of 1942. Although these early experiments were with a 250lb bomb it was not long before the Kitty was carrying 500lb and 1,000lb bombs – and not just single bombs. Billy Drake was amongst the fighter pilots now faced with a change of role and tactics: "Our AOC, 'Mary' Coningham, wanted us to changeover to the ground-attack role. He had recently had it demonstrated to him that the Kittyhawk could carry a useful bomb-load, and as fighter-bombers he felt we could do more to assist the army than in the past. This was a completely new role for most of us in the RAF, and we became the forerunners of the tactical ground-attack units of the DAF. Initially we carried a 250lb bomb beneath the fuselage, usually fitted with an extension rod to the fuse in the nose, so that it would explode just above the ground surface, allowing maximum damage to be caused to soft-skinned vehicles and personnel. So began a sharp learning curve. As we were no longer just escorting bomber formations, or undertaking sweeps or patrols over the front line, we quickly learned that navigation had become much more important in allowing us to find our targets. We also had to learn to deliver our bombs in a medium-to-steep dive of 30–45 degrees, using the gun-sight." (*Billy Drake, Fighter Leader* p44.)

It was also a time of reorganization, in part because over 300 fighters and nearly 200 bombers had been transferred to the Far East, the war situation looking even worse there. "Nevertheless, the reduced force was trained to a high pitch and remoulded in the light of practical difficulties encountered during the second Cyrenaican campaign. Fighters were gathered into a new operational Group (No. 211) and at the same time were organised for administrative purposes into wings of four squadrons. Each wing could be located on a single airfield and these four-squadron bases simplified arrangements for offence, defence and training. At the same time problems of direct support for ground troops and the ever-recurring difficulty of recognition of friendly units from the air were partly solved by an increase in positive liaison facilities between army and air force headquarters, and by the decision to arm as many squadrons as possible with fighter-bombers which could intervene in confused ground battles and be certain of attacking only enemy forces. The small light-bomber forces were also regrouped in wings each of two squadrons and stationed at Bir el Baheira only twenty miles from Gambut, where the fighters were concentrated. This proximity allowed joint tactics to be evolved. Additional reasons for the concentration of the fighters at Gambut, rather than the more forward airfields at El Adem and Gazala, were the prevalent dust storms and the increasing frequency of enemy attack in those areas. Communication problems were easier in the Gambut area, the existing early-warning organisation was adequate, and fighters could still operate over the front lines." (*RAAF history*.)

For the land forces on both sides it was a time of re-equipment and training. The Germans continued to improve their small unit tactics, as well as command and control, and assaults on defensive positions, including night operations. By the end of May they were undertaking divisional-scale manoeuvres. The ability to find and resupply combat units at night – and because of Allied air power this was best done at night – had been a weakness in the previous campaign, and attempts were made to put new procedures in place.

The intensive Axis campaign against Malta had certainly paid off in respect to convoys to Africa and in the period January to March only 16,000 of 190,000 tons was lost, and in May only 10,000 from the 170,000 tons shipped. The loss of Malta's air and submarine strike capability was enabling Rommel to build up his strength and stock of supplies. The Allied anti-shipping effort was, of course, still underway although now primarily from North Africa.

Chapter Two

Gazala to El Alamein

"Supplies are the fundamental premise of the battle and must be given priority of protection." (Rommel)

In the blistering summer heat of the North African desert the two-year back-and-forth attack and counter-attack of the German-Italian and Allied armies looked set for a decisive final action. It is June 1942 and the British forces are in headlong retreat having at one point appeared to be on the cusp of victory at Gazala. The Desert Fox was up to his usual tricks.

The next stage of the battle would be different in that Rommel was better equipped than ever, and the British had adopted a new defensive strategy for the Gazala Line based on "boxes" that had all-round defence and, in theory, could withstand a siege as they were self-contained with infantry, artillery and tanks – and could be supported by air. They were also surrounded by, and monitored, extensive minefields, the idea being that any German advance could be slowed or held up whilst counter-attacks were set up by the mobile armoured reserve. The effective air strengths of the two sides were similar at the start of the battle.

The 8th Army's defensive line ran from the sea some 45 miles south to Bir Hacheim, with a number of heavily defended boxes along this line, all protected by minefields and, in theory at least, mutually supporting, and being capable of all-round defence. General Ritchie had placed XIII Corps in these forward positions, with the 1st South African Division in the north, the 50th Infantry Division next along the line, and 1 Free French Brigade holding the box at Bir Hacheim, the left flank, although to counter a southern sweep another box had been placed to the south-east of Bir Hacheim, held by the recently arrived 3 Indian Motor Brigade. Behind this 'front line' other boxes were located at Knightsbridge (22 Guards Brigade) and El Adem, with

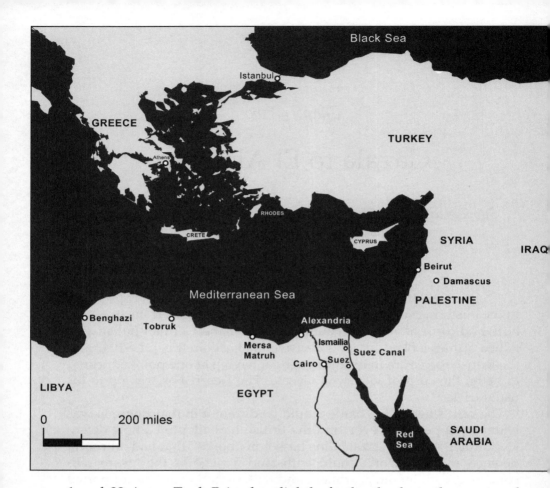

1 and 32 Army Tank Brigades slightly further back, to the west and south of Tobruk, positioned to support the boxes or counter any enemy thrust, whilst the main armoured strength of XXX Corps was even further back, with 1st Armoured Division at Trigh Capuzzo, to cover the central sector, and 7th Armoured Division covering the southern sector.

It looked like a sound disposition to counter any sudden enemy move, whilst also providing opportunities to renew the Allied offensive. Numbers also appeared to be in the Allied favour, with a superiority of 742 tanks to 570 tanks (of which 360 were German and 210 Italian), 500 artillery pieces to 350 and 700 aircraft to 500, and 125,000 men against 113,000. So, the Allies were confident that Rommel would be taking a massive risk if with such inferiority he attacked well prepared and manned positions.

But, this was Rommel, and he had proven many times that sitting waiting to be attacked was not his style. He had pushed the Allies back to this point and, as was typical of the Desert War, the pause was caused by the need to build-up supplies, especially fighting vehicles and tanks. With the increased pressure that had been placed on Malta, which reduced its ability to participate in offensive strikes against Axis shipping, the much-needed supplies had once more started to flow to Rommel from the supply bases in Italy, by no means all that he needed or wanted, but enough for him to plan his return to the offensive. Given that the sea protected one flank for the Allies, and the desert to the south of Bir Hacheim was a tricky proposition, he had two options – a frontal attack, risking the extensive minefields and pre-positioned anti-tank and artillery protection of the boxes, or a bold sweep south to create pincers against the various Allied positions. His decision would be based on two things: intelligence of the Allied dispositions, and his appreciation of the character and psychology of his opponents. "The British command was to be made to expect our main attack in the north and centre of the Gazala line. We hoped to persuade them to deploy their armour behind the infantry positions in this sector. The idea of a German frontal attack against the Gazala position could not appear so very far-fetched to the British command, as it was quite within the bounds of possibility that we would prefer it to the risky right hook round Bir Hacheim. If we failed to mislead the British into concentrating the whole of their armour in this sector, then we hoped that they would send at least part of it up there and thus split their striking power." (*Rommel Papers.*)

Having made his determination that the Allied dispositions were potentially flawed, he decided on the bold southern sweep for an armoured thrust, but this would need to be masked so that the Allied armour was caught off-guard. So, a convincing build-up for a frontal attack would need to persuade the British that he was going to hammer at the front door. He hoped this would keep the British looking straight ahead, with air recce focused in that direction, and with some armoured units repositioning to support the boxes in the line of the expected attack. This "attack" was to be made by the Crüwell Group, comprising the Italian X and XXI Corps and the non-motorized element of the German 90th Light Division. Allied air reconnaissance was effective and Rommel planned to use this to his advantage; all movements by the main attack force, the bulk of the Afrika Korps and the Italian XX (Motorized) Corps, would be made in daylight towards staging areas that appeared to support a build-up for an attack on the northern and central parts of the line, but then at night they would move south to their real staging areas, whilst other vehicles maintained the semblance of activity in the original areas. It was a risky move, especially as the night move by columns was over ground that was largely unknown.

The move worked as planned, the Korps being aided in finding the right direction by observing flares dropped over the Bir Hacheim box by the Luftwaffe. During the final manoeuvring to the jumping-off point, the columns had to cope with a sandstorm; this was the period of the khamsin (a dry, hot, sandy local wind affecting Egypt), although this also helped hide their presence as they positioned near Rotondo Segnali. The plan was for the three German formations, 15th Panzer, 21st Panzer and 90th Light (motorized elements), to drive up between Bir Hacheim and Bir El Gobbi, spreading out to pincer, outmanoeuvre or engage opposition, whilst the Italian Ariete, one of the best Italian formations, assaulted Bir Hacheim. The code-word "Venice" was sent at 1700 hours on the 26th May and Crüwell Group started its diversionary attack against 50th Division. However, the attacks were weak and made little impression on the defences, to the extent that they were virtually ignored! Fighting quickly died down, and within hours the Allies were aware of the real danger, as armoured car recce had "bumped into" the lead Panzer units and reported the threat. However, the reports were not believed; this was assessed as the diversion, designed to draw British armour to the south, away from the "real" threat. "At 20.30 hours I ordered 'Operation Venezia' and the 10,000 vehicles of the striking force began to move. My staff and I, in our place in the Afrika Korps's column, drove through the moonlit night towards the great armoured battle. Occasional flares lit up the sky far in the distance – probably the Luftwaffe trying to locate Bir Hacheim. I was tense and keyed-up, impatiently awaiting the coming day. What would the enemy do? What had he already done? These questions pounded my brain, and only morning would bring the answers. Our formations rolled forward without a halt. The drivers often had difficulty in maintaining contact with the vehicle ahead. Shortly before daybreak we took an hour's rest some 10 or 12 miles south-west of Bir Hacheim; then the great force started to move again and in a swirling cloud of dust and sand, thrust into the British rear. Enemy minefields and decoys gave some trouble, but an hour or two after daybreak all formations of the Panzer Army were in full cry for their objectives. 90th Light Division reported their arrival at El Adem as early as 10.00 a.m. Many of the supply dumps of British XXX Corps, for whom this area had acted as supply base, had fallen into their hands. At about midday the British command reacted, and a furious battle developed." (*Rommel Papers.*)

The effective air strengths of the two sides were roughly equal at the start of the battle, although this would rapidly change in favour of the Allies. As the battle around "Knightsbridge" developed, the DAF was called on to establish air superiority and to support the ground forces; for most squadrons this meant intensive operations, with, for example, the three "sister" squadrons (3 RAAF, 112, 274) averaging 350 sorties a day between 27th and 31st May. By the early hours of the 27th, the Germans were east of the Gazala line and facing north, ready to push towards the coast, with the 90th Light, aiming at El Adem, on the right and the 21st Panzer on the left, aiming to pincer behind Knightsbridge. Because of its open flank position, the former had been reinforced with extra armoured cars from the other units to provide an extensive warning screen.

Advancing in the centre, the tanks of 15th Panzer were unexpectedly engaged by a hull-down British tank unit that would normally have been picked-up by armoured car recce. The Grants of the 4th Armoured Brigade had the 75mm main armament and the range at which they were engaged was a shock to the Germans, who rapidly lost several tanks. It was but a brief hold-up, as the Germans brought forward some 88s to engage the enemy and swung a panzer platoon around the flank. The British tanks rapidly withdrew, but much of the 8th Hussars and 3rd Royal Tank Regiment (RTR) were lost in the engagement, whilst the remnants of the Brigade moved back on El Adem. The commander of 3rd RTR, General "Pip" Roberts, subsequently wrote of this action: "We continued to move forward slowly, closing up on the light squadron and looking for a suitable hull-down position. There they are! More than 100, yes, 20 in the first line, and there are six, no, eight lines; a whole ruddy Panzer Division is quite obviously in front of us! Damn it. This was not the plan at all – where the hell are the rest of the Brigade? However, no indecision is possible because no alternatives present themselves. 'Hello Battalion – Orders: B and C Squadrons [Grants] take up battle line on the small ridge 300 yards to our front. A Squadron [Honeys] protect the right flank.' The Grant squadrons were instructed to hold their fire until the Boche tanks were within 1,200 yards or had halted. The leading enemy tanks had halted about 1,300 yards away; all our tanks were firing, there was no scarcity of targets. Our instructions were to hold on as long as possible." Then, after a short while ... "Peter [adjutant] tell Brigade we cannot hang on here much longer, either there will be nothing left, or we will be cut off, or both ... But C Squadron on the left are all going back, or what is left of them. Hello C Squadron, what's the matter, you're going the wrong way. Sorry, replied C Squadron Commander, but I can't see a damn thing with blood in my eyes, and all my periscopes are smashed. Also, I have no more ammunition. OK – well done, carry on. It was found later that this tank had 25 hits on it. But the situation was now getting serious ... on the right, B Squadron seemed to have three tanks still firing, but they obviously could not have much ammunition left; no sign of 5th RTR coming up on either our right or left. There are certainly 20 Boche tanks knocked out in front of us, if not more, but if we are to reorganize at all we must go – and pretty quickly." (Quoted in *Royal Tank Regiment*, George Forty.) Meanwhile, 21st Panzer was headed towards the box held by the 3 Indian Brigade; outgunned and inexperienced, an initial firm resistance collapsed, and the box was overrun, as was one at Retma held by 7 Motorized Brigade. Driving onwards to Trigh Capuzzo they were well positioned to engage an advance by the 44th Royal Tank Regiment, which had been ordered south. In a typical engagement, the line of German anti-tank guns, concealed in a wadi, rapidly destroyed 18 of the British tanks.

Ariete had less success against the French at Bir Hacheim; the first advance stalled in the minefield and was engaged by the defenders' guns, and even when some tanks broke into the box, the Foreign Legion defenders destroyed them and their supporting infantry. The Italians could make no impact on the box and were ordered to move around it, to the east, to maintain the integrity of the overall armoured thrust. By midday the situation looked promising for Rommel's attack, with the four prongs still more or less intact and, with the exception of Bir Hacheim, achieving most of their objectives. It also seemed that the British were in confusion, and where engaged had been defeated and tumbled back. That impression was not quite true, as 15th Panzer found out when it tried to move forward and was hit in both flanks; one armoured thrust in the late afternoon got in amongst the support echelon, destroying or dispersing precious lorries (the Germans had started the attack very short of transport vehicles), and thus disrupting supply to the combat elements. The local commander put together a scratch force to form a defensive line, which crucially included a battery of 88s; once more these superlative guns proved invaluable and decimated the British attacks, which insisted on frontal assault rather than manoeuvre. At least 12 tanks were destroyed, and the assault stalled. Nevertheless, it was clear that the flanks of the attack were vulnerable, and that the British were not just sitting back. This led to some consolidation of the attack elements, with 21st and 15th Panzer closing up south of Acroma, and a slowing of the original time-table. Critically, the German supply path had been disrupted, by the hold-out of Bir Hacheim, which meant a longer route, by marauding British forces, and by air attack, and without supplies, especially fuel and ammunition, the armoured thrust was vulnerable.

"Looking back on the first day's fighting, it was clear that our plan to overrun the British forces behind the Gazala line had not succeeded. The advance to the coast had also failed and we had thus been unable to cut off the 50th British and 1st South African Divisions from the rest of the Eighth Army. The principal cause was our underestimate of the strength of the British armoured Divisions. The advent of the new American tank had torn great holes in our ranks. Our entire force now stood in heavy and destructive combat with a superior enemy. I will not deny that I was seriously worried that evening. Our heavy tank losses were no good beginning to the battle [far more than a third of the German tanks had been lost in this one day]. The 90th Light Division under General Kleeman had become separated from the Afrika Korps and was now in a very dangerous position. British motorised groups were streaming through the open gap and hunting down the transport columns which had lost touch with the main body. And on these columns the life of my army depended." (*Rommel Papers*.) Rommel ordered a continuation north for the 28th, with 15 Panzer via Acroma, some 9 miles away, and 21 Panzer to Eleut el Tamar. The latter was highly successful, cutting up a number of British formations, and reaching the escarpment overlooking the Via Balbia – which ran along the coast. The 21st were short of fuel and ammunition but had not suffered significant losses. The 15th, however, was in a bad state, having been more heavily engaged since the attack was launched, and being virtually out of fuel and ammunition, and being down to less than 30 "runners" in its armour. It was unable to take its objective. The battle was poised; the Germans, depending on how you look at it and what happened next, were either well placed to exploit what Napoleon would have called a "central position" able to attack either way, or, they had stranded themselves (surrounded) with inadequate fuel and ammunition and were ripe for being annihilated. There were indeed strong British armoured forces being manoeuvred ready to do just that, and unless the Germans could resupply then the gamble would prove an expensive failure.

Rommel well understood the problems of supply and had discovered a route that he considered viable, and he was also hopeful that shorter routes would soon be open as mine-clearing operations continued, seemingly undisturbed by the British. Stragglers (armour and supply vehicles) that had been dispersed in the British attacks also found their way back to their units. Nevertheless, it was still finely balanced, and an aggressive British operation could have been the end: there were later comments that the British wasted the 28th in missed opportunities. This has been a much-debated point – both at the time and since – with much criticism aimed at General Ritchie. During a period of convalescence, Rommel wrote: "Lt-Gen Ritchie became the subject of severe criticism. But was it in fact true that the British defeat was the result of their commander's mistakes? I think that my adversary, General Ritchie, like so many generals of the old school, had not entirely grasped the consequences which followed from the fully motorised conduct of operations and the open nature of the desert battlefield. Despite the good detailed preparation of his plans, they were bound to go wrong, for they were, in essence, a compromise. However, in spite of the precarious situation and the difficult problems with which it faced us, I looked forward that evening full of hope to what the battle might bring. For Ritchie had thrown his armour into the battle piecemeal and had thus given us the chance of engaging them on each separate occasion with just about enough of our own tanks. This dispersal of the British armoured brigades was incomprehensible. In my view the sacrifice of the 7th Armoured Division south of Bir el Harmat served no strategical or tactical purpose whatsoever, for it was all the same to the British whether my armour was engaged there or on the Trigh Capuzzo, where the rest of the British armour later entered the battle. The principal aim of the British should have been to have brought all the armour they had into action at one and the same time. They should never have allowed themselves to be duped into dividing their forces before the battle or during our feint attack against the Gazala line. The full motorisation of their units would have enabled them to cross the battlefield at great speed to wherever danger threatened. Mobile warfare in the desert has often and rightly been compared with a battle at sea – where it is equally wrong to attack piecemeal and leave half the fleet in port during the battle." (*Rommel Papers.*)

Rommel remained bullish and his orders for the 29th were for the capture of Acroma, with renewed assaults on the west of the Gazala line by the Italians. However, the orders were changed before the start time to one of defence, with 21st Panzer to consolidate around Point 209, 15th Panzer to prepare for an assault by 7th Armoured Division and maintain the integrity of the northern flank, and 90th Light to hold a line south-east of Bir el Harmat. Meanwhile, Rommel was still searching for a better supply route to his now beleaguered forces – and found it. The Italians had made two paths through the minefields and following one brought Rommel to the 15th Panzer; he was followed by supplies and the Ariete Division; he also called on a battle group from 21st Panzer. It was just in time and when the 2 Armoured Brigade advanced from Knightsbridge it met elements of three enemy armoured groups – if it had attacked the previous day it may have destroyed the vulnerable 15th Panzer. The 22 and 4 Armoured Brigades gradually joined the battle, but it was piecemeal and uncoordinated, and losses were heavy.

This enabled 15th to move forward and close a pincer on a significant part of the British front lines; however, it was still an uncomfortable situation in respect to supplies, so Rommel reversed his front, and 'advanced' (withdrew) westward, protecting his rear against any attempt at British intervention, his intention being to withdraw to a resupply point and then turn back once more. It went awry when the Germans bumped into a box held by the 150 Brigade of 50th Division; this was a strong box with minefields and guns and proved the value of these all-round defence boxes. The Germans could not afford to be held up; behind this new "front" the 90th were under increasing pressure from 1 Tank Brigade at Bir Harmat, and with clearing skies, the RAF was out in force attacking columns and any concentration of armour. The British too had their problems, not least their experience of being mauled by anti-tank guns every time they had engaged in the previous days, perhaps leading to a reticence on the part of some commanders to commit to daring action. One tank commander recalled: "... ordered to mount an attack against a German line, consisting of mainly anti-tank guns, all well dug in. It was hoped to 'crash through' the Germans' lines." His commander protested vehemently at this tactic and was removed from his post for his troubles. The attack went ahead as ordered. "As we approached the crest of the rise, the order was given to speed up and the tanks on either side of us followed suit. But we were the first to reach the skyline, at least of those in our immediate vicinity, and as we came into full view of the enemy, so the shells arrived. Clouds of smoke and dust soon blinded my vision and I never saw one of the many anti-tank guns that now started to take their toll. In the first second we must have received at least four direct hits from armour piercing shells. The engine was knocked out, a track was broken, and one shell hit the barrel of the 75mm gun and broke it. Then quite a heavy high explosive shell dropped on the mantlet of my 37mm gun and pushed it back against the recoil springs. That shell landed inches above my head, but the armour plating held firm, and I suffered nothing more than a 'singing in the ears'. But a splinter hit the subaltern in the head, and he fell to the floor of the turret dead. I found that my gun would not fire. Almost every tank in that battle met with the same treatment, and the whole line was halted on the crest of that small ridge. I half climbed out of the gunner's seat so that I could see over the top of the turret, and the sight that met my eyes was terrifying. These Grant tanks carried a large supply of ammunition for the 75 mm gun stowed underneath the main turret. If an armour piercing shell happened to penetrate the armour and hit the ammunition, the result had to be seen to be believed. Sgt Adams' tank was halted less than 10 yards from me, and as I looked across I saw him, and his crew start to bale out. He had one leg out of the cupola when suddenly his tank just disintegrated; the turret, which weighed about 8 tons, went sailing into the air and landed with a dull thud in front of my tank, the sides of the tank split open with the force of the explosion and exposed what remained of the inside – a blazing jumble of twisted metal. Not a member of the crew had a chance of survival.

"Benzie's squadron went into this action with a strength of twelve tanks. In under a minute all but one were in flames, and all along the line it was more or less the same story. Why my tank was not on fire was a mystery to me, we had been hit often enough. But we were now manning a useless lump of metal, we could not move, and our guns were out of action. Our orders were clear, 'No baling out unless the tank is on fire.' Anyhow, by now it was almost safer to stay where we were, because the whole area was still under heavy shell fire, although the anti-tank gunners were blinded by the pillars of black smoke that swirled up from each burning tank. I bent down and removed the wireless headphones from our dead tank commander and put them on. At least the wireless was still working, and I called up Regimental Headquarters. 'Why, are you still alive? Thank God somebody is?' I explained our position, and the Adjutant said he would send up a tank to try and tow us back when things had quietened down."

While the British considered their next move, perhaps confident that the battle had turned in their favour, Rommel's resupply gamble had paid off and on the night of the 30th his forces were resupplied and ready for action. "In the afternoon, I drove through the minefield to X Italian Corps HQ for a meeting with Field Marshal Kesselring, the commander of X Italian Corps, and Major von Below (Adjutant to the Führer), during which I informed them of my further plans. With the Afrika Korps screening the British minefield against all attacks from the north-east we were first going to clean up the whole of the southern part of the Gazala line and then to resume the offensive. In the course of this operation, we intended to destroy the 150 British Brigade at Ualeb and then the 1 Free French Brigade in Bir Hacheim." (*Rommel Papers.*)

The 31st was another wasted day by the British, whereas the Germans focused on eliminating the 150 Brigade box; by the end of day they had established themselves in a dominant position that led to the final destruction of the box on 1st June. It had been an heroic defence by 150 Brigade, supported by a few tanks of 44 RTR. Rommel noted on this day that "The great crisis of the battle is over." With this pivotal box overrun, Rommel now had a clear supply route and a bridgehead in which to consolidate and then advance once more. His intention was to drive north to the coast, but first he wanted to secure the southern wing and eliminate the Bir Hacheim box, a task given to the 90th Light and the Italian Trieste Division.

The week of 2nd to 10th June was a battle of attrition in two main areas, Bir Hacheim and Knightsbridge. Rommel's plan to split his armour, the 21st going north and the 15th holding to await developments, was blocked by a series of British attacks, although these had limited success and both sides had to stop to reorganize and resupply. Meanwhile, Ritchie was planning a major armoured thrust by 2 and 4 Armoured Brigades, a total of some 400 tanks, along with another force aimed at the Ariete Division in the south. The offensive opened on the 5th with an artillery barrage, closely followed by armour. It all started well, especially against the Italians, but, once again, German gun lines wreaked havoc on the British armour, and both 15th and 21st Panzer began to drive forward in a pincer movement. This "Battle of the Cauldron" was a fierce conflict across a relatively limited area of desert; the withdrawal of the tanks left the Allied infantry exposed and they were quickly overrun. The Panzer pincer closed behind the British and the advance had also disrupted and dispersed the HQ of 5th Indian Division and 7th Armoured Division, making command and control near impossible, as well as neutralizing the Bir el Harmat box. What should, with 400 tanks and support, have been a British success had turned into a disaster. By the early hours of 6th June, the British losses included over 100 tanks, two infantry brigades and four artillery regiments, and the initiative was firmly back with the Germans. Auchinleck later stated that this "unsuccessful counter-stroke was probably the turning point of the whole battle."

Rommel later wrote: "This defeat had done considerable damage to the enemy's offensive power. As I had foreseen, the British command had decided against committing any major force from the two Divisions in the Gazala line to form a second point of pressure on the 21st Panzer Division. Nor had any units of the 2nd South African Division been committed. In a moment so decisive they should have thrown in all the strength they could muster. What is the use of having overall superiority if one allows one's formations to be smashed piece by piece by an enemy who, in each separate action, is able to concentrate superior strength at the decisive point?"

The Free French were continuing to hold Bir Hacheim and a great many air sorties were flown in support, as the Germans were subjecting the defenders to air assault by escorted Ju87s. Billy Drake had his first air combat with 112 Squadron whilst leading 10 Kittyhawks in a fighter-bomber sortie on 6th June: "Near the target we spotted four Bf109s below us. What luck, we dived on them and claimed the lot shot down – three confirmed and one probable, the latter being my personal contribution to events. We then bombed Axis vehicles claiming one in flames and six damaged. Not a bad result, we felt." (*Billy Drake, Fighter Leader* p45). He later changed the probable to a definite with confirmation from ground forces that the 109 had crashed. Most of his total of 23 confirmed kills (and three shared) were scored in the Western Desert with 112 Squadron. By the end of the day the Squadron had flown 38 sorties, and in addition to the aerial victories, claimed five MT destroyed and 12 severely damaged; the total could have been more but as the Squadron recorded "The dust and confusion of the tank battle below gave them little opportunity to intervene effectively." Rommel now wanted to destroy the box at Bir Hacheim and a strong combat group was put together for this task, the final attacks commencing on the 7th. There seemed little likelihood of any relieving force and overnight on the 6th a number of lanes were cleared through the minefields and assault groups moved into position. Despite artillery and air support the attacks were once more halted. Meanwhile, the RAF was providing air support for the defenders, and the debut mission for 6 Squadron's Hurricane IIDs – armed with two 40mm guns and designed for tank busting – took place on the 7th with Sqn Ldr F. Hayter leading five other pilots to attack tanks and MT near Bir Hacheim. One returned early with engine problems and the other five were unable to find the target. Pilots reported very wide dispersal of tanks amongst MT, such dispersal not being favourable to the functions of the Hurricane IID." (6 Sqn ORB.) The following day two ops were flown, both by sections of three aircraft. Claims were made by all three pilots in the first section, but in the afternoon only Plt Off Bosly returned, claiming attacks on two large MTs resulting in one flamer. Flt Lt Allan Simpson recounted the sortie: "Our mission was to relieve the pressure on them from tanks, which were lobbing shells from a few thousand yards away. As we neared the target, we dove to pick up speed and attacked level from about 1,000 yards at ten feet off the deck; later that summer, some of the boys took off their tail wheels by hitting tank turrets; one bent his propeller on a tank." He was hit and wounded during the run-in: "My initial reaction was to cost the enemy as much as possible, and so I continued my attack on the German Mark III tank, then lined up another at which I got a good run, and then a truck." He then decided it was time to get out of the area as it looked likely that the aircraft would not fly much longer and he was not sure how badly wounded he was. His account, in *All the Fine Young Eagles*; pp139–140, provided more – and fascinating – detail on his action, but the end result was that he baled-out, was picked up by ambulance and a few days later was back in Egypt.

Stronger attacks on the 9th were also beaten back, despite artillery and dive-bombing; indeed, the Luftwaffe commitment caused Kesselring to prompt Rommel to throw more forces at Bir Hacheim, as it was proving a drain on Luftwaffe resources. "Meanwhile, we several times had trouble with Kesselring. He was being severely critical of the slow progress of our attack on the French. What mainly upset him was the fact that he had had to keep Luftwaffe formations continuously employed over Bir Hacheim, where they had suffered severe losses. He insisted that an immediate attack should be launched on the French by all our armoured formations. This was completely out of the question, for tanks cannot be sent into minefields which are protected against clearance by strong-points. Moreover, Ritchie would not have remained inactive on the other fronts while this was going on. Such a move would have led to disaster. We did our best to pacify Kesselring, who probably had little idea of the difficulties we were up against." (*Rommel Papers*.)

The French were very appreciative of the RAF support, and on the 10th they sent a signal to the AOC (Air Officer Commanding): "Bravo! Merci pour le RAF!" to which the AOC replied: "Merci pour le sport!" Despite such support – and bravado – the defence could not continue, and on the night of 10th June the remaining defenders withdrew, which meant the end of the original defence line. The Luftwaffe and Panzer Army were still finding it difficult to collaborate or agree, although on the evening of the 9th General Waldeau reported that over 1,000 sorties had been flown to date supporting the Bir Hacheim operation. It was agreed that a major effort would be made on the 10th, with three waves of attacks. The first attack had to be curtailed because poor visibility (haze and dust) made it hard to distinguish friend from foe. The second and third waves were more successful and by the end of the day 140 tons of bombs had been dropped by the Ju87s and Ju88s, which had been covered by large numbers of fighters. The Germans had now taken the southern and central parts of the line, and the British had reorganized the line from Gazala to Knightsbridge. It proved fruitless and over the next few days the Germans manoeuvred, advanced, engaged and destroyed defensive positions and the few weak Allied counter-attacks, which once again were more like cavalry charges than coordinated armoured operations. The capture of high ground overlooking the Knightsbridge box meant the end for that position, and the Guards units joined the by now general withdrawal of the 8th Army. The panzers now swung north to cut the Via Balbia and trap the units at Gazala, the main aim being to cut-off and destroy the two British divisions in this sector. The attack was led by 15th Panzer with two reconnaissance battalions on their right flank, and Trieste Division on the left wing, and 90th Light Division on the right wing. This was a powerful force and Ritchie moved 2nd Armoured to Bir Lefa to counter the encirclement. On the following day the Germans threw a gun line forward, expecting the usual British charge, whilst 15th Panzer sent a flank attack. Heavy fighting took place, with the British tanks suffering significant losses. By afternoon the British were poorly placed as pincers from 15th and 21st Panzer were racing to cut them off. The British were retreating, but on the 13th they once again fell into a German gun-line trap, losing large numbers of tanks. "The slaughter of British tanks went on. One after the other of the 120 or so which they probably now had left remained lying on the battlefield. A murderous fire struck from several sides into the tightly packed British formations, whose strength gradually diminished. Their counter-attacks decreased steadily in momentum." (*Rommel Papers*.)

The Knightsbridge box was abandoned on 14th June and the Allies rapidly moved back to the borders of Egypt; the RAF was leapfrogging to airfields as they retreated – and then frequently attacking the Luftwaffe now established at airfields that the RAF had themselves recently been using! The mobility of the squadrons was essential and the groundcrew had to be quick off the mark to avoid being overrun – and to ensure that nothing useful was left behind for the enemy. Billy Drake described the way that 112 Squadron leapfrogged: "The whole of the Squadron's ground echelon was divided into two parties, A and B. As the A party moved back to a new landing ground, the B party continued to service, refuel and re-arm the aircraft as long as possible. The last to leave each airfield were the pilots and aircraft, who usually took off for an operation over the front as the B party withdrew, then landing at the new base further back, where the A party had already set up and were waiting for them." (*Billy Drake, Fighter Leader* p47.)

"Throughout this black fortnight, when all that our forces had so painfully won seemed to be slipping away, the Desert Air Force fought hard and continuously. During the Knightsbridge battle Bostons, Hurricanes and Kittyhawks went out hour after hour on a shuttle service of bombing and strafing, returning only to refuel, re-arm and take off again. The landing grounds shimmered in the June heat under a constant cloud of dust kicked up by the take-offs. Beneath it, ground crews worked each hour of daylight and far into the darkness; they abandoned their tents and dug themselves holes in the ground beside their aircraft in the dispersal areas, flinging themselves wearily into these holes to get a few hours' sleep when exhausted. After dark they muffled their heads in blankets and worked on their aircraft by the light of pocket torches; and they continued to work through bombing raids in which the enemy was using peculiarly unpleasant anti-personnel missiles known as 'butterfly bombs'. And while these men toiled on the ground through the midsummer heat, the pilots and aircrews flew, fought and flew again, without time to shave their beards or change their clothes. Certainly, they earned Auchinleck's acknowledgment that "It should be made clear that R.A.F. support for the Army has been unstinted at great sacrifice throughout the present campaign." (*NZ in RAF*.)

Although the British tank actions have been seen as "futile charges", they did, despite their losses, prevent the Axis forces from closing the Via Balbia and cutting off large numbers of troops; instead, large numbers of troops were able to escape and make the long retreat to Egypt. The boxes at El Adem and Acroma were still being held but the overall situation and perceived lack of armour, although tank strength was probably still greater than that available to Rommel, meant that these boxes had no role to play, other than delaying the Germans. Tobruk, due north of El Adem, was next on Rommel's plan. British command morale appeared weak and Rommel played on this in his strategy to take Tobruk rather than bypass it and undertake another siege. Pushing his armour forward to persuade the British that his forces were committed to the pursuit, he then broke away much of the armour for an assault on Tobruk, leaving the 90th Light to keep the pressure on the retreating British, and push on to Bardia, as he was confident that the enemy commanders would not turn and fight or act in an aggressive fashion. The assault on Tobruk commenced in the early hours of 20th June 1942, the south-east corner of the Tobruk bastion being subjected to bombing and artillery fire. Despite the minefields and some effective artillery fire, the advance pressed forward, quickly seizing key points; within hours it was clear the garrison was destroying supply dumps – an indication that the defence was already a lost cause. In less than two days of operations, the fortress of Tobruk, with its garrison of over 30,000 men, had fallen and the Germans gained a bounty of equipment, especially trucks, and supplies. It also gave them another receiving port for supplies from Italy. In an Order of the Day, Rommel stated: "The great battle in the Marmarica has been crowned by your quick conquest of Tobruk. We have taken in all over 45,000 prisoners and destroyed or captured more than 1,000 armoured fighting vehicles and nearly 400 guns. During the long hard struggle of the last four weeks, you have, through your incomparable courage and tenacity, dealt the enemy blow upon blow. Your spirit of attack has cost him the core of his field army, which was standing poised for an offensive. Above all, he has lost his powerful armour. Now for the complete destruction of the enemy. We will not rest until we have shattered the last remnants of the British Eighth Army. During the days to come, I shall call on you for one more great effort to bring us to this final goal." (*Rommel Papers.*)

In recognition of his success, Rommel was promoted to Field Marshal. Operations in North Africa were notionally under the supreme command of the Italians, and an order had been received to halt the pursuit on the line Sidi Omar-Halfaya-Sollum, and despite his desire to press on Rommel stopped the advance at Capuzzo. On 22nd June Rommel, General Ettore Bastico (the notional commander of all Axis forces in North Africa) and General Albert Kesselring (Commander-in-Chief South) met in Rome to agree strategic priorities. Bastico initially insisted on complying with the halt order, but he was persuaded to allow the pursuit to continue, largely because Rommel convinced both Bastico and Kesselring that with the supplies he had captured and with the disorganization of the enemy, there would never be a better opportunity. Rommel also knew that he had to keep pressure on the British to prevent them rapidly rebuilding their offensive capability. The panzers rolled on, attempting to cut-off the retreating enemy who, it was now clear, was racing back to its next prepared defence line at El Alamein. The Axis forces drove hard, so hard that mechanical failures increased, reducing the number of combat vehicles in particular, but with no fear of a counter-punch this was not critical. Then tanks were also outrunning fuel supply, a more serious issue, which at one point brought 21st Panzer to a halt – until they took petrol from support vehicles to keep the combat vehicles running. The Allies relied heavily on the RAF to delay the enemy, a fact recognized by Rommel: "My formations were being repeatedly assailed by heavy RAF bomber attacks. Our own Luftwaffe was re-grouping at the time and could not put up any fighters. The Afrika Korps, with its 50 remaining tanks, was the most frequent target of the RAF's attacks. On the morning of the 26th June, swarms of British aircraft continued the attack and succeeded in destroying a supply column, which caused the Afrika Korps a serious petrol shortage for a time."

On the 26th the RAF attacks had indeed caused a major delay in resupply, allowing the ground forces a small respite in which a rearguard took up position at Mersa Matruh; it made little difference and was soon broken and when 90th Light cut through to the coast, a number of British formations were cut-off. Auchinleck took direct command of 8th Army; to try to hold the Germans west of Matruh, a series of attacks was put in by 1st Armoured, which had no real effect and cost 18 tanks. The British had also decided that Matruh could not be defended and that it was best to continue back to the Alamein position. Many British positions had been bypassed and their garrisons now sought ways back to the British lines, which added to the overall confusion, especially as the Germans were using large numbers of British trucks; indeed, a number of Allied troops headed towards "friendly trucks" only to discover too late that their occupants were German.

The resistance of early June became the collapse of late June, and the Allied forces tumbled back eastwards, the DAF hopping back to airfields and mounting of attacks on those airfields it had just left. The intensity of operations remained high, with 112 Squadron noting on the 26th that: "The majority of pilots flew four sorties each and were thoroughly tired by nightfall. The length of the sorties varied between an hour and 45 minutes. Just as the last mission returned there was a panic and several pilots had to forego their dinners. In the engagement that followed, Fg Off Whitmore shot down a Me.109F, and Plt Off Cudden was posted missing. The Squadron moved that night to LG106 (El Daba), the enemy approaching somewhat rapidly." Plt Off Cudden returned a few days later in an Army ambulance. Brian Thompson recorded on 22nd June: "Heard today that 25,000 [Allied] prisoners had been taken in Tobruk – bad show – things are not too good. Wonder what in hell is our army trying to do – lose the war?" The important airfield at Fuka was taken, and Mersah Matruh was captured on the 29th June, although by now the Axis force was all but spent. Nevertheless, the advance continued, they were in Egypt, morale was high and the main objectives of the campaign – the Suez Canal and the British naval base at Alexandria – seemed within reach; indeed, the Canal was only 60 miles away. But, one major natural obstacle lay before them, a series of deep wadis that meant that the British had been able to construct strong fortified boxes across the 40 miles or so of desert that were practicable for assault; to the north this line was protected by the sea and to the south by the Qatarra Depression.

In a letter to his wife on the 29th, Rommel wrote: "Now the battle of Mersa Matruh has also been won and our leading units are only 125 miles from Alexandria. There'll be a few more battles to fight before we reach our goal, but I think the worst is well behind us."

As the beaten remnants of the 8th Army moved through this position they passed fresh troops holding the boxes, before reaching staging areas where they were reorganized, resupplied, and, in many cases, fed back into the line.

30th June: "A most immediate signal from AHQ Egypt to the effect that every available aircraft is immediately to be made serviceable, to be armed and, where applicable, made ready to carry bombs. Major inspections to be ignored during present crisis." At the end of June, the German propaganda machine was stating that Rommel would be in Cairo "within days" – and many on both sides believed the message. Following a conference in late June between Rommel and Kesselring, the former was all for an immediate push on Egypt. Kesselring was less convinced: "... first came a report on the situation from Rommel, who declared that there were practically no enemy forces of any significance opposing him and that his army could reach Cairo within 10 days. Even though I realized that Rommel had more insight in the situation on the ground than I, my objections would have to be raised. Any further advance, even if there was only a minimum of combat activity, would result in a maximum loss of armoured and motor vehicles. The necessary supplies would not become available for a long time. Even though there might be no sizeable British ground force reserves in Egypt, one could be sure that the first reinforcements from the Near East were already moving up. I felt confident to speak for the Luftwaffe. My flying forces would face the Nile in a completely exhausted condition with aircraft that needed overhauling and without sufficient supplies. They would be opposed by fully combat-ready units which could be further reinforced in the shortest time. As an airman I considered it madness to attack head on an airbase that was fully intact. Because of the decisive importance of the part played by aviation I had to reject from this point of view alone the continuation of the offensive that had as an objective the conquest of Egypt and the seizure of Cairo."

Oil was a critical strategic asset both in its production and its distribution, and it was a key objective of Allied bombing from 1942 onwards. Whilst Rommel was pressing into Egypt and looking forward to capturing the Suez Canal, an event took place that was to have a significant impact on the Middle East campaign. A USAAF unit had been created, as HALPRO (The Halverson Project), in 1942 to attack Japan from China, but whilst transiting the Middle East the mission was changed and it was attached to No.205 Group. The reason for holding the bombers in the Middle East was to provide a strike force for attacking the important oil facilities at Ploesti "at the earliest possible time". The mission was flown on 12th June. Thirteen bombers left Fayid between 2230 and 2300 hours on 11th June "instructed to proceed individually to the target, attack at high level, and then continue, if possible, to an aerodrome near Ramadi, Iraq. At the objective there was broken overcast at 10,000 to 12,000 feet which practically obscured the targets. All 13 planes reached the objective. The attack, which was a surprise, was made at dawn. Most of the aircraft bombed from below the clouds. About 10 bombed the Astra Romana Refinery at Ploesti [the biggest and most important]." ("The Ploesti Mission", USAF Historical Study #103.) The attack seemed to do little damage, but equally well no aircraft were lost to enemy action, although four ended up in neutral Turkey, where the crews were interned. It was still an amazing mission – 2,600 miles. The Ploesti attack was followed by participation, on the 15th, in an attack on Taranto, but at that point the unit still expected to head off to China. However, by mid-June the USAAF had agreed to provide strategic bombers to the theatre and US Army Air Forces in the Middle East (USAAFIME) was formed under General Russell Maxwell. "It was not the intention of the War Department that the planes of HALPRO should be employed in local tactical operations unsuited to the technical characteristics of heavy bombers. Only the extreme need of weakening the enemy close to the front, so that the effects of the attack would be felt at once on the battle area, justified the use of these bombers for this purpose." ("The AAF in the Middle East", USAH Historical Study #108.) The 15th June operation around the Malta convoy was also significant in that it saw the first United States Army Air Force (USAAF) mission in the Mediterranean theatre. Amongst the Allied bombers attacking the Italian fleet were seven B-24 Liberators from HALPRO operating out of Egypt alongside No.205 Group. By the end of June, several B-17s had also arrived, as well as Maj-Gen Lewis Brereton, on secondment from 10th Air Force (India). The first B-17 mission (9th Bombardment Squadron) took place on 2nd July, a night mission to Tobruk with B-24s. The Flying Fortresses of the 9th and 436th BS had arrived at Lydda from the USAAF's 10th Air Force in India. The 98th BG arrived in late July and by early August its B-24s were attacking port targets in North Africa. All the US bombers concentrated at Lydda in Palestine; with the risk of Allied defeat in Egypt, Churchill was pressing for additional American combat units, both air and ground. The heavy bomber force in the Middle East was also boosted by the arrival of two Bomber Command Halifax squadrons – 10 and 76 Squadrons sending detachments to Aqir. The units were unsure of their role or how long they would have to stay, and the route out via Gibraltar was not without incident, with two aircraft written-off. The squadrons became No.249 Wing in No.205 Group and the first mission, a single Halifax of 10 Squadron, was flown on the night of 11/12 July, the target being Tobruk. For the remainder of July night raids on Tobruk remained the routine for both squadrons, with aircraft using Shallufa as a forward airfield when required.

During the first three days of July, Rommel attempted to breach the Allied lines; 90th Light took the box at Bir el Schine and fought off an armoured counter-attack, but they were heavily attacked from the air and nearing exhaustion. Rommel switched to the central sector by the Ruweisat ridge, but the New Zealanders had attacked and broke Ariete Division, a situation only restored by a panzer counter-stroke. It was clear to Rommel that no more could be achieved without re-organisation and reinforcement, so the offensive was halted on the 4th. He planned to take units out of the line for refit, replacing armoured units with Italian non-mobile infantry units, but making extensive use of tank and 88mm gun decoys to confuse the British. He was still having supply problems and continued to rely on captured equipment. "Unfortunately, the refit of our formations made very slow progress, due to the fact that for some unaccountable reason the few ships engaged on the Africa run were still not arriving at Tobruk or Mersa Matruh but at Benghazi or Tripoli. This meant that all supplies had to be carried by transport columns or our few coastal vessels over a distance of either 750 or 1,400 miles. This, of course, was more than we could manage." (*Rommel Papers.*)

Meanwhile, precautions were being taken for the possible increased attacks on, and even loss of, key installations such as Alexandria harbour. According to the Admiralty Mediterranean War Diary for 2nd July: "The Commander in Chief's Operational Staff transferred to Ismailia being established in Navy House. A few officers went by air but the remaining joining by road in convoy under the direction of the G.S.O. (Lieutenant Colonel Mosely). All arrived by nightfall without incident. The Chief of Intelligence Staff and Staff also reached Ismailia. Accommodation in Ismailia was very limited and the resourcefulness of the Naval Officer in Charge in finding accommodation for all was appreciated. The decision to establish the Commander in Chief's Operational Staff at Ismailia was taken due to the efficient communications at Ismailia, and the facilities for close touch with General Headquarters, Cairo, and H.M. Ships at Port Said. 201 Naval Cooperation Group less an operational staff moved to Abu Sueir about 12 miles from Ismailia. Staff Officer (Intelligence), Mediterranean, and Staff Officer (Intelligence), Alexandria, were established at Port Said. JAVELIN reached Port Said with the Commander in Chief's officer records of a most secret nature."

The Wellington squadrons of 205 Group continued their maximum effort operations: "Double sorties by tired aircrews, flying aircraft that were equally tired and kept serviceable only by the superhuman exertions of ground crews working without rest. Once Rommel had been checked in the first week of July, the immediate task was to prevent supplies reaching the enemy. Tobruk was the main supply port and from July onwards it became the target for all the aircraft that 205 Group could put into the air ... The enemy had built up one of the most vicious concentrations of heavy and medium AA defences ... one particularly dangerous and effective battery of heavy guns was christened 'Eric' by the crews. In their minds they pictured 'Eric' as a fat, bespectacled, but very cunning Hun, who waited, clock in hand, ready to give the order for his battery to fire when the night bombers arrived. A coloured cartoon of 'Eric' hung on the wall of the briefing room and many jokes were made about this fictitious character. While over the target, however, crews treated 'Eric' with due respect." (*RAF Middle East Review No. 4.*)

Rommel tried one more throw of the dice; on 9th July an initial attack was going well when a British counter-stroke destroyed the Italian Sabratha Division on the northern sector. The situation was restored by the 15th Panzer but over the next few days 8th Army targeted other Italian Divisions, wreaking havoc on Trieste, Brescia and Trento Divisions and creating gaps in the line. German counter-attacks once more restored the situation, but it was clear that no offensive was possible. "This British drive along the coast had brought about the destruction of the bulk of the Sabratha and a large part of the Trieste, and important sectors of country had fallen into enemy hands. We were forced to the conclusion that the Italians were no longer capable of holding their line. Far too much had already been demanded of

them by Italian standards and now the strain had become too great."
(*Rommel Papers*.)

Despite the success against the Italians, it was a low point in British
fortunes after the ups and downs of advance and retreat. The difference though was that the DAF was now able to mount hundreds of
sorties – day and night – blunting Axis advances, destroying logistics
and the all-important fuel supplies, and generally wearing down
the Axis forces: Rommel – "The enemy air force by its continual day
and night operations has caused considerable loss among our troops,
delayed and, at times, cut off our supplies ... the supply situation is
tense owing to continual attacks on German supplies at Tobruk and
Matruh." Also, when the Luftwaffe had concentrated on the airfields
at Gazala, Tmimi and Sidi Barrani they had been subjected to heavy
night attacks by No.205 Group, which flew 60 or 70 sorties a night.

It was a defeat for sure, but it could have been a disaster: "But the
greatest achievement of Desert Air Force came during the retreat to
El Alamein; for while the Eighth Army was moving back some
400 miles in a fortnight, it not only escaped destruction on the ground,
but it also escaped decimation from the air. This second fact was the
more remarkable since, for days on end, the coastal road presented
the astonishing spectacle of a congested mass of slowly moving troops
and transport, a target such as pilots' dreams are made of. A little
attention from Stukas and Messerschmitts and the lorries must have
piled up in endless confusion. But the enemy bombers did not appear,
and the Eighth Army reached El Alamein virtually unmolested from
the air – during one period of three days when the congestion was
greatest, its casualties on the road from air attacks are recorded as
being just six men and one lorry. This incredible immunity was partly
due to the inability of the Luftwaffe to keep up with Rommel's
advance but, when due allowance is made for this fact, the German
dive-bombers could still have wrought havoc among our retreating
forces had their activities not been vigorously discouraged by the
Royal Air Force. Much of the work of its squadrons was done out of
sight of our troops; highly effective attacks, for example, were made on
the Gazala airfields as soon as they were occupied by the enemy, so
crippling the German fighter effort from the start. Later, enemy squadrons were twice caught on the ground, at Tmimi and Sidi Barrani, at
critical moments during the pursuit. And such fighters as the Germans
did manage to bring forward were kept so busy trying to protect their
own forces that they had little leisure to attack ours." But the Army

realised the protection the RAF was giving it. "Thank God, you didn't let the Huns Stuka us," General Freyberg told Tedder, "because we were an appalling target." And even though Desert Air Force was continually forced to retire from its forward bases, the effort in the air was increased and not diminished. During the first week of the German attack Coningham's squadrons flew 2,339 sorties, but in the last week, when the El Alamein line was withstanding the initial shock, they flew 5,458. At the same time, the proportion of aircraft serviceable, so far from declining as the fight continued and casualties mounted, actually showed a slight improvement. All this was made possible by the strenuous and indeed heroic efforts of the air and ground crews, by the boldness of their leaders and the remarkable efficiency of the organisation that had been created. Weeks before, Coningham had had plans prepared for retreat as well as for advance and the landing grounds to the rear had been stocked with petrol and bombs. His squadrons were therefore able to make a steady withdrawal, fighting all the time. And as they moved back, repair and salvage units stripped the airfields of all useful equipment and supplies. The result was that the Luftwaffe advanced on to empty desert while the Royal Air Force moved back on to well-stocked bases from which it could operate with greater intensity.

Meanwhile, on the Egyptian frontier the defence lines were strengthened, and reinforcements started to arrive. The RAF was able to operate from their well-established bases, and with short supply lines, which enabled a high sortie rate. Additional American air assets were also arriving; the experienced 98th BG arrived in mid-August and with 12th BG and 57th FG attached to RAF units in the desert, the American contribution to what they called the Egypt-Libya campaign became well established. With more units came another command change, with the formation of the IX Bomber Command and IX Fighter Command, and when Lt Gen Frank Andrews took command of USAAFIME in November the organization became the Ninth Air Force.

Despite his desire to press on, Rommel elected to hold his position, arrange his units for any counter-attack, and plan for the final attack that would see final victory in this theatre. This decision was based on a visit by Kesselring at which they discussed the weakness of the Italian formations, the need for more German combat units, a larger Luftwaffe presence – it had been clear for some weeks that the RAF had achieved a level of air superiority – and, most importantly, a regular supply of fuel and equipment, as they now had control of ports closer to their front lines. It was a gamble and the build-up would need to be quick, as the Allies were now back at their logistic hub and so could resupply quickly. They also discussed Malta and although Rommel had once believed that the capture of the island was of little consequence, he had been convinced that only by neutralizing Malta could the Mediterranean supply routes be secured.

Chapter Three

Malta: Cornerstone of Allied Mediterranean Strategy

In October 1941 Albert Kesselring had been appointed as C-in-C South and in his memoirs recalled his briefing during a meeting with Hitler, Goering and Jeschonnek: "The unfavourable situation of our supply line to North Africa, I was told, must be remedied by the neutralization of the British sea and air key-point, the island of Malta. When I objected that we ought to make a thorough job of it and occupy Malta, my interruption was brushed aside with the flat statement that there were no forces available for this." He arrived in Rome on 28th November 1941 and was soon even more convinced that "Every day showed more plainly the naval and air supremacy of the British in these waters. Meanwhile Malta had assumed decisive importance as a strategic key-point, and my primary objective at the beginning was to safeguard our supply lines by smoking out that hornet's nest. Time was required to build up the ground organization in Sicily, to bring forward our air formations and the supplies needed to smash Malta's naval and air bases, as well as to secure the cooperation of the Italian air force for our offensive. For the moment it was impossible to do more than reinforce the air umbrella over the most indispensable convoys." (*The Memoirs of Field-Marshal Kesselring*.) Führer Directive 38 was issued on 2nd December where Hitler: "commanded that sections of the Luftwaffe now released from the East, to the strength of about one Fliegerkorps and the necessary air defence forces, be transferred to the South Italian and North African Area. I put Field Marshal Kesselring in command of all the forces to be used for this task, as C-in-C Southern Area. His tasks are:

1. To achieve air and sea mastery in the area between Southern Italy and North Africa and thus ensure safe lines of communication with Libya and Cyrenaica; the suppression of Malta is particularly important in this connection

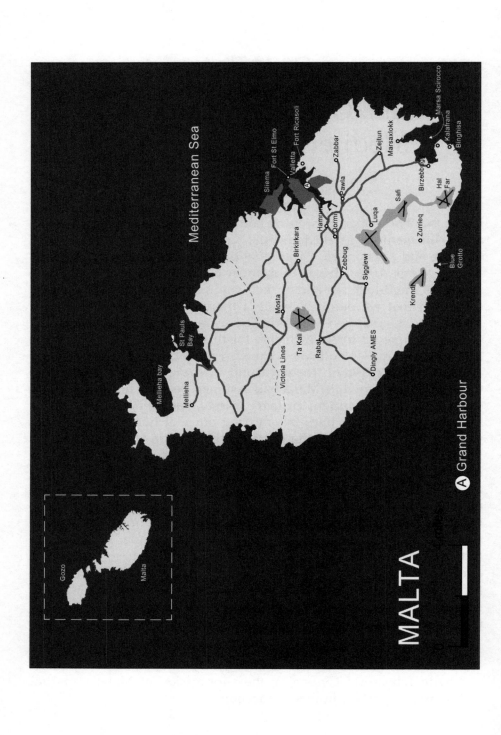

Mediterranean Sea

Mellieha bay
St Pauls
Bay
Mellieha

Sliema
Fort St Elmo
Valletta
Fort Ricasoli
Zabbar
Zejtun
Marsaxlokk
Marsa Scirocco
Kalafrana
Binghisa

Pawla
Hamrun
Qormi
Birkirkara
Luqa
Safi
Birzebbuga
Hal
Far

Mosta
Zebbug
Siggiewi
Zurrieq
Krendi
Blue
Grotto

Victoria Lines
Ta Kali
Rabat
Dingly AMES

Gozo
Malta

MALTA

miles

A Grand Harbour

2. To cooperate with German forces operating in North Africa and with the forces of her Allies
3. To paralyze enemy traffic through the Mediterranean and to stop British supplies reaching Tobruk and Malta; this is to be effected by close cooperation with German and Italian naval forces."

Thus, in December 1941, an air armada of some 600 aircraft (German, including Kesselring's Luftflotte 2, and Italian) was assembled in Sicily under the command of Kesselring with orders to destroy Malta to safeguard Axis shipping. The arrival of II Fliegerkorps from Russia, with strong bomber elements, as well as 109s of JG53 (three Gruppen) along with II./JG3 gave the Axis forces a massive superiority over Malta's air capability. The airfields in Sicily were crammed with aircraft, a tempting target but the Maltese had little capability to make significant attacks. The new air campaign was launched in late December, the initial focus being Malta's airfields, with Hal Far, Luqa and Ta Kali being subjected to heavy attack. With the arrival of large numbers of aircraft and experienced crews it looked inevitable that Malta would be overwhelmed.

Although Malta's naval striking capability (surface and submarine) was limited, the triad of Gibraltar-Malta-Alexandria provided the Allies with an overall offensive capability that was effective despite the Axis domination of the land areas around the Central Mediterranean. By mid-December 1941 Luftwaffe recce aircraft, usually Ju88s, had started to appear over Malta again, and on the 19th the first combat took place, when an early morning recce Ju88 was followed up by three more Ju88s seeking to attack recently-arrived ships. They were intercepted by 249 Squadron, who claimed one shot-down, with one Hurricane damaged. And so it continued for the rest of the month; the relative peace and quiet of Malta was over, and the RAF was facing superior enemy fighters and combat-experienced German pilots. The Germans were now appearing multiple times a day, four attacks on the 26th and five on the 29th; the latter proved to be a bad day with three combats during the five raids.

The attacks intensified in January and the defenders were gradually being beaten down, the number of fighters reducing to a handful each day, flown by exhausted pilots. The weather in January meant that only Luqa, which had a surfaced runway, could be guaranteed as operational. Although some offensive missions were flown from Malta in January, to all intents and purposes by February any effective offensive was over. In early 1942 Malta was pounded heavily and enemy fighter patrols around the island made anti-shipping strikes virtually impossible, and consequently anti-shipping operations from North Africa became even more critical. Shipping remained the only effective way to get large quantities of supplies to Africa to support an offensive, but within weeks of receiving increased supplies Rommel was on the move and driving the Allies backwards at a rapid rate. Capturing airfields on the way, but very few supplies, and ably supported by the reinforced Luftwaffe the panzers seemed unstoppable and the Germans moved on Egypt. The loss of airfields across North Africa impacted the war in the Central Mediterranean making it harder for the RAF to interdict supply convoys. Success or failure – for both sides – was on a knife edge; Rommel needed large quantities of supplies, especially fuel for his panzers, and having failed to capture Allied dumps he was in a difficult position. To a large extent it was about to become even more a war over fuel supplies. The anti-shipping campaign was thus to play a significant, indeed perhaps crucial, part in the Allied success; never was logistics more critical – or more vulnerable. Even though there had been little confirmed success by Allied aircraft in January, although the Royal Navy's submarines were proving effective, the constant patrolling and the various attacks had contributed to Axis shipping taking longer routes.

Meanwhile, on 13th February a signal from C-in-C to Hitler stated: "The most significant factor at this time is that not a single heavy British ship in the Mediterranean is fully seaworthy. The Axis rules both the sea and the air in the Mediterranean. However, enemy submarines still menace our shipping, and there is still a shortage of transport vessels and escort forces, and the oil situation continues to be critical." No mention of any air threat or, for once, the need to deal with Malta. As we will see from a report a month later, the Germans saw they had a window of a month or so for these favourable conditions. The failed convoy MW9 from Alexandria on the 9th was evidence of this dominance. None of the three merchant vessels made it to Malta; *Glen Campbell* was damaged and returned to Tobruk, whilst *Clan Chattan* and *Rowallan Castle* were so seriously damaged that they had to be sunk by the escort ships. Nevertheless, it was not all one way, and Malta's Albacores scored successes on the 3rd (*Napoli*) and 14th (*Ariosto*) of the month, both recorded as being shared with a submarine. However, overall February was another month in which most enemy shipping was sunk by submarine or surface vessel.

Malta's airfields were plastered in February, with Luqa the main target being on the receiving end of 142 attacks of varying magnitude. As this was the main bomber airfield it was clear that it was no longer a suitable location for Wellingtons. AVM Lloyd sent a somewhat despairing signal to Tedder on 23rd February: "February 22 clearly showed inadequacy of our fighter force here. Continuous alerts. Attacks on our aerodromes all day. Apart from material damage to buildings, aircraft, aerodromes and runways which is very serious, loss of working time very grave. Loading of mines on to 37 Squadron aircraft, for example, had not been completed by nightfall. It also largely accounts for bad serviceability among fighters and reconnaissance aircraft. I could get only one reconnaissance aircraft all day. Had two ASV Wellingtons at beginning of day but by night only one, which is not enough for an operation of the importance of that pending last night. Our few fighters did gallant work but the pace and numbers too hot for them, also when they did get in machine gun fire did not kill. Enemy fighters in great numbers and in pairs were sweeping round Island so that in addition to attacking bombers, Hurricanes had to escort out and in reconnaissance aircraft. Sea rescue unable to rescue pilot shot down close to Island owing to impossibility or providing adequate cover for High Speed Launch. All attacks well escorted together with high cover." Having described the problem, he went on to define the solution, all of which points had been made before: "Am confident if we could shoot down a score this daylight nonsense would stop. To do this must have Hurricanes with cannons as it is very distressing for our pilots to see bombers go off carrying so much lead [lack of lethality of the 0.303in machine guns]. Must also have Spitfires in adequate numbers for high cover. Same sort of thing on slightly reduced scale continuing today [23rd]."

March was to prove a very hard month for Malta; enemy sorties increased to nearly 5,000, which meant that bombing or air activity was frequent day and night. Despite all the recent arrivals, the average daily RAF fighter serviceability was only 12 aircraft. The intensity of air attacks is reflected in the fact that the RAF lost 46 aircraft on the ground and only 12 in the air (with nine pilots killed, a higher ratio than usual). The RAF also had 28 personnel on the ground killed, and a further 34 injured. The Wellingtons of 37 Squadron scored an early success with an attack on Palermo harbour on the night of 2nd March. The attack seems to have been particularly accurate and to have been responsible for sinking 13,000 tons of shipping (three ships, *Cuma*, *Tre Marie* and *Securitas*).

After numerous requests and an agonizing wait, the first Spitfires arrived in Malta on 7th March under Operation SPOTTER/QUARTET. First combat patrols were flown on the 10th, the Spitfires climbing to 19,000ft to provide high cover against fighters, whilst the Hurricanes were to focus on the bombers, the same tactic that had been success-fully employed in the Battle of Britain. The Ju88 formation was after Luqa and was intercepted after bombing; the first confirmed Spitfire victory over Malta went to Flt Lt P. Heppell, shooting down a 109 of JG53. A German naval report of 14th March was clear that the "favour-able situation in the Mediterranean, so pronounced at the present time, will probably never occur again." The report was urging immediate action. "The Naval Staff thinks it is desirable on the part of the Führer to issue orders that preparations for an offensive against the Suez Canal be begun. The need for the occupation of Malta is pointed out. Advantage should be taken of the present state of its defences, greatly weakened by German attacks. If Axis troops do not occupy Malta it is imperative that the German Air Force continues its attacks on the island to the same extent as heretofore. Such attacks alone will prevent the enemy from rebuilding Malta's offensive and defensive capabil-ities. If our attacks are not continued, the enemy will immediately and hurriedly begin to rebuild Malta."

The supply situation on Malta was dire and unless a convoy could be run the consequences were likely to be critical. In late March Cunningham assembled an Alexandria to Malta convoy that com-prised four supply ships plus a significant naval escort. The overall plan included suppression of as many as possible of the air bases that could send bombers to attack the convoy, and that included bases in Africa and on the islands of Rhodes and Crete, as well as Sicily, when (and if) the convoy closed on Malta. The convoy sailed from Alexandria on 20th March. Malta was trying to prepare for the arrival of its next batch of Spitfires, repairing airfield surfaces and dispersals and trying to work out a defence plan to protect the new arrivals, and the remaining resident aircraft, from immediate attack. More raids arrived on the 21st, adding to the damage on the airfields (and else-where) and destroying or damaging more aircraft on the ground. Meanwhile, convoy MW10 had had a tense but undisturbed day, clear-ing the first danger zone – south of Crete – without being attacked from the air. They had been spotted, however, so an attack was only a matter of time. Air attacks, primarily by Ju88s, started on the morning of the 22nd and coincided with the appearance of an Italian surface force. The convoy commander elected to send the supply ships and their close escort on to Malta and then turn to engage the surface fleet and prevent it getting in range of the supply ships. Of the supply ships, the first two, *Pampas* and *Talabot*, entered the harbor in the early morning of the 23rd. *Breconshire* was hit a number of times and eventually had to drop anchor, whilst *Clan Campbell* was sunk. Having been left dead in the water some 10 miles from Malta, *Breconshire*, and her 10,000 tons of supplies, was a sitting target. Attempts were made on the 24th and 25th to tow the ship to harbour and when that failed to use HMS *Plumleaf*, a tanker, to try to pump off the valuable fuel cargo. Throughout, she was given a strong "escort" that was there to provide AA cover. On the evening of the 26th a Ju88 put four more bombs into the *Breconshire*, and fires raged – but still she didn't sink. However, by the following morning it was clear she was doomed, and as the cargo exploded she finally sank.

The latest push by Kesselring to get Hitler's support for the Malta plan (C3 to the Italians and Herkules to the Germans) came at an apt time, as Admiral Raeder had recently proposed his new "Great Plan": "[It] called for a series of mutually supporting attacks between Germany and Italy in the Middle East, and Japan in the Indian sub-continent that were intended to knock Britain out of the war. Raeder called for the Axis forces to take Malta and drive on across the North African desert to the Suez Canal. Once that had occurred, it would be possible for the German and Italian forces in the Mediterranean to link up with Japanese forces in the Indian Ocean via the Red Sea – a situation that Raeder claimed would not only cause the collapse of the British Empire, but also create the preconditions for the defeat of the United States." In his view, the victory in the Mediterranean depended on maritime power and Air-Navy-Army cooperation and mutual dependence. To ensure the latter, "The key is a central base from where to operate, and the utmost important base in the Mediterranean is the fortress of Malta." Raeder demonstrated with statistical data that the Axis losses had greatly reduced after the arrival of Kesselring's air forces in the Mediterranean. Malta was not the final objective, but surely the most important and the most urgent. Hitler agreed with the Grand Admiral on the necessity to take actions against Malta." ('The Axis and the intended invasion of Malta in 1942: A combined planning endeavour', Major Alessandro Vivarelli, 2014.)

Kesselring held a conference at II Group HQ to finalize plans for the neutralization of Malta: "The basic idea of II Group's orders was to surprise and neutralize the enemy's fighters, or at least to cripple them so much that they would not be any considerable danger to the ensuing bombing assault, while the three airfields were to be attacked at short intervals with heavy bombs, light anti-personnel bombs and machine-gun fire in order to destroy the aircraft on the ground and to render the runways at least temporarily unserviceable. Daylight attacks were to be concentrated and incessant and given such powerful fighter protection that the British fighters would be kept away from our bombers and pursued until they were wiped out. At night continual nuisance raids by single aircraft were to hinder clearing up the wreckage and repairs. An additional part of the programme was the sinking of the few supply ships making for the port by dive-bombing attacks, and the blocking of the harbour entrance by dropping mines." (*Memoirs of Field-Marshal Kesselring.*) The main assault began on 2nd April and was to last for approximately six weeks, and, according to Kesselring, was a great success. The numbers of RAF fighters dwindled every day despite the best efforts of maintenance crews; the attrition rate on aircraft was unsustainable. Malta had enough pilots but nothing for them to fly.

Axis intelligence had been caught unawares by the April arrival of Spitfires, but within days, the intensive air bombardment had put the Spitfires out of action. "Spitfires arrived Luqa and Ta Kali 20th but unfortunately followed 90 minutes later by raid, 40 tons on Ta Kali, 12 tons on Luqa. Put every serviceable Spitfire into the air. Subsequently total tonnage dropped on Luqa and Ta Kali during 20th after arrival Spitfires 48 tons Luqa, 98 tons Ta Kali; 21st 125 tons Ta Kali and 28 tons Luqa; 22nd 154 tons Ta Kali and 46 tons Luqa. Both places were a complete shambles in spite of soldiers working day and night. Have made every effort to get Spitfires off ground but after arrival Spitfires following sorties made for each of three raids a day: 20th – 6 and 15; 21st – 10, 12 and 10; 22nd – nought and 6. We shall be able to maintain an effort 6 or 8 Spitfires each sortie with luck. Enemy escorts heavier. We have lost eight in combat and nearly all are hit, some seriously. 9 Spitfires destroyed on the ground and 29 damaged sufficient to affect serviceability." (HQ RAF ME to Air Ministry 23rd April.) So even the arrival of nearly 50 Spitfires still only enabled six or eight to face each of the large-scale raids, and attrition would likely mean even fewer within a matter of days.

April had brought over 6,700 tons of bombs raining down on Malta, with the docks receiving 3,156 tons and the three airfields receiving 2,395 tons (Luqa 804, Ta Kali 841, Hal Far 750), which was over three times as much as the March figure of 2,147 tons. April was the worst month for casualties, with 300 civilians killed, and a further 630 wounded, and 24 Service personnel in Heavy AA sites killed (and a further 80 wounded) – this was by far the highest number of casualties to these gun sites. In one of his reports, AVM Lloyd noted: "Conditions had become extremely difficult. The poor quality of the food had not been noticed at first, then suddenly it began to take effect. In March it had been clear enough but in April most belts had to be taken in by two holes and in May by another hole ... Our diet was a slice and a half of bread with jam for breakfast, bully beef for lunch with one slice of bread, and except for an additional slice of bread it was the same fare for dinner. There was sugar, but margarine appeared only every two or three days; even drinking water, lighting and heating were all rationed. And things which had been taken for granted closed down. The making of beer required coal, so none had been made for months. Officers and men slept in shelters, in caverns and dugouts in quarries ... Three hundred slept in one underground cabin as tight as sardines in a tin and two hundred slept in a disued tunnel. None had any comfort or warmth. Soon, too, we should want hundreds of tons of fuel and ammunition ..." A third Spitfire reinforcement flight was arranged for 9th May, with both *Wasp* and *Eagle* involved. This time 64 aircraft were to be flown off and upon arrival at Malta were to be immediately escorted to prepared blast pens for re-fuelling and re-arming. Everything possible was done to avoid the failure of the April reinforcement, when the majority of the Spitfires were destroyed on the ground within days of arriving. This was a crucial operation involving the largest single reinforcement flight.

Gliders were noticed on airfields in Sicily and it was clear that the Germans were preparing the final assault. Around this period, Kesselring and Rommel agreed that the dual objectives should be Malta and Tobruk and that one without the other was "not enough". "The protection of the sea lanes and receiving ports came within my province, and I therefore suggested to Hitler that the capture of Malta should have precedence, as a preliminary to a ground assault on Tobruk. Although Hitler agreed with this sequence, he later changed his mind. At Berchtesgaden at the end of April he endorsed Rommel's intention to launch the land operation from El Gazala first." (*Kesselring Memoires.*) On 10th May the Italian Air Staff issued a "Memoranda on the Malta Situation". This started with a review of the invasion plans that had been under development since February and the principal aims of operations since Spring:

- Neutralisation of AA defences by forcing the batteries to intensify their fire in order to exhaust their ammunition and to tire their personnel
- Elimination of enemy aircraft by concentrating first on the fighters and then on the bombers
- Close cooperation between the Luftflotte 2 and the Sicilian Air Force
- Dislocation, at all costs, of the supply routes to Malta

The plans for an invasion of Malta had been in hand since February 1942 and in his memoirs, Kesselring says, of his points made at the Tobruk meeting: "The assault on the island must be the next step. The allocation of forces in the plan had been so calculated that failure was out of the question. Two parachute Divisions under General Student had been brought in, including the Italian 2nd Parachute Division [note: in other records this was the 185th Folgore Division]. Troop-transport aircraft, heavy freight-carrying aircraft and Giants for tank transport were also available in ample quantities. In addition, there were two to three Italian Assault Divisions, elements of the battle fleet to shell the island fortifications and to escort the troop transports and assault aircraft, and air formations in rather greater strength than had been used for the original attack. The draft plan for the operation broadly had the following shape:

1. Attack by airborne troops to seize the southern heights as a jumping-off base for an assault to capture the airfields south of the town and the harbour of La Valetta, shortly preceded by a bombing raid on the airfields themselves and anti-aircraft positions.
2. Main attack by naval forces and landing parties against the strong-points south of La Valetta and, in conjunction with parachute troops, on the harbour itself, synchronized with bombing raids on coastal batteries.
3. Diversionary attack from the sea against the bay of Marsa Scirocco." (*Memoirs of Field Marshal Albert Kesselring.*)

The Italian Air Ministry's Plan for the Occupation of Malta (Operation "C3") stated: "The Italian Air Staff put forward to the Chief of the General Staff the view that the capture of Malta was primarily an air operation and that the ground and naval operations were necessarily of a supporting nature." Considering the lack of amphibious assault areas – Malta is a rocky island with cliffs and few bays or beaches – air assault was certainly the only option. "It was assumed that a total force of not less than 1,000 aircraft of all types would be needed in order to maintain strong and unceasing attacks and at the same time to carry out the following tasks, in cooperation with the naval forces:

- Blockade of the island
- Protection of transport
- Transport operation
- Protection of naval forces
- Attacks on shipping

The table below is based on Minutes of a 24th February meeting:

Planning Phase and Activities to be conducted
- Phase I (until 10 March). Studies of the Comando Supremo are conducted by the joint staff with the support of Regia Marina (Admiral Vittorio Tur), Regio Esercito (General Vittorio Sogno), and representatives of the Japanese Naval Mission to Italy. After a general orientation, four separate courses of action are developed and examined through a war game session. As a result, one solution is brought forward as the basis for the final concept to be approved by the chief of Comando Supremo at the end of phase II.
- Phase II (10–30 March). Representatives of Regia Aeronautica and OBS (Kesselring's headquarters) join the planning staff, in order to check the feasibility of previous plans and define the kind of support provided by the Germans. The phase ends with the approval of the final concept of operations, and the issue of orders for the constitution of an expeditionary command in charge of the final preparation and conduct of the operation.
- Phase III (1–30 April). Constitution of the expeditionary command, development of a detailed plan for the operation, in co-ordination with Comando Supremo, OBS and the three services.
- Phase IV (1 May–31 July). Plan refinement and preparation.

Source: "The Axis and the intended invasion of Malta in 1942: A combined planning endeavour", Major Alessandro Vivarelli, 2014.

It is worth noting that the Japanese were also involved in the planning, as their experience of amphibious operations was considered to be valuable, although they were in favour of sea assault before air assault and so were at odds with the German and Italian viewpoint. The aircraft projection was for 578 aircraft from the Reggia (240 fighters, 140 bombers, 30 torpedo-carriers, 18 dive-bombers, 30 assault aircraft – which were defined as CR.42s with glider bombs, 120 transport aircraft) and a further 500 from Luftflotte 2. The original plan that envisaged an assault in early May had two options, the preferred one being a 'coup de main' by air assault just after twilight. However, "With the change in the situation on the Island, due to the transfer of fighters there and the supply of arms and ammunition by the minelayer *Manxman*, the 'coup de main' plan was scrapped, and the possibilities of an attack in force were considered." This revised operation would "consist of a quick succession of violent attacks so as to gain a beachhead for the landing of forces, afterwards developing into an operation leading to the possession of the whole island. The number of paratroopers available for the operation was considered adequate to resist for several hours to establish a good footing for further operations." It was decided that the operation should take place at full moon and in favourable weather conditions, with the main landing at Marsa Scirocco and the secondary landing, of light forces, on the SW coast. There was concern over British naval interference: "In order to combat the possible intervention of naval forces from Alexandria and Gibraltar, it was arranged that all the bomber and torpedo-bomber units, together with fighter units and assault aircraft if necessary, which were stationed in Sardinia, Libya and the Aegean as well as the torpedo-bomber units based on Sicily, should attack these forces." These Italian forces were listed as:

- Sardinia: 36th T-B Stormo, 51st Bomber Gruppo, 24th Fighter Gruppo
- Aegean Rhodes: 104th T-B Gruppo, 161st Fighter Gruppo
- Aegean Gadura: 41st T-B Gruppo, 47th Bomber Stormo
- Libya K2: 131st T-B Gruppo, 133rd T-B Gruppo, 3rd Fighter Gruppo
- Libya K3: 150th Fighter Stormo
- Libya: 35th Bomber Stormo, 50th Assault Stormo, 2nd and 4th Fighter Stormo, and 12th and 160th Fighter Gruppo
- Sicily Pantelleria: 130th and 132nd T-B Gruppo

In April, Cavallero requested a German staff officer with expertise in air and sea landing operations, and the training of parachute units. On 11th April, Major-General Bernhard Ramcke arrived in Rome; his experience with the Crete operation and his dedication to airborne operations, as well as an appreciation of combined operations, made him a valuable asset to the planning phase. "His tasks were not limited to the education of his Italian counterparts on the challenges and risks inherent in the conduct of airborne operations. Ramcke was expected to establish a more far-reaching and enduring cooperation with the Italian armed forces, to achieve a high level of training and standardization within the Italian airborne units." ("The Axis and the intended invasion of Malta in 1942: A combined planning endeavour", Major Alessandro Vivarelli, 2014.)

With the overall plan settled: "General Sogno issued a training guidance based on two main pillars; the build-up and training of airborne units (parachute and air landing), and the conversion of generic infantry formations into a specifically organized, trained, and equipped landing force. Regio Esercito also established a three-phase training calendar (from 20 March through the planned execution date), with a progression from individual and small unit tactics to the conduct of large-scale airborne and seaborne landing exercises. The achievement of a high level of inter-service cooperation (Army-Air Force and Army-Navy), and the interoperability of Folgore and La Spezia Divisions with the German counterparts were of paramount importance. Since mid-April, both Folgore and La Spezia benefited from the training assistance of Major General Ramcke and his pool of instructors. Training had been in progress since 1st March 1942 and the two Divisions soon impressed the German trainers with the high level of morale of the officers and men, all volunteers. In Tarquinia, Folgore's units progressively filled their ranks, and underwent an intense program, based on daily jump training, demanding physical activities, field tactical exercises, hand-to-hand combat, and survival skills. In close coordination with Regia Aeronautica, large-scale exercises were conducted in Sardinia, and later in southern Italy, whose central theme was the execution of parachute jumps followed by tactical actions, with the intent to recreate the conditions expected in Malta. In the meanwhile, La Spezia, the third divisional formation of Student's projected airborne corps, faced the demanding task of converting from an infantry to an air-landing Division. The undertaking was exceptionally tough, given the absence of any doctrinal or procedural precedent in Italy.

The initial guidance that Regio Esercito provided to VII Corps in March 1942 included the definition, in coordination with Regia Aeronautica, of standardized procedures for the rapid loading and unloading of personnel, vehicles and equipment from the airplanes, as well as the conduct of frequent air transportation tests to verify the conditions of the freight under different flight conditions." ("The Axis and the intended invasion of Malta in 1942: A combined planning endeavour", Major Alessandro Vivarelli, 2014.)

Training the amphibious assault force was a bigger problem as, except for specialist units in FNS (Force Navale Speciale), most were infantry units with no such experience. Indeed, this was one of the main concerns amongst Italian planners as to the risks of the operation. Doctrine had to be written and passed down as operational procedures, and units had to undergo intensive training in all aspects of such operations and cooperation with the Navy. A series of exercises included day and night operations against pre-alerted Italian defences, such as when 4,500 men landed along the cliffs south of Livorno. As an observer, the Japanese Admiral Abe stated that "I came back to Rome convinced that you can accomplish brilliantly, having observed your tenacious exercises, conducted with indomitable spirit and severe discipline ..."

On 30th May the Supreme Command had issued an order that to prepare for Operation "C3", all air transport with Italian North Africa was to be suspended from 1st June. The Naval Supreme Command seemed less than enthusiastic and, in their study, concluded: "The operation was, without doubt, one of great difficulty, because the defences could be considered one of the most highly concentrated in the World. It was estimated that the coastal defences of the Island consisted of 85 naval batteries, including 19 of heavy calibre; various types of defensive obstructions in the most important bays, besides those in the port of Valetta; submerged barbed wire entanglements along the beaches; all kinds of defences (both active and passive), including high tension wire entanglements and mines on the beaches. In addition, there were airfields encircling the archipelago. As the batteries were either in caves or in well-protected gun emplacements, they were not very vulnerable either from the sea or the sky."

After the quiet period of late May to late June, some on Malta thought the worst was over – but this was not quite true, although the island was now well-placed to defeat what would be the last assault. Whilst the Italians had been moving units to Sicily, the Germans also reversed their draw down and sent reinforcements of two bomber Gruppen (KG77) and one Fighter Gruppe (I/JG77) to Sicily. The fighters had come from the Eastern Front and were flown by very experienced pilots, under the leadership of Hpt Heinz Bar. July was thus set to be a hectic month for Malta, and it started on 2nd July with a number of heavily escorted raids by the Italians, with both sides suffering losses, but the balance in favour of the defenders. More such raids followed, and on the 6th the German Ju88s were back. The day had been a busy one, with the defenders doing well; the Luftwaffe raid was the last of the day and it too was mauled by the Spitfires, KG77 losing at least three aircraft, one crew being picked up by HSL 128. George Beurling scored his first confirmed victories on 6th July, claiming two M.202s, as well as damaging a bomber. On his fourth sortie of the day he claimed a 109 from JG77 destroyed. He continued to be successful over the next couple of days, and was awarded an immediate DFM, the citation reading: "Sergeant Beurling has displayed great skill and courage in the face of the enemy. One day in July 1942, he engaged a number of enemy fighters which were escorting a formation of Junkers 88s and destroyed one fighter. Later during the same day, he engaged 10 enemy fighters and shot two of them down into the sea, bringing his total victories to eight." (AMB 7613.)

The main Axis offloading ports at Benghazi, Tripoli and Tobruk (since its capture in June) remained high on the list of targets for the Allied bombers, especially from Egypt, still including the USAAF units. In addition to ports, the bombers also went after supply dumps and any major concentration of equipment. The original B-24 force was joined in such attacks by B-17s of the 9th and 436th Bombardment Squadrons, the longer range of these bombers enabling them to operate from bases in Palestine. Later in July the disparate USAAF units became the 1st Provisional Heavy Bombardment Group, and continued attacks on shipping, ports and other installations, although Benghazi and Tobruk remained the most frequent targets. It was a similar picture for the bombers of No.205 Group, with a concerted series of attacks on Tobruk harbour from early July, which resulted in damage to the port and shipping. AVM Keith Park CB MC DFC took over as AOC on 15th July, having arrived on Malta on the 14th. His experience in the Battle of Britain led him to make some changes to the tactical use of his fighters, something he could do as he now had significant numbers of Spitfires. His basic tactic was for fighters to climb as fast as they could and gain height on the way to intercepting the enemy bombers to the north of Malta; this relied on reasonable warning time – and the climb performance of the Spitfire, but it had the effect of taking the fight to the enemy and disrupting the raids before they reached Malta. Whilst Malta was delighted with its Spitfire Vs, some were already angling for the new Spitfire IX, but this was quashed in a signal to ACAS Ops on 21st July: "I consider it would be premature to endeavour to clear the Spitfire IX for use in Malta when it is not yet cleared for operation in this country and its reliability is not yet established." The detail went into lack of tropicalisation and the fact it could not be flown off carriers in same way that the Spitfire V could.

The middle of July saw two carrier operations planned for delivery of Spitfires, with the carrier HMS *Eagle* assigned for two trips, by the end of which she should have delivered over 60 Spitfires. This would make up for losses suffered since the June resupply and enable Park to expand his offensive operations. Operation Pinpoint saw 32 fighters sent from the UK to Gibraltar in convoy OG85, with the freighters *Empire Shackleton* (18 aircraft) and *Guido* (12 aircraft) delivering the Spitfires to Gibraltar on 25th June. The aircraft were assembled, and test flown at North Front airfield, Gibraltar, and ground crews and pilots mustered in preparation for the run to Malta. Just over two weeks later the Spitfires and their pilots were embarked on *Eagle* for what would be that carrier's seventh such run. The carrier sailed on 14th July with an escort provided by the cruisers *Cairo* and *Charybdis*, and five destroyers (*Antelope, Ithuriel, Vansittart, Westcott* and *Wrestler*).

In reasonable weather the convoy made good progress and expected to reach the flying-off point the following day. However, they had been spotted leaving, one of the drawbacks of Gibraltar being that agents could easily observe British naval movements and report via Spain. The agent report of preparations to sail meant that the Italian monitoring submarine was well-placed to pick up and shadow the convoy. The escort ships were all experienced and were as alert as ever, and HMS *Wrestler* had recently, on 2nd May, been involved in sinking *U-74*. Under the command of the experienced Kptlt Helmut Rosenbaum, the Type VIIB submarine *U-73* had been operational in the Mediterranean since February 1942, surviving an air attack on 22nd March which meant that the submarine had to limp to La Spezia for repairs. Its eighth war cruise, this time operating out of La Spezia, Italy, commenced on 1st July and although the original patrol area assigned was off the coast of North Africa, the orders were changed, and Rosenbaum took his boat to the west of Sardinia. A second U-boat, *U-561* under the command of Oblt Robert Bartels, was in the same area, and both had been directed to positions from which they could locate and engage the convoy, their orders being to target the aircraft carrier.

In the early hours of 15th July, the convoy was steaming eastwards, the escorts were fanned out and the carrier beginning its preparations for the launch of its Spitfires. There was no sign of enemy activity, the radar screens were clear of aircraft, and reconnaissance reports showed no indication of the Italian naval build-up that would threaten the operation. Rosenbaum's *U-73* had manoeuvred between the escorts and had not yet been picked up; he knew that as soon as he fired his chances of escape were slim – but he also knew the importance of his target and that the risk was worth it. Having suffered torpedo failures on previous missions, he was determined to make best use of his first salvo from his four bow tubes. Assuming he could get into the right position he had decided on a three-torpedo first salvo, keeping the fourth tube ready. *U-73* had one of the new Torpedo Data Computers (TDC) that solved the torpedo triangle and calculated the gyro angle and the torpedo spread angle, so even allowing for one torpedo failure he should ensure two hits. As an experienced submariner and one with a number of successes in *U-73*, Rosenbaum knew the importance of a patient set-up, even though the risk of detection increased minute by minute. The carrier, which he had identified as HMS *Eagle*, was indeed a tempting target as he calculated its speed and heading, and final adjustments were made to the firing computer. There was still no reaction from the escorts, but the whole crew knew this would soon change. The order to FIRE having been given, the first torpedo left its tube, followed at three-second intervals by the second and third, their fan angle having been determined by the TDC.

On board *Eagle*, the torpedo tracks were spotted and an evasive manoeuvre executed, but the heavily-laden carrier was not manoeuvrable enough and two of the three torpedoes struck home, the third narrowly missing the stern. The explosions rocked the ship and within moments she had started to list to port. Despite the escorts now racing towards the spot, to hunt the attacker and to offer assistance to the carrier, there was nothing they could do to save the situation. Rosenbaum fired his fourth torpedo as soon as the first ones had hit, and the carrier had become an easy target; this one was aimed amidships and found its mark. The list increased, and it was clear the ship was doomed; whilst the cruisers and two of the destroyers continued to search for the attacker, the other two destroyers moved to positions from which they could pick up survivors, a risky operation with at least one U-boat still in the area. The end came quickly for *Eagle* with secondary explosions rupturing even more of the hull. *Wrestler* picked up a target and launched depth charge patterns; this was *U-561*, Bartels having stationed himself as a back-up for *U-73*, and the submarine was soon in trouble. Other escorts moved to the area of the attack, which enabled Rosenbaum to escape. He transmitted: "Convoy – 4 destroyers, 2 cruisers, one aircraft carrier, probably one battleship. Fan shot at aircraft carrier. 3 hits from 500m distance. Loud sinking noises. Everything OK." The rescue operation for the crew of *Eagle* resulted in 250 men being plucked from the sea, which included six of the Spitfire pilots and a number of other RAF personnel. Although *Wrestler* claimed a U-boat destroyed, *U-561* was only heavily damaged and was able to limp back to La Spezia. For the convoy all that remained was a final sweep of the area for survivors and a return to Gibraltar.

The loss of the Spitfire reinforcement caused an immediate signal from AOC Malta requesting information on how soon a new attempt could be made. A week later this was followed by "Spitfire situation becoming critical, wastage rates cause for concern, lack of spares. Forward operations curtailed to preserve aircraft for defence." The planned second July reinforcement operation was cancelled; the loss of *Eagle* meant that the only immediately available carrier was *Argus*, which had left Gibraltar's Force H in late June for the UK. More importantly, a major supply operation for Malta was planned, and risking another carrier before that was not considered an acceptable risk. The reply to AOC Malta, via AOC Middle East, was "do the best you can"; there would be no additional aircraft until August and Operation PEDESTAL.

Meanwhile, the Axis air assault forces were gathering in Sicily. The experienced and energetic Kurt Student had been given command of the airborne element of Operation HERKULES, the German code name for the Malta attack, with his XI Fliegerkorps. He arrived in Rome at the end of April to join the planning team. His experience in the successful but costly Crete operation, and the fact that he and his planners had both time and detailed information with which to plan the assault, meant that the Malta operation was meticulously prepared, but still risky and with the inevitably high cost. The small size of Malta and the extensive photograph coverage, as well as detailed geographical knowledge, meant that the planners had comprehensive knowledge of the terrain, defences and capabilities of Malta. Student later stated: "We knew much more about the enemy's dispositions. Excellent aerial photographs had revealed every detail of his fortifications, coastal and flak batteries, and field positions. We even knew the calibre of the coastal guns, and how many degrees they could be turned inland." (*Luftwaffe War Diaries, Bekker.*)

The German 1st Parachute Division, under the command of General Richard Heidrich, comprised the 1st, 2nd and 3rd Regiments, plus an artillery regiment, Pioneer battalion, flak battalion and the HQ staff. They were joined by the newly formed 4th Parachute Division. The 4th was also boosted by bringing General Ramcke's four battalions out of the line at El Alamein. Major Friedrich von der Heydte, known as "The Baron", was commander of the 2nd Battalion under Ramcke and he and his men were jubilant at the thought of returning to their designated role – and leaving the damned desert behind. It also meant re-equipment rather than the "make-do" of North Africa. The Italian element, the 184th Airborne Division Nembo, was around 7,500 strong, with one artillery and three infantry Regiments, plus support units. It was also very well equipped with infantry weapons and light anti-tank weapons, including the excellent Breda M38 heavy machine gun and the Breda M35 20mm anti-aircraft gun, that was also effective against ground targets. In joint exercises witnessed by Kesselring, he expressed himself impressed with the morale and capability of the Italians.

The second phase of the air assault would comprise the air landing, and an additional wave of paratroops on coastal targets. The air assault elements comprised the Italian 80th Infantry Division, of approximately 11,000 men, and the German 4th Parachute Division. The Italian 80th Infantry Division La Spezia had formed in 1941 for the specific purpose of spearheading the air landing element of the invasion of Malta. Under the command of Generale Fernando Gelich it comprised two infantry regiments (125th and 126th), the 39th Bersaglieri Battalion, a machine-gun company, one anti-tank and two artillery battalions, plus the usual support units. With the on-off nature of the invasion of Malta, some units had deployed to North Africa to gain combat experience, but by early summer 1942 they were all reunited for the final preparations. Their task was to combat air land on Luqa, backing up the paratroops and securing the airfield.

A comprehensive air fleet was assembled to transport these forces, comprising ten Groups of Ju52s, the workhorse of German airborne and transport operations, with over 500 aircraft. Under the overall authority of the Air Transport Chief (Mediterranean), the units included 3rd Group/1st Special Duties Wing, 4th Group/1st Special Duty Bomber Wing, 400th, 600th and 800th Special Duty Bomber Groups, all at Brindisi, and 1st Group/1st Air Landing Wing. Units that had been in Greece and Crete were now concentrated in Italy and Sicily. The Italians added a further 200 transports, a mix of SM75s, SM81s and SM82s. The glider force of some 500 gliders comprised a mix of DFS230 and Go242 gliders, with a small number of Me321 Gigants (around 25) that were capable of carrying 200 troops or armoured vehicles. Equally important was the short distance between airfields and drop zones, which meant that in theory each transport could make four trips in one day. The amphibious assault was based on 50,000 Italian troops in two sea lifts, the first wave being XXX Corps, around 28,000 men, and the second by XVI Corps. The Friuli and the Livorno Divisions, each some 10,000 men, were the main elements of XXX Corps, although specialist troops from the 1st Assault Battalion and the San Marco Marines were involved, the latter having trained in ocean swimming and beach assaults, and as part of the FNS special operations they were also trained in demolition of underwater defences. The plan was for the high ground overlooking the designated landing area in Famagosta and Marsaxlokk Bay on the S/SE corner of Malta to be occupied by the air assault forces, at least to the extent of suppressing the main defences. Once ashore, the ground force would advance north-west to link up with, support and complete the conquest of the Hal Far-Safi-Luqa airfield complex, and then onward to Ta Kali, leaving the second seaborne wave to take over their positions and to encircle Valetta. The Axis commanders hoped to avoid urban fighting in Valetta, relying on the Allies surrendering once it was clear the island had been lost. The second wave was slightly stronger, as one element, the Superga Division, was to land and seize the island of Gozo, whilst the main force, based around the Assieta and Napoli Divisions would land at Marsaxlokk. The second wave would also include armoured units and heavier artillery.

To transport the sea assault forces, a sizeable collection of landing craft was assembled at ports in Sicily. Italian shipyards had been constructing MFP (Marinefährprahm) Type A craft from German plans, and around 70, known as Class MZ motor barges – or "sea mules", were ready by the end of June, supplemented by a further 40 sent from Germany. Each of these craft had a capacity of around 200 troops. The Germans provided a variety of other suitable craft, including a small number of Siebel ferries, the importance of which was their armament of 88mm and 20mm cannon. This still amounted to a fairly small lift, and the bulk of the troop and supply transport was from merchant shipping, which included a number of ferries and passenger ships, as well as cargo ships and even converted trawlers. The challenge was in getting men quickly from ship to shore, which involved a variety of smaller vessels, including over 200 German *Sturmboote*. These small but fast boats could carry six equipped troops and whilst really designed for river crossings, they were highly suitable for the Malta task – as long as the defenders had been suppressed. There was also an assortment of some 300 large and small inflatable craft, some motor powered and some with oars. Some of the merchant ships had undergone structural improvements, including having wood bumpers to enable them to 'berth' at the rocky cliffs, and boardwalks and stairs to assist the ascent. The *Seeschlange* (sea snake) floating ship-to-shore bridge was also tested and ready; originally designed for use in the invasion of England, it had been modified to make it a more stable jetty alongside which ships could tie-up and off-load troops and equipment. The final tests had taken place in the Naples area so as not to arouse suspicion and it had moved to Sicily at the end of July.

As with any assault operation, the convoy would be vulnerable en route and in the assault phase, so a powerful surface force was assembled to provide close support and to provide blocking forces against potential intervention by the Royal Navy. It was not possible to send German surface warships to the area, but there had been an increase in the number of U-boats, and as part of Operation Herkules the German and Italian submarines were tasked to provide blocking positions against Alexandria and Gibraltar. As mentioned earlier, the air forces had also been distributed with an anti-shipping role in mind, as well as direct attack on these two naval bases. It was critical that no Royal Navy forces got within range of the assault convoy.

On 1st August the PEDESTAL convoy cleared the Straits of Gibraltar. The same day, the Beaufighters of 248 Squadron swept over airfields in Sicily in an attempt to disrupt the Axis air effort, claiming six aircraft destroyed, but no Spitfires took part, the conservation policy having been put in place in late July. The Force initially included no less than four carriers: *Victorious* with 38 aircraft (18 Fulmars, 14 Albacores, 6 Hurricanes), *Indomitable* with 44 aircraft (22 Hurricanes, 12 Albacores, 10 Martlets), *Argus* with 18 aircraft (16 Hurricanes and 2 Fulmars), and *Furious* with the 38 Spitfires for Malta. The composition of the forces was:

Force W:
- Battleships 2: *Nelson* and *Rodney*
- Carriers 3: *Argus, Indomitable, Victorious*
- Cruisers 3: *Charybdis, Phoebe, Sirius*
- Destroyers 12: *Antelope, Eskimo, Ithuriel, Laforey, Lightning, Lookout, Quentin, Somali, Tartar, Vansittart, Wishart, Zetland*

Force X:
- Cruisers 4: *Cairo, Kenya, Manchester, Nigeria*
- Destroyers 12: *Ashanti, Bicester, Bramham, Derwent, Foresight, Fury, Icarus, Intrepid, Ledbury, Pathfinder, Penn, Wilton*
- Tug 1: *Jaunty*

Force R:
- Oilers 2: *Brown Ranger, Dingledale*
- Corvettes 4: *Coltsfoot, Geranium, Jonquil, Spiraea*

Operation BELLOWS:
- Carrier 1: *Furious*
- Destroyers 8 (Force H): *Amazon, Keppel, Malcolm, Venomous, Vidette, Westcott, Wrestler, Wolverine*

Minesweeping Force:
- Minesweepers 4: *Hebe, Hythe, Rye, Speedy*
- MLs *121, 126, 134, 135, 168, 459* and *462*

At 0715 on the 2nd the escorting Sunderland reported enemy aircraft, and from 0830 onwards Ju88s started shadowing the convoy. One was shot down and one damaged. The launch of the 38 Spitfires from *Furious* started at 1230 (Operation BELLOWS); one aircraft had a problem shortly after take-off and had to land on *Indomitable*; the remaining Spitfires formed up and headed for Malta. When the first group arrived at Malta, the airfields at Luqa and Ta Kali were under attack and the hoped-for escort was obviously not going to appear. Fuel reserves were low, and the formations were left with little option but to risk an approach to whichever airfield looked most viable. The first four made it down safely at Luqa and were quickly tucked away in revetments, where refuel/re-arm parties were waiting, as were replacement pilots. The next group were less fortunate and were bounced by 109s, losing two in quick succession, with no chance for the pilots to escape. Two others were damaged but were able to crash-land, where the wrecks were quickly pushed out of the way. It was a similar story for the remainder, and total losses amongst the 36 Spitfires that had made it as far as Malta were 16 aircraft and 10 pilots. Even 20 Spitfires were a welcome addition at Malta.

Meanwhile, the second day started well for Force H when *Wolverine* rammed and sank the Italian submarine *Dagabur* north of Algiers. The convoy was still being shadowed and the aerial defence capability of the convoy comprised 34 Hurricanes, 10 Martlet and 16 Fulmar fighters, which were tasked to maintain a constant air patrol of 12 fighters, which were reinforced as needed. Just after 0900 the bombers were back, with 30 Ju88s attacking, losing two aircraft for no result. Attacks by aircraft and U-boats continued, with another submarine sunk, the Italian *Cobalto* being rammed by *Ithuriel*. Fleet fighters were heavily engaged especially in the evening, with large numbers of enemy fighters and then a heavy and coordinated attack by dive-bomber and torpedo-bombers between 1800 and 1850. *Indomitable*, *Foresight*, and *Rodney* were all hit or damaged, although only *Foresight* was sunk (by the Navy as it had suffered severe damage).

"We were ordered to take off from Decimomannu and had to face off some enemy naval units that were escorting a large supply convoy." On that morning the weather was poor, with low clouds and showers. The fierce gusts forced the pilots to make continuous trim corrections to maintain the right course: below the sea had a leaden look. As we approached the target, tension on board was rising. No words, only glances between the crew and the constant search for something out there, either ships or enemy fighters. "Finally, at around midday we located the enemy and immediately started to aim at a British cruiser on escort. We could not ask for a better position for an air attack: the sun on our shoulders and the naval artillery that was not even firing a single shot. We descended to lower altitudes but as the crew was activating the pointing device and dropped the first bomb, our target suddenly changed its course to the left. It is unnecessary to say that our bomb splashed heavily into the water! From that moment on, the enemy artillery unleashed all their fire mouths! There were explosions everywhere around us and from the initial formation of five, only two of us managed to come back to the base. We were also attacked on our way back when a lonely Hurricane spotted us and repeatedly shot enraged bursts that fortunately missed our aircraft by no more than 5 metres. Then I immediately diverted my plane into a large and thick formation of clouds after having dropped the remaining bombs: this manoeuvre meant our salvation." Luigi Gastaldello SM79 pilot, 32nd Stormo.

At 1855 Force Z, the main fleet, turned back west, whilst Force X, the convoy escort, pressed on – with only limited air cover provided by a few Beaufighters. The whole of the Axis air and submarine attack was now focused on Force X. At 2000 on the 3rd *Nigeria* and *Cairo* were torpedoed by U-boats, the latter having to be sunk, and the former being escorted back to Gibraltar. In the hour between 2000 and 2100 heavy attacks were made. During this attack *Empire Hope* was bombed and abandoned, *Clan Ferguson* was torpedoed and blew up – she was loaded with 2,000 tons of aviation petrol and 1,500 tons of explosives amongst other items – however 96 survivors reached the Tunisian coast to be interned by the French. The *Brisbane Star* was torpedoed and fell out from the convoy. At midnight, MTBs lying in wait off Cape Bon commenced their attacks and just after 0100 on the 13th two Italian boats torpedoed the cruiser *Manchester*. Stopped, it was subsequently decided that she should be scuttled which was done at 0500, most of her survivors reaching the Tunisian coast and internment. Within an hour, the scattered merchant ships of the convoy were picked off by the small, fast MTBs, with *Almeria Lykes*, *Glenorchy*, *Santa Elisa* and *Wairangi* being sunk.

Meanwhile the surface threat from Italian cruisers had greatly diminished; lack of fighter cover resulted in their withdrawal eastward and being harassed by reconnaissance aircraft from Malta. The final blow for the Italian cruisers came when submarine *Unbroken* damaged the cruisers *Bolzano* and *Muzio Attendolo*. No further threat was posed by Italian surface warships. At 0700 on the 4th the remainder of Force X, with the three remaining MVs, was 120 miles west of Malta, but still faced attack. Just after 0800 a bomb hit *Waimarama* causing such an explosion that it destroyed not only the ship but the bomber responsible; *Ledbury* rescued 45 men. This was followed 90 minutes later by a most determined dive-bombing attack by Stukas directed principally at the tanker *Ohio*. She was near missed several times and struck by a Ju87 which she had shot down, her steering gear being disabled; an hour later more attacks further damaged and stopped her. *Port Chalmers* was set on fire, though she continued with the convoy.

The final air attack came at 1130, and another ship was lost, the *Melbourne Star* which had a mixed cargo of 12,800 tons, one of the larger loads in the convoy. More importantly, the tanker *Ohio* was once more targeted and in her damaged condition was unable to man-oeuvre effectively; whilst Ju87s made dive-bomb attacks, a trio of Italian SM79 torpedo bombers ran in. At least two torpedoes hit the tanker, and this was her end; fortunately, she did not explode and most of her crew were able to escape before she broke up and sank.

At 1230 the convoy came under short range air protection from Malta and proceeded without further problems. They arrived at Malta at 1600. There was some good news when *Brisbane Star* arrived at 1430 on the 5th "after a cruise around the Gulf of Hammamat and success-ful interview with local French authorities". The French had tried to persuade the Captain to enter port and surrender, an option supported by some on board as the ship had a number of wounded, but the Captain refused and made a night dash to Malta. This was only small consolation as the all-important tanker had been lost, as had nine out of the twelve merchant ships. Less than 30,000 tons of supplies made it through; the table below shows the full extent of the losses.

MV Name	Tonnage	Fate
1 *Glenorchy*	9,000	Sunk
2 *Empire Hope*	12,700	Sunk
3 *Waimarama*	12,850	Sunk
4 *Santa Elisa* (USA)	8,400	Sunk
5 *Clan Ferguson*	7,350	Sunk
6 *Deucalion*	7,500	Sunk
7 *Dorset*	10,600	Sunk
8 *Almeria Lykes* (USA)	7,800	Sunk
9 *Rochester Castle*	7,800	Damaged, arrived Malta
10 *Brisbane Star*	12,800	Damaged, arrived Malta
11 *Port Chalmers*	8,500	Undamaged, arrived Malta
12 *Melbourne Star*	12,800	Sunk
13 *Ohio* (tanker)	9,500	Sunk

Only 20 Spitfires and less than 30,000 tons of supplies – and no tanker. The convoy had been costly and had produced little result. Two of the ships that made it were so badly damaged they would need months of repair work. The immediate future looked bleak and life on Malta would become even more difficult. The Italians and Germans con-tinued to build up forces in Sicily and Southern Italy for the invasion of

Malta; with the 8th Army pinned back within the borders of Egypt, the airfields of North Africa were also part of the overall air strategy, as were islands such as Pantelleria.

According to Kesselring "the allocation of forces in the plan had been so calculated that failure was out of the question." And yet there were still many in the Axis command that were wary; Malta was small and vulnerable but its rocky coastline and limited open land (pretty much only where there were airfields) meant that sea and air assault was going to be difficult. For the Germans, the heavy losses in the air assault on Crete continued to influence their thinking. There was a strong body of opinion in favour of simply neutralizing Malta's ability to strike rather than to risk invasion. There was concern about the capability of the Italians and that the burden of the assault would have to be borne by German units. Kesselring and Rommel flew to Berlin to meet Hitler; they found the Führer in an ebullient mood: news from the Eastern Front was good and Hitler had read reports of the defeat of the Malta convoy. The discussion turned to the strategy for the Middle East war – assault Malta or press to the Suez Canal. Rommel had invariably favoured the latter, whilst Kesselring favoured the former, and both revisited their same arguments. Hitler was adamant that both could be achieved now that additional forces, air and ground, could be assigned to the area, and that to ensure the build-up of force for the decisive push on Egypt, it remained important to neutralize Malta. There remained little confidence in the Italians being able to keep Malta suppressed if German air elements were moved to North Africa, so the best option was occupation – neutralize Malta once and for all.

Meanwhile, in London a similar debate was underway. Churchill and Alan Brooke (Chief of the Imperial General Staff) had recently returned from the Second Washington Conference (19th–25th June), where one of the main topics for the politicians and the military staffs had been a Second Front to help the Russians – and for which Stalin had been calling for some time. The Americans and Russians wanted this to be "somewhere in Europe", but the Americans were persuaded by the British that this was not viable in 1942 and that the best option was in the Mediterranean Theatre, where a decisive intervention could lead to victory in North Africa and an assault on Axis Europe through invasion of Italy. It was not an easy sell to the Americans, especially as they knew Stalin would be unimpressed with this "side show". Nevertheless, Churchill won his argument and it was agreed that an Anglo-American invasion of North Africa via Vichy French Algeria some time in late 1942 was the most viable option and would also enable American ground forces to gain combat experience. In what would turn out to be one of the War's most apposite command appointments, General Dwight D. Eisenhower was appointed Commander-in-Chief of US Forces in the European Theatre of Operations. As a side note, this was also the meeting at which the two leaders agreed to combine their atomic weapon research.

In the middle of July Marshall, King and Harry Hopkins led a team from the US to discuss future Anglo-American operations, and whilst there had been agreement in Washington that North Africa would be the location for an assault, Alan Brooke was concerned: He noted in his diary "It will be a queer party as Harry Hopkins is for Africa, Marshall wants to operate in Europe, and King is determined to strike in the Pacific!" His own views had been clear for some time and started with liberating North Africa and securing command of the Mediterranean, after which an assault on Italy to force them from the Axis. Malta was also on his mind, as a key strategic asset, and intelligence intercepts had showed increased traffic concerning possible invasion options. As Brooke expected, the American Chiefs of Staff (COS) pushed for Europe – the new proposition being an assault on the Cherbourg peninsula in late 1942 as a preparatory move for an attack in 1943. As his diary notes, "The memorandum [from US COS] drew attention to all the advantages but failed to recognize the main disadvantage that there was no hope of our still being in Cherbourg by next spring!" Whilst this was progressing, the British COS meetings were proving equally frustrating, not least the lack of any good news or prospects in the Middle East for 1942, and an increasing frustration with Auchinleck's seeming lack of offensive spirit. The prospects were indeed worse than was being revealed to the Americans, Churchill having warned Brooke "Not to put Marshall off Africa by referring to Middle East dangers in 1943." Roosevelt in the meantime had signalled to Churchill that he was supporting the Africa option and was attempting to influence his COS. By mid-July agreement had been reached: "They all agreed to giving up immediate attacks in the Continent, to prepare plans for attack on North Africa." (*Alanbrooke diaries*.) With this week of "activities" behind him, Brooke prepared for a lightning tour of the Mediterranean and Middle East, his first stop being Gibraltar. He toured the Gibraltar defences and was impressed by the amount of tunneling; he was keen to get to Malta to see the Governor, Lord Gort: "I knew he was in a depressed state, feeling that he had been shoved away in a corner out of the real war, and in danger of his whole garrison being scuppered without much chance of giving an account of themselves." He arrived in Malta early on the 2nd and met with Gort and Park; in his diary he commented that: "The visit had been worthwhile, and I think I brought new hope to Gort. The conditions prevailing at Malta at that time were distinctly depressing, to put it mildly! Shortage of rations, shortage of petrol, a hungry population that rubbed their tummies looking at Gort as he went by, destruction and ruin of docks, loss of convoys just as they approached the island, and the continual possibility of an attack on the island without much hope of help or reinforcements." The new hope was the information relayed regarding the planned Anglo-American landings; as Park pointed out, this was good news but the immediate issue for him as AOC was lack of aircraft, although with limited petrol and ammunition the aircraft shortage was only one of his problems. With CIGS (Chief of Imperial General Staff) and his party having moved on to Cairo, Lord Gort met with his commanders to discuss the situation on Malta. The meeting comprised Maj-Gen Ronald Scobie (GOC), Maj-Gen Clifford Beckett (Artillery and AA Defences), Brigadier William Vaudrey (Fixed Defences), AVM Park (AOC), and Admiral Ralph Leatham (Vice-Admiral Malta).

In 1942 the average strength of the Malta garrison was 1,100 officers, 17,000 other ranks, just under 9,000 local troops plus 2,000 members of the Malta Auxiliary Corps, whilst the RAF had just over 4,300 personnel and the Navy around 1,600: a total military strength of around 35,000. The main land forces were in 11 British Battalions and three Maltese Battalions, three regiments of Artillery, and a small number of tanks (Matilda and Cruiser), organized into four operational Brigades. The fixed gun defences comprised some 130 coastal guns, the largest being seven 230mm (9.2in) guns. The large guns were in four locations and were manned by the 4th Heavy Coast Regiment Royal Artillery at Fort Bingemma (western end of Victoria Line – one gun), Fort Madalena (NE end of the Victoria Lines – two), Fort San Leonardo (two) and Fort Benghisa (two); the latter covered the approaches to Marsaxlokk Harbour. The 10 150mm (6in) guns were likewise in four batteries, manned by the Royal Malta Artillery, at Fort Delimara, Fort San Rocco, Fort Tigne and Fort Campbell, whilst Fort St Elmo (an impressive 12 guns covering Valetta harbour) and Fort Ricasoli (six guns, also covering Valetta and Grand Harbour) housed quick-firing 6pdr guns. As with all of Malta's military structure, the Lascaris War

Rooms were the nerve centre for defence and offence, with dedicated sections such as the Anti-Aircraft Guns Operations Room and the Coast Defence Room. This underground facility was immune from air attack and as long as communication and information continued to flow it was capable of directing the defence of the island.

The infantry defence of Malta was outlined in a command document: "Beach posts continue to be fully manned by KOMR units whose primary role is to be fully alert at all times and to give the alarm of any landing from the sea, however, small. Secondary role is to resist such invasion to the last man and the last round. OPs at selected viewpoints all over the Island to be kept manned at all times to watch out for parachute attack. British Bns (or those parts not already committed to airfield defence) to be centrally placed on 'Action Station' to move towards any threat which may develop in their area. Troops allotted to the defence of airfields to patrol by night dispersal areas and groups of pens and to take immediate offensive action against raiders without waiting for elaborate counter-attack plans. In the kind of attack which is envisaged, time will be all important; a matter of 10 minutes one way or the other may decide the whole issue, and if sufficient of our aircraft were to become grounded in an hour's violent and confused fighting, the situation in this part of the Mediterranean might be very seriously affected."

Kesselring called a conference of his commanders to finalize the plans for the invasion of Malta; the air element was critical to the overall plan both in preparing the way, supporting the assault, and ensuring that the Royal Navy could not intervene. The overall strategy called for four phases:

Phase 1: Preparation through the neutralization of Malta's defence capability, especially the fighter force and air defence capability.

Phase 2: Air assault by paratroopers and gliders against key targets, especially the airfields

Phase 3: Amphibious assault and second element – air landing – of the air assault

Phase 4: Consolidation and final conquest

Concerns were once again expressed over the viability of the amphibious assault, given the lack of landing areas and the nature of the Maltese terrain; the air assault was expected to be costly, but its commanders were convinced that it was viable and that their forces could move from some of their landing areas to support the amphibious assault by neutralizing several key batteries. Overall, there was a sense of relief that at last the problem of Malta would be resolved.

After the conference the planning staffs finalized detailed plans and issued orders to the various units. Phase 1 was expected to last 10 days, during which all of Malta's airfields would be subjected to intensive bombing and strafing, day and night. This was considered very achievable, as the chance of Malta receiving any reinforcement of fighter aircraft was minimal; however, within the second part of this phase, days 6–10, the crews were to concentrate on aircraft on the ground and avoid damage to airfield surfaces. It was expected that the number of fighter aircraft would by then be minimal and the focus could switch to other air defence assets, especially anti-aircraft batteries and their control systems. This was also the period for intensive attacks on shore batteries and other ground defence locations, especially in the planned approach and landing areas. Phase 1 was scheduled to start on 15th August and the end of Phase 4 was scheduled for September – a total period of just over four weeks. It was also recognized that pressure would need to be put on Allied locations that might attempt to intervene, with the Royal Navy at Gibraltar and Alexandria being the key concerns. Pressure was put on the Vichy French to launch air attacks on Gibraltar, the few that had been made up to now – way back in 1940 – had been token and ineffective. To bolster this, the Ju88s of KG30 were sent to Oran, Meknes and Tafaroui. The primary targets were airfields and any shipping, the aim being to neutralize Gibraltar's ability to assist Malta. The Italian four-engined P108 bombers based on Sardinia with the 274th BGR (LR Bomber Squadron) were also assigned to the Gibraltar operations. The submarine cover off Gibraltar, and between Gibralter and Malta, was also to be increased in the days preceding Phase 2, as was the U-boat screen in the Atlantic area off Gibraltar.

The Axis anti-shipping squadrons, especially the torpedo-bombers, were positioned in Sardinia ready to attack any Allied naval operation. To cover the threat from the Navy at Alexandria, a similar strategy was adopted. The He111s of KG26 were alerted for two roles – attacks on the military installations in the Cairo and Alexandria area, and mining of the Suez Canal; once again, the intention was to prevent intervention with the Malta operation. Sea-mining, by submarine and aircraft, was to be increased in the period leading up to Phase 2, with key minefields kept active until Phase 4. The U-boat screen of Italian and

German submarines was increased. Finally, air units in North Africa were to intensify attacks on the Allied defences to suggest an imminent land assault. The fighter forces had also been strengthened, with the 109s of JG53 in Sicily (Catania, Comiso, Gela) being joined by JG77; between them they had an average of 200 serviceable fighters. The Italian contribution to the fighter force included the three Re2001 squadrons of 2 Gruppo on the island of Pantelleria, and the Mc202s of 7th Gruppo.

A British assessment on the risk of invasion had concluded that:

- Seaborne operations: Major naval units from Taranto destined to pick up and escort transports from other ports or harbours would require a minimum of 20 hours to effect the operation and appear off Malta. Destroyers from Syracuse, Augusta and Messina, and E-boats operating from any of the bases mentioned, for the purpose of landing small landing parties, could do so comfortably in the hours of darkness.

- Airborne operations – Invasion: If based on the Rome-Naples airfields (350–450 miles) and obliged to return thither for a second or third lift, Ju52 aircraft would be operating at extreme range with extra tanks and would be airborne 2½–3 hours each way. If towing gliders the speed would be reduced to approx. 100mph. Ju52s operating from any airfield in Western Sicily could reach Malta in less than 1½ hours and from SE Sicily in 1 hour. Gliders could be released 30 miles from Malta at 10,000ft under reasonably favourable conditions and reach this island in anything from 15 to 30 minutes according to the type used.

The study concluded that any such preparations would be quickly spotted by RAF reconnaissance, Malta warned, and intensive bombing of the airfields undertaken.

Meanwhile, Alanbrooke was in Cairo meeting with Auchinleck, in part to discuss the next strategic steps and in part to reflect Churchill's lack of confidence in the current commanders, especially Ritchie. After his initial meeting with the Auk, he joined him at a C-in-C's conference that included Tedder (air) and Cunningham (naval) to discuss priorities and needs, although this was to some extent courtesy and his real reason for the visit to Cairo became clear on 4th August when he proposed a number of command changes, most significantly that of Montgomery as new commander of the 8th Army. In his diary he noted: "I had been surprised that the Auk was prepared to accept Monty in command of 8th Army. I had expected some opposition, but I felt some serious doubts whether an Auk-Monty combination would work. I felt that the Auk would interfere too much with Monty, would ride him on too tight a rein, and would consequently be liable to put him out of his stride. As I was very anxious to put Monty in command of 8th Army, I felt this might necessitate moving the Auk to some other command." (*War Diaries.*) In the evening, Churchill addressed the commanders at the Embassy, reviewing the overall Middle East situation and stressing the importance of the planned Anglo-American landings and that there must be an offensive from Egypt to ensure German forces could not be switched. Auchinleck queried the timeline given by Churchill, stressing that his forces would not be ready, especially if a new commander was due to take over 8th Army.

Wednesday 15th August 1942 was the usual hot summer day on Malta and Sicily. Before dawn the groundcrews at airfields across Sicily and southern Italy had been preparing for a massive three-wave attack on Malta. Meanwhile on Malta's fighter bases, squadrons had been reporting their aircraft serviceability, which was never as high as Park would have liked. The Hal Far Hurricane units (185 and 229 Squadrons) reported a total of 15 serviceable on the morning of the 15th, with 1435 Flight reporting four Beaufighters ready for action, whilst the Ta Kali Spitfire Wing (249, 601 and 603 Squadrons) had 25 serviceable, and Luqa had 10 Spitfires (126 Squadron), and two Marylands and two Spitfires with 69 Sqn. The early morning Maryland recce by 69 Squadron had gone off as usual to check on the Italian ports for signs of convoy activity, whilst the unit sent a Spitfire recce to Sicily on the round robin of airfields. Recent photos had showed a build-up of aircraft in Sicily, including more Luftwaffe units.

The radar stations at Dingli (AMES 504) and Gozo (AMES 521) reported large raids building over Sicily and southern Italy but what they did not see until too late were the wave-top formations of Bf109s that were already inbound to Malta and approaching the coast. The German plan was for an initial fighter-bomber sweep at first light, followed by a second sweep 30-minutes later, just ahead of the first bombing wave. The targets for all three attacks were the airfields at Luqa, Ta Kali, Hal Far and Krendi. Although German and Italian Ju87 dive-bomber losses had been high, the Stuka (Picchiatello to the Italians) was considered key in the pinpoint dive-bombing that would be required in support of the invasion. Both Italian Ju87 units (96th and 97th Gruppo) took up residence on Sicily, where they were joined by StG3.

In the first attacks on 15th August, the 40 Bf109s approached Malta from the west, the first group passing north of the Dingli radar station, hugging the contours as they aimed towards Rabat, one formation sweeping left around the town and the other around the right, so that they hit Ta Kali from two directions. The second formation coasted in near Krendi, ignoring that airfield as they split and headed to Luqa and Hal Far. With little warning, the anti-aircraft guns had no chance of reacting to the first runs, as the fighters searched out aircraft in their pens, strafing aircraft, vehicles and personnel.

At Ta Kali several Spitfires were claimed as damaged, and a few vehicles were hit; as quickly as they had appeared, the 109s had gone, exiting south and running out over Krendi, strafing any activity they saw on the airfield. One fighter was lost to anti-aircraft fire and one was seen to clip a wall with its wingtip and spiral in with no chance of the pilot escaping. At Luqa it was a similar story, a number of aircraft claimed as damaged, one Maryland destroyed, and various buildings strafed. The stone pens in which aircraft where tucked away made it difficult for the attackers. Running out over Safi, along the line of the taxi-way that joined the airfields to Luqa, the fighters continued to strafe any suitable targets, albeit with little result. The second group ran over Hal Far from west to east, catching two Hurricanes being towed and claiming them both as destroyed. Two 109s were claimed by the defenders, although one of these was only damaged and made it back to Sicily.

Within minutes the attack was over; little damage had been done on Malta, but the Lascaris War Room was now alert to more raids, with radar reports of groups forming up over Sicily and Southern Italy. The Spitfire and Hurricane squadrons were duly alerted, and the decision taken to operate standing patrols in a blocking line to the north and east of the airfields, as there was no chance for aircraft to scramble and influence the outcome of an attack. The existing fighter plan had called for the squadron on standby to be airborne within two minutes and the immediate readiness squadron to be off in three minutes, but even this assumed some notice. The plan was therefore changed to have two sections of four aircraft on standing patrol "whenever an attack is expected", with the remainder of the standby squadron on two minutes and the immediate readiness squadron on three minutes. Any standing patrol was potentially wasting Malta's precious aviation fuel, and this operational plan could not be maintained for long.

Four Hurricanes of 185 Squadron were airborne from Hal Far 30 minutes after the all clear had been sounded from the first attack; two climbed to 2,000ft and two to 10,000ft and positioned themselves on patrol lines just off the east coast, while four Spitfires of 249 Squadron from Ta Kali took up similar stations to the NE. The remaining immediate readiness aircraft of both squadrons were at two minutes, and at Luqa 126 Squadron was at immediate readiness. Sector Control passed the news that enemy formations were building over Sicily, and that low-level targets had been intermittently seen heading south from Sicily. Plt Off Jones was leading the low pair of 249 Squadron and picked up a number of 109s heading towards the coast but was not able to tell how many. Having called the tally, he led his wingman in an arcing intercept of the left-hand fighter he had seen. Meanwhile, the high pair had also picked up the attackers, and having determined there was no high cover, they too dropped into the fight. Jones positioned his chosen victim, closed the range and fired a two-second burst, seeing strikes in the area of the cockpit and engine. The 109 immediately flipped over and went into the sea. Turning his attention to the next 109, it was now clear the fight was on, as the enemy fighters were manoeuvring. A quick glance showed his No.2 was still present and his tail seemed clear. A quick burst as his target pulled a tight turn and he was on the receiving end, as shells passed over his starboard wing. Pulling hard he saw two 109s behind him and no sign of his wingman. By this time the other Spitfires had joined in, but it was an uneven contest, as they were engaged with eight 109s.

Meanwhile, the Hurricanes of 185 Squadron had been vectored to intercept another formation. This turned out to be a formation of Ju88s with a 109 escort; the first pair executed a head-on attack on the Ju88s, causing the formation to break but with no apparent result. By then the escort was on them and as one pilot recalled; "It always used to be said that if you could actually recognize a 109 in the mirror, it was too late. Now, I could identify not one but four of them in line astern, coming in from five o'clock and a little aft in a fast curving arc. As I whipped my aircraft into a tight diving turn towards the attack, a salvo of 20mm cannon shells hammered into my starboard wing. Flames started to lick the engine cowlings and it was clearly time to get out!" Having baled out successfully, he was picked up by one of Malta's HSLs (High Speed Launches).

As the Spitfires of 249 were engaged with their groups of 109s, others from that formation swept on to their targets, catching a number of

Spitfires in the act of scrambling from Ta Kali; the first two aircraft were airborne and turning when the attackers appeared, but one was immediately engaged and shot down, whilst two others were destroyed on the ground. As with the first raid, the 109s strafed anything that moved and any aircraft they saw. At Luqa the Ju88s ran in sprinkling small calibre bombs across large parts of the airfield, the aim being to disrupt the airfield's operational capability. The fighters strafed any suitable target of opportunity. Other formations attacked the other RAF airfields, causing minimal damage and casualties.

By now, the first main raid of the day was inbound, and was estimated at 100+ aircraft in two groups. With 185 and 240 squadrons back on the ground from their previous action, the scramble against this raid consisted of the Hurricanes of 126 Squadron and Spitfires of 610 Squadron, with 603 Squadron being moved to immediate readiness. Whilst the Spitfires climbed for height – or as much as they could get with the notice they had – the Hurricanes positioned at 12,000ft; each squadron had sent 12 aircraft and it was not long before they were engaged. The first group of Ju88s was seen at 15,000ft, and seemed to be heading for Luqa; they had a close escort of Italian Re2001 fighters, and there was a top cover of a "large number" of 109s. The weight of this attack, and that of the other similar bomber formation, was on the three main airfields – Ta Kali, Luqa and Hal Far – and all suffered damage and some casualties. In the air combat, three Hurricanes and two Spitfires were lost, with three pilots safe, with claims made for six German aircraft (two Ju88s and four 109s) and two Re2001s. A final daytime raid appeared a few hours later, and this time it included formations of escorted Ju87s attacking the radar stations at Dingli, Ghar Lapsi, Ta Silich and Gozo; some damage was caused at all the locations, with Gozo (AMES 521) being off air for the rest of the day. One Ju87 was lost. The other formation focused on Ta Kali, where additional damage was caused, including the destruction of one Spitfire and damage to a number of others. As darkness fell, the final raid of the day was made by Italian bombers, the target being Grand Harbour. It had not been a good day for Malta's defenders; not only was the scoreboard against them but the number of damaged aircraft meant that groundcrew would have to work hard to produce a reasonable number of serviceable aircraft for the following day.

The next two days were similar and even though the defenders could see the pattern there was little they could do about it; to put more aircraft on standing patrols would burn up more fuel and wear aircraft and pilots out more quickly. The anti-aircraft defences were also using up ammunition at an excessive rate and scoring few successes. As August 18th dawned, Malta had a total of 70 serviceable fighters, including six Beaufighters of 1435 Flight, which were kept for night operations. The squadrons had no shortage of pilots and no shortage of ammunition; the shortage was spares and aviation fuel. A submarine had arrived overnight with a number of critical spares for the fighters, and this was for now the only way that such critical items could be reliably delivered, although on a small scale. The submarine also took out of Malta a number of bomber and torpedo-bomber aircrew that were "surplus to requirements" as, for now, Malta was on a purely defensive basis. By the end of the day the defenders had lost four more aircraft, with several others damaged, two of which became sources of spares as they were declared not worth repairing. Tedder at HQ RAF Middle East sent a Most Immediate signal to the Air Ministry: "Request advise what are immediate prospects further deliveries of Spitfires to Malta. Would urge supreme importance of achieving further big delivery of Spitfires. I cannot make good from here any of fighter wastage incurred at Malta."

The response was not promising: "In view of the great commitment involved in the operations necessary to supply Malta with Spitfires must warn you of need for conserving Spitfires consistent with the vital operational needs of Malta. Malta should avoid as far as possible accumulation of unserviceable Spitfires firstly by concentrating on keeping serviceable those Spitfires which require least repair work, secondly by attempting to fly to Egypt those which require considerable repair, but which can be made airworthy for flight. By this means damage to these aircraft would be avoided and a reserve of serviceable Spitfires would be built up in Egypt on which Malta could subsequently draw." With Rommel having pushed the Allies back into Egypt, there were no airfields in North Africa that could be used as staging points for aircraft from Egypt to Malta. The Spitfire V with a long-range 90-gallon jettisonable tank had a maximum range of around 1,000 miles if the tank was jettisoned once empty, so in theory aircraft could make the trip – but with no margin of error – it also meant arming only some of the guns and with a minimum of ammunition for self-defence. Tedder discussed with Park the possibility of replacement Spitfires from Egypt, and the option of sending more Beaufighters.

August 19th was a better day in that only two aircraft were lost, and thanks to the work of the groundcrew, the number of serviceable aircraft actually increased. The bad news was that the Stukas had continued to focus on the radar sites and by the end of the day, three were badly damaged. The anti-aircraft artillery had claimed four enemy bombers, but the ammunition expenditure had once more been high, and orders were received to reduce the rates of fire. Although the risks were high, the decision was taken for the fast minelayer HMS *Welshman* to make a solo run from Alexandria to Malta with a mixed cargo of aviation POL and anti-aircraft ammunition. The tactic had worked before and the ship left Alexandria at last light on the 19th; passing bomb alley, south of Crete, she was spotted by a reconnaissance aircraft which shadowed her at a distance. A formation of SM79 torpedo bombers duly appeared but *Welshman* was able to defend herself, claiming two of the attackers and avoiding the torpedoes that had been launched. However, she was also being tracked by *U-617* and not long after the aircraft attacks she fell victim to the submarine, being critically damaged. The crew escaped to the boats and the ship was scuttled.

One of the major concerns for the invasion planners was the reaction of the Royal Navy; with strong forces in Alexandria and Gibraltar, the potential for the Royal Navy to critically interfere with the landing operations had to be taken into consideration. The intense battles around the Pedestal convoy had heavily damaged the carrier *Indomitable* and caused the loss of a number of combat ships, reducing the Gibraltar fleet combat capability. On the plus side, some Italian ships had been sunk (heavy cruiser *Bolzano*) or damaged (light cruiser *Attendolo*) by the submarine *Unbroken*. As C-in-C Mediterranean Fleet since April 1942, Admiral Sir Henry Harwood had difficult choices to make. Unlike his predecessor, the aggressive Nelson-like Admiral Sir Andrew Cunningham, Harwood, a favourite of Churchill's, had less operational experience, having spent the previous two years in staff appointments, although before that he had led the cruiser squadron that hunted down the *Graf Spee*. Since the outbreak of the war, the Royal Navy had achieved a morale superiority over the Italian Navy, whose senior commanders were invariably "less than enthusiastic" joining in combat with their opponents. They were especially wary of any night combat, as the Allied superiority in such warfare had been clearly demonstrated at the Battle of Cape Matapan in March 1941, the night action causing no damage to the British but significant loss to the Italians. Despite the Italian lack of radar and night capability, the Navy had made little progress in fitting appropriate equipment. It was also noted, though, that Cunningham had not remained on station to follow-up on his victory, as he did not want to be exposed in daylight to the Axis air strength. Both sides therefore faced a dilemma; for the Italians it was how to protect the invasion fleet and for the British it was how to intervene but not suffer the same losses to aircraft that had happened around Crete.

As it became increasingly clear that Malta was under threat of assault, and that air assault would play a major role, infantry units and anti-aircraft units were moved around, in part to provide more fire-power covering the airfields, as these would inevitably be primary targets for the air assault, as they had been in Crete. Nevertheless, with limited supplies of ammunition and medium weapons, the defenders still had limitations and the decision was taken to rely on mobile combat groups rather than entrenched positions.

In London it was clear from ULTRA intercepts and other intelligence that an invasion of Malta would take place in the second half of August; it was also clear that the only force capable of influencing the outcome was the Royal Navy, although reliance was also placed on strategic bombing of the invasion ports and airfields. Churchill was adamant that no risk was too great to preserve Malta and he applied pressure on the Chiefs of Staff to take appropriate action. The loss of air bases in North Africa and the fact that Malta's air strength was reduced to fighter self-defence meant that there were few Allied land-based aircraft able to reach the Malta combat area. As Malta was no longer able to attack the Axis airfields and ports, the strategic bombing forces were increasingly tasked against these targets. The squadrons of No.205 Group had been the main strategic bombing force and had been kept busy attacking a wide range of targets, but especially ports and airfields; with the retreat into Egypt they had moved into airfields in the Canal Zone, which meant the Wellingtons had limited range having lost their forward airfields. The Group had been joined by two B-24 Liberator units, 159 and 160 Squadrons, which had originally been intended for the Far East but were retained in the Middle East. They were soon joined by American strategic bombers.

With the loss of Malta's air striking power, and the clear evidence of build-up of air and naval forces in Sicily and Italy, the decision was taken to undertake an intensive bombing campaign from the Middle East and England, using RAF and USAAF heavy bombers. It had been a long time since Bomber Command had mounted a major raid on Italy, such as that by 76 bombers to Turin on 10/11 September 1941, and since Harris had taken over as C-in-C in February 1942 he had focused his increasing bomber strength against German cities and industry. The directive from the Air Ministry for an Italian campaign was not well received, especially as in June Harris had mounted his Thousand Bomber raids to demonstrate the potential of his Command for concentrated and consistent bomber ops. Nevertheless, such a campaign was put in place to commence in mid-July with a series of attacks on the ports at Genoa, La Spezia and Naples. Airfield and port targets in Sicily and southern Italy were assigned to No.205 Group and the Americans.

The 2nd Battalion of the Devonshire Regiment had been part of the Malta garrison since 1939 and was part of 1 (Malta) Brigade from July 1942; in addition to their role in defending coastal districts and airfields against attack, the Brigade's units also contributed to the building of aircraft pens, repairing bomb damage, and manning AA guns. There was now an increased emphasis on inspecting the anti-invasion defences and procedures, and the British and Maltese units took part in various exercises, although ammunition for live-firing was restricted. The AA units, were of course, in constant practice, but for the coastal guns and for units holding static defence positions, as well as the "mobile" forces, there were scenarios for air assault and sea assault. As with the other infantry units, 2 Devons also shared the privations of the Maltese people and spent much of their time clearing up bomb damage, not only for military infrastructure but also reported to help with the civilian infrastructure particularly around Valetta.

Assault: 20th August 1942

The first wave of Italian paratroopers left their bases in southern Italy in the early hours of 20th August 1942, whilst a short time later the mass of Ju52s in Sicily was airborne with the men and equipment of the 1st Parachute Division, accompanied by gliders towed behind He111s. It was an average of 200 miles for the Italian formations and 140 miles for the Germans, and the plan was for both formations to arrive over their targets around 0630; this meant that forming up in darkness was a challenge although they had been practising for weeks, but it would deliver the troops in the early daylight hours that would give them the best chance of successful landing in the difficult Malta terrain and for them to seize their initial objectives by the end of the day. The air formations were escorted by fighters, although the threat of fighter interception was considered minimal and most fighter effort had been assigned to a dawn attack on the landing zones, in which Ju88s and Ju87s would target known strong points and AA defences. In the Lascaris War Room it was clear from the intelligence reports and radar plots that the enemy forces were massing for an assault on Malta; this had been expected for some days, as signals intercepts from both Italian naval codes and ULTRA had revealed the scale of the build-up and the general timescale. As usual, additional reconnais-sance sorties had been mounted to try to mask the source of Allied intelligence, although this had become increasingly difficult in the face of the attacks on Malta's airfields: 69 Squadron Spitfires had flown regular missions over Sicily, whilst the Marylands covered areas of interest in Italy. It had cost the Squadron three aircraft in a four-day period, but it had been vital work.

At around 0600, the first waves of fighters and bombers appeared over Malta; Hurricanes and Spitfires had been scrambled some minutes before but were overwhelmed by the scale of the attack. A mixed force of eight Hurricanes from 126 and 185 Squadrons picked up a Ju88 for-mation with its escort of 109s and in the ensuing combats claimed two bombers and a fighter for the loss of three of their own aircraft. The Spitfires of 601 and 603 Squadrons were up from Ta Kali just before their airfield was hit, and they too were soon in a one-sided contest, although they were able to bounce a formation of Ju87s, claiming three before the escort joined in. Of the ten Spitfires that were airborne, five were shot down. Whilst the combats were underway, those enemy aircraft not engaged had pressed on to their targets. At Ta Kali, the Ju87s targeted AA defence positions, supported by fighter strafing, whilst the fighters also strafed targets of opportunity such as vehicles and aircraft. At Luqa, and Hal Far it was a similar story, but with Ju88s in the bombing role. The airfields at Safi and Krendi were also targeted, whilst other formations of dive-bombers took on the radar stations, causing extensive damage.

As the surviving RAF fighters landed and taxied back to their pens, another wave of fighters appeared over the airfields and at around the same time the first German paratroopers were tumbling out over Ta Kali and Luqa. According to one report: "They were dropped from about a height of 200ft, the parachute appearing to have some special device for making it open rapidly as small puffs of smoke or white powder were seen above the top of each parachute as it opened. In most cases each parachutist had one or two parachutes accompanying

lots of 2 Squadron SAAF discuss the next support mission.

auforts of 39 Squadron at Gianaclis; the anti-shipping squadrons needed to be based close to
e coast.

Allied aircraft destroyed on the ground at Sidi Barrani – air power played a key role in the desert war.

The Ju87 Stuka initially caused fear amongst Allied ground forces, but with the increase in Allied fighter cover the dive-bombers proved vulnerable.

Lack of roads and long distances impacted the way the desert war was fought.

Admiral Sir Andrew Cunningham was a dynamic and aggressive leader of the British Mediterranean strategy.

British artillery, especially the 25-pdr, played a significant role in all the desert battles.

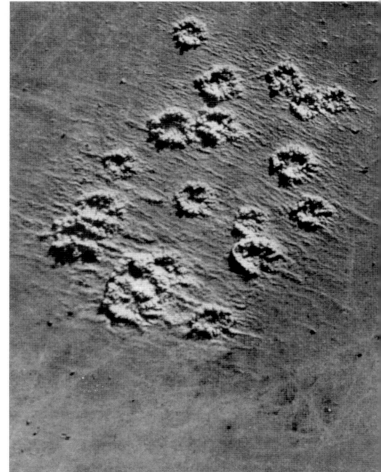

Allied bombers attacking dispersed enemy Motor Transport, a difficult target as the chance of a hit was low, but the overall disruption was significant.

German. Tank.
Desert 1.9.4.2.

the early period of the conflict, German armour – tanks and self-propelled guns – was superior to at used by the Allies, as was their tactical employment.

llied pilots checking map of their patrol area.

The Luftwaffe duo – Ju87 and Bf109.

Malta was considered a strategic key in the overall campaign, primarily as an air base from which to interdict Axis supply routes. This 1960s shot still shows the wartime airfields, although most of the runway structure is post-war. The island in the distance is Gozo.

ibraltar was a key naval and air base within the Allied strategy, supporting Malta and the
iddle East.

Hurricanes of 261 Squadron were part of the air defence of Malta.

The delivery of Hurricanes and Spitfires to Malta by carrier was crucial, and the loss of carriers and their cargo impacted Malta's ability to defend itself.

Kali, one of Malta's main airfields, looking heavily damaged. Intense air attacks brought Malta's operations to a halt and paved the way for invasion.

Malta landscape; air assault on the rocky terrain of Malta was risky and relied on taking the airfield sites.

Operation TORCH involved convoys assaulting three landing areas.

neral Patton, commander of US II Corps, aboard ship prior to the invasion.

rman Tiger tank; the appearance of these powerful and almost invulnerable tanks was a major
ck to the Allies.

Bostons over Tunisia; the medium bombers provided support for ground operations.

As part of the Race to Tunis, Allied forces landed at Bône harbour.

tish 6-pdr anti-tank gun in position near Tebourba.

servation post in the mountains of Tunisia; the terrain played a major role in tactical operations.

Hurricanes of 253 Squadron over exotic North Africa; the Arabs were familiar with invaders who came and went and were quick to adapt to changing situations.

General Alexander briefing correspondents on the situation in Tunisia.

ontgomery consults with Horrocks and other commanders.

itish infantry dug-in, with a Bren ready to counter air attack.

The desert was a harsh combat environment; British tank commander catching up on paperwork.

German assault on the defences of Tobruk.

him carrying machine guns and ammunition. The enemy were therefore able to produce intensive MG fire within about two minutes after the parachutists had been dropped. Hitherto most of us have expected our anti-parachutist detachments would be able to shoot up parachutist detachments at leisure as they dropped from a height." One problem with this technique was the large number of injuries, and some fatalities, during training. That expectation was also a concern for the attackers, as it had been the case during the Crete drop that a large number of paratroopers had become casualties very quickly in the face of well-positioned and determined defenders. However, in this instance the Germans had far better intelligence on the defences, unlike the more fluid situation with Crete, and they had adapted their tactics to minimize some of those risks. Furthermore, although Malta had a reasonably strong garrison, it had numerous threat areas to cover, the communication along the lanes of Malta would be slow, and the Battalions had been on garrison duty and most soldiers and commanders had little actual battle experience.

As the units of the 1st Regiment hit the ground they were engaged by small arms and machine-gun fire, but less concentrated and effective than they had expected. Battle formations formed up and within minutes machine-gun sections were engaging the defenders, enabling the combat units to move towards their objectives. The drop had been extensive across Ta Kali, to ensure that enough effective units were on the ground to secure the landing areas for the gliders of the follow-on wave. There had been little anti-aircraft fire as the first wave approached, but it was still important for the known AA gun positions on the north and west sides of Ta Kali, to ensure that the second wave, and the vulnerable gliders, would face a minimal threat. Within the first hour enough men of 1st Regiment had grouped and were able to secure half of the airfield, but opposition was increasing and there were a few pockets of resistance taking advantage of the numerous stone aircraft pens as 'strongpoints'. It would be another two hours before the scattered forces were fully in action.

Meanwhile, it was a similar situation at Luqa, although two Ju52s had collided and crashed before the drop zone, and AA fire here was more intense. The men of the 2nd Regiment were soon in action and driving the defenders off the western side of the airfield. A combat unit had also dropped near the radar station at Tas Salvatur, quickly overwhelming the poorly-equipped defenders. One paratrooper later recalled: "I was sure when we jumped we would have only infantry to deal with. My first surprise was to be greeted by a number of Bren carriers.'' The Bren carriers were on the airfield as utility vehicles to push aircraft off runways to avoid them being blocked, but with the invasion alert they had been returned to their original function and caused difficulties for the lightly-armed paratroopers. However, this was a temporary setback as the attackers were in too great a number and had control of too large an area for the small number of Bren carriers to have much impact. The defending British Battalion was thinly spread and called for the reserve Battalion that had been assigned to support against air assault. They also called for artillery support, but the guns were short of ammunition and were only able to fire limited shots.

The third assault formation, comprising the 3rd Regiment of 1st Parachute Division and elements of the Italian 184th Division, had Krendi and Hal Far as their objectives, as well as the coastal guns and defence positions overlooking the planned sea assault area on the coast near Krendi. The Italians dropped at Hal Far and the Germans at Krendi, the latter also aiming to link up with their colleagues at Luqa. The radar station at Lapsi, on the coast near Krendi, was quickly taken and the attackers established a blocking position overlooking the road running from Ix-Xaqqa to Krendi, with other combat units pushing south-east along the cliff tops towards the harbour of Wied iz-Zurrieq, a distance of just over two miles. The plan was for the Italians to capture Hal Far, set up a blocking position at Birzebbuga and also push west to join up with the 3rd Regiment at Blue Grotto bay. Once again, the initial assault went well, although some paratroopers were lost when they were despatched too early, falling into the sea close to cliffs at Hal Far. The airfield defence battalion was initially thrown into confusion but was able to regroup and establish a defence line on the eastern edge of the airfield, calling on reinforcements from the forces around Marsaxlokk.

In the Lascaris War Room confusion reigned; the scale of the air assault and the number of locations that were reporting attacks, including areas in the north, such as St Paul's Bay and the Baida Ridge where no attacks were underway, meant that decisive action in one area would produce crisis in another. The Mobile Reserve, 1st Durham Light Infantry, at Gebel Ciantor was well-placed to intervene at Luqa or Krendi, and they were ordered to move towards Luqa, whilst leaving a defending force to protect nearly Dingli. The Battalion was underway within minutes of receiving its orders and heading down the road towards Siggiewi, from where it could deploy towards Luqa or Krendi. The advance units, bicycle mounted, quickly occupied the village, but immediately came under machine-gun fire from the German blocking force near Tas Salvatur.

With attackers and defenders engaged at numerous locations, the land battle would inevitably turn in favour of the more numerous and better-armed defenders in a short space of time. Casualties amongst the paratroopers mounted, and at Ta Kali they were driven back from the south-east corner of the airfield by a counter attack supported by two tanks. However, having exposed themselves the tanks became a prime target for German air attack, and were soon destroyed by Ju87s. The Stukas were active across all the battle areas, providing the aerial artillery to break up any attempted counter-attacks. They also caught parts of the DLI as they headed towards Siggiewi. The area was also alive with 109s, who also strafed troops and defensive positions. The German planners had realized that the second wave of air-drop and glider troops had to follow-up as quickly as possible, whilst balancing the time taken for the first wave to secure areas of the airfields on which gliders could safely put down, as these were the only areas on Malta that glider landings were possible. All airborne ops carried a high risk, and unlike with Crete, where the air landing by glider had been the first wave, they were now coming in to landing zones that hopefully had been secured.

As the 109s cleared the landing zone, they were closely followed in by the first wave of assault gliders, which had been launched from 10,000ft some miles off the coast. The bulk of the gliders were DFS230s, towed by Ju52s and the formations had been established to ensure the best concentration on the ground – some carried nine riflemen, making ten in total when the glider pilot became an infantry soldier, whilst others had either a machine-gun or mortar crew in addition to a smaller number of riflemen. The mortars were crucial weapons to get into action as quickly as possible, as these provided an important addition to the firepower of the combat units. The gliders were able to stop in 20–30 yards and their well-trained occupants could disgorge and be in action within minutes. At Ta Kali the airfield area secured by the previous wave was soon dotted with gliders; some had been engaged by the defenders' machine-guns, and more British (and Maltese) artillery units were coming into play. Whilst the overall situation still looked reasonable, it was still a dangerous time for the attackers and it was essential that they pushed on as quickly as possible; it was also clear that the village of Rabat, almost on the edge of the airfield, was becoming a strongpoint for the defenders, whilst the high ground beyond the village was being used by artillery. The village had been occupied by the 8th Manchesters, supported by three tanks and a battery of 25-pounders, with orders to advance and recapture the airfield. However, the threat had been recognized and a concentrated dive-bombing attack by Ju87s was delivered which disorganized the build-up for the counter-attack, destroying many buildings in the ancient town of Rabat, and causing heavy civilian casualties.

The landings at Luqa had gone well, although one area of the landing zone was brought under artillery fire and several gliders were destroyed – but not enough to influence the overall flow of reinforcements. With the additional men and more support weapons (machine guns and mortars), the German combat units advanced across the airfield and towards the village of Luqa, which was their second objective and where they were to establish a blocking line. Casualties were generally low, as the defenders gave ground and retreated towards the Malta Sports Club race course, where an interim defence line for Valetta had been established and was occupied by the 2nd Queen's Own Battalion and the 3rd King's Own Malta Regiment. RAF personnel on Luqa had been ordered to destroy aircraft and stores as they retreated and had joined the defence line at the racecourse. Major van der Heydte, commander of the 2nd Battalion of the 4th Parachute Regiment, had landed in the second wave at Luqa and took command of the left flank of the advance. Having been part of the Crete operation, he was fully aware of the dangers of allowing the defenders time to recover and regroup – what was needed was constant pressure, keeping the enemy on the back foot. Under cover of a mortar barrage, his men rushed forward, establishing new firing positions with their machine-gun sections to disrupt any attempt at resistance; at one point his command unit became isolated and was in danger of being overrun, but reinforcements arrived, and his attackers were themselves captured. After some heavy fighting on the eastern edge of the airfield, his advanced troops moved into Luqa village, which they found was deserted. Setting up strong defensive positions, they sent patrols south towards Tas Salib and Gudja.

Even with the additional forces from this second wave, the situation at Ta Kali and Luqa was not yet secure for the Germans, as a concerted British push to Siggiewi and Zebbug would enable the British to hold a central position between the two airfields and threaten to overwhelm and defeat the attack on Ta Kali. This would require decisive action by the commanders and in the confused battle that had been developing across much of Malta, there was a lack of clear decision-making at Lascaris; too many conflicting reports, and too much uncertainty as to likely development meant that no decisive orders were sent to the Battalions that were not yet engaged. The Italian second wave to Hal Far comprised the La Spezia Division's 125th and 126th Regiments and the 39th Bersaglieri, all of whom were air landed, with the transports being preceded by and escorted by dive-bombers and fighters. The first wave troops had secured the western half of Hal Far, providing the transports with good landing runs, although the runways were under artillery fire. Despite this fire, most transports and gliders landed without incident, albeit not always in their designated zones, which meant some mixing-up of units. The 125th was sent to drive the advance to the east, to secure the rest of the airfield and then move on to Birzebbuga, whilst the 126th and 39th were assigned the task of moving towards the Blue Grotto to link up with the German forces from Krendi. This left the important task of advancing along the link taxiway to Safi to the 184th's paratroopers and to secure the coastal areas on which the seaborne landings were due the following day.

The advance west met with little resistance until the Italians neared Zurrieq, where they ran into well sited machine guns supported by artillery. Whilst the 126th deployed to advance direct on the village, the 39th swung south to outflank the position. By the end of the day the Italians had secured the village and linked up with the Germans at the Blue Grotto. By the evening of the 20th, the Axis forces were well established and had seized most of their objectives; casualties had generally been light and at his command HQ in Sicily, Student was in general pleased with the progress made. His reserve force of paratroopers, along with his command HQ and a second airlift that would include the small number of Me323s with armoured vehicles, was scheduled for early on the 16th. The risk was overnight; the defenders could still, with decisive action, drive the attackers away from one or more objectives; his main fear was that the British would overwhelm Luqa and thus drive a wedge between the forces at Ta Kali, which would be isolated, and those at Hal Far. This very option was being debated by Gort and his land commanders; they still had several fresh Battalions, especially in the north of the island, that could be used for such a counter-stroke, but it would need to be delivered under cover of darkness because of the enemy air superiority. There was also concern that a further landing might be made in this area.

The Germans and Italians consolidated their positions overnight, waiting for dawn and the seaborne landing and the third and final air landing operation. Overnight the bombers were active over Valetta, with the dual aim of keeping the defenders occupied and continuing to provide a level of uncertainty as to the next offensive moves. As part of the Axis deception plan, targets around Mellieh Bay and St Paul's Bay on the northern side of the island were attacked, to suggest that this might be one of the sea assault areas and thus keep defenders looking this way and not re-positioning south of the old Victoria Lines. Indeed, one invasion fleet was moving in that general direction, but its target was Gozo, where the Superga Division of XVI Corps was to go ashore. It had been spotted by a Sunderland operating from Alexandria, which had reported its position, course and composition. The convoy was still under air cover provided by 110s and the Sunderland was engaged and damaged but managed to escape.

Meanwhile, the main fleet, with its extensive escort screen was moving into position east of Malta. It had been picked up by a screening British submarine, which was tasked to track and report the fleet and, once closer to Malta and if opportunity arose, to attack the largest troopship that presented itself. A number of other submarines from the 10th Submarine Flotilla were also in the area; as Malta's Manoel Island (HMS *Talbot*, opposite Sliema) had been the Flotilla's base until the heavy air bombardment caused them to move out; they were keen to contribute to Malta's defence. HMS *Thrasher* and HMS *Utmost* were stationed to the north-east of Malta and as reports of the invasion convoy were received they manoeuvred for a moonlight attack. Under the command of Lt Cdr Hugh Mackenzie, *Thrasher* had been very active in summer 1942, claiming a number of successes, the most recent being on 29th June when she sank the Italian sloop *Diana*. In the early hours of 16th August, Mackenzie, having slipped past behind a destroyer, lined up on a merchant ship. The log recorded: "0355 fired three torpedoes from the stern tubes at the merchant vessel, that was estimated to be of about 5,000 tons, from 2,000 yards. Two hits were obtained. 0400 – retired to the Northward, destroyers carried out a search. One passed overhead but failed to gain contact and no depth charges were dropped." His victim was the 1,589-ton *Padenna* and she was soon listing and doomed, although able to launch her boats. At around the same time, the destroyer escort on the other side of the convoy picked up a contact and launched depth charges; this was HMS *Unseen*, under the command of Lt Anthony Langridge, which was trying to break through the escort screen. Although able to avoid the escorts, she was chased away and unable to make an attack.

The first Italians were already ashore, detachments of FNS units having been dropped off by submarine and light craft near the Famagosta Beach (main landing area) and Larnaca (Marsaxlokk Bay) landing sites, and the Cipro (Gozo) landing site. The main effort at the Famagosta site was scaling the cliffs, which was achieved with little difficulty and no opposition. Reaching the top of the cliffs the combat units headed for their objectives. They overran several defensive points before the alert was given, but at Ras il-Bajtar they ran into a strongly held position and were held up. The defenders were part of 2nd KOMR and in accordance with their orders they reported the incursion and then held their ground.

The key position along this stretch was Fort Benghisa; this medieval strongpoint guarding the Bay had always been an important part of Malta's defence, and it now housed the coastal guns of 10th Heavy Battery RA; it also housed AA guns. With the airborne assault at nearby Hal Far, the fort's defenders were expecting an attack. They had been subject to dive-bomb attack in recent days, albeit with little effect as the fort's ancient walls and more recent reinforcement made them difficult targets. Nevertheless, they were fairly isolated and other than a few pill-box positions there was not an interlocked defence system in this area. The fort was a key objective for the commandos and they were able to breach the outer barbed wire without being detected. The attackers had excellent intelligence on the layout and garrison of the fort and were able to focus their attention on the key points to ensure local superiority. Making extensive use of grenades to create confusion and clear likely defence spots, the commandos made steady progress and within an hour had secured the fort. Having seized the fort, the Italians were able to link up with the airborne forces in the area of the Blue Grotto. The FNS units that went ashore in Marsaxlokk Bay had Kalafrana and the area from Benghisa Point to Pretty Bay (Birzebbuga) as their objectives, which included having to clear underwater obstacles and defences. RAF and Navy personnel had been evacuated from the Kalafrana base, but it had been handed to elements of 2nd KOMR along with a detachment of the 1st Lancashire Fusiliers; a number of mobile Bofors guns had also been moved to the area. Some Italian commandos scaled the cliffs at Benghisa Point whilst others took their assault boats into Pretty Bay, routes through the cleared underwater obstacles having been marked. Reaching the top of the cliffs, the commandos quickly secured the area and moved towards Kalafrana. Meanwhile, the landing at Pretty Bay was coming under intense fire and casualties were mounting. Lightly armed, the commandos advancing from Benghisa could do little to help their colleagues, and there was no opportunity for the Marine Light Infantry to land in the face of the defensive fire; for now, this assault was stalled.

The British had been considering their naval options to support Malta, but in the absence of air cover it was risky. The Gibraltar force now had only one carrier, HMS *Furious*, which meant that air cover would be minimal even if she embarked all the designated Fulmar and Sea Hurricane squadrons. Even the main combat strength of Force H had been depleted with ships removed for other tasks. There was the added problem of the build-up for the planned Allied assault on North Africa and any diversion of effort to Malta or significant ship loss would impact that operation, an operation that had deep political as well as military overtones. This left only the Alexandria force. The loss the previous December of two of the main capital ships, the battle-ships *Valiant* and *Queen Elizabeth*, both of which were damaged in the daring raid by Italian manned torpedo crews, had seriously weakened the fleet. To send a cruiser and destroyer force would be a risk, but it was determined that a force should set out – the main question was when, as it had to minimize the air risk whilst putting the ships in a position to defeat any blocking force and engage the invasion convoy. Calculating that the invasion fleet would approach from the north of Malta towards the most likely landing beaches, and based on the Axis air threat, the strategy was for the cruiser and destroyer force to approach from the east under cover of darkness with the aim of picking up the convoy on radar and thus achieving a tactical advantage. This would mean moving through 'Bomb Alley' between Crete and North Africa in daylight, and having to fight off determined air attack. The best the RAF could do was to provide Beaufighter escort for part of the way, and to undertake a bombing campaign against the main threat airfields. The fleet would also be shadowed by Sunderland flying boats and a force of RAF and USAAF heavy bombers preceding the fleet, being guided to the enemy convoy by ASV Wellingtons. A force of torpedo-armed Beauforts and Wellingtons was on standby to launch anti-shipping strikes.

The Italian Battle Fleet centred around the battleships *Littorio* and *V.Veneto* with associated cruisers and destroyers set out from Naples, being joined by units out of Augusta, to take up a blocking position on the likely passage from Alexandria to Malta, whilst remaining in range of air cover. Further out was a screen of German and Italian submarines. This meant that any fleet from Alexandria would run a gauntlet of submarines and air assault before finally coming up against the Italian Battle Fleet. An Italian submarine reported the departure of the British fleet from Alexandria, and with the time, course and composition known, the Axis planners prepared the air response. The anti-submarine sweep by RAF aircraft had picked up two submarines, one of which they attacked and forced to the surface, where it was rammed and sunk. However, with the Germans holding most of the North African coastal airfields, it was not long before the ships were under air attack. With the Beaufighters still present, the ships had some cover, but the AA cruisers were kept busy and were expending ammunition at an alarming rate. The first wave of dive bombers caused no significant damage, whilst the defenders claimed four enemy aircraft, two falling to Beaufighters. With the departure of the Beaufighters, the fleet was now more exposed, and was soon under attack once more, by aircraft from bases in Crete and North Africa, including dive-bomber and torpedo-bomber attacks. The light cruiser HMS *Coventry* was attacked by Ju88s and was hit a number of times, catching fire; once the surviving crew had been evacuated, the ship was sunk by HMS *Zulu*. Around the same time, another cruiser, HMS *Manchester*, was hit by two torpedoes and was soon listing heavily. The ship was abandoned and scuttled, a decision that later led to the Court Martial and dismissal of her Captain. Whilst avoiding one torpedo attack, the destroyer HMS *Sikh* was disabled by another torpedo, causing her to become stationary; an easy target, she was soon bracketed and hit by dive-bombers, causing uncontrollable fires. Two other destroyers were damaged and would be unable to continue with the fleet. With this loss of ships and with many miles to go under the threat of air attack, the decision was taken to withdraw to Alexandria.

With the arrival of daylight, the Luftwaffe was back once more over Malta, attacking pre-defined targets in support of the main seaborne assault, as well as the tactical targets identified by the troops on the ground, and targets of opportunity. There was no air opposition, and other than over Valetta and Grand Harbour should they stray that far, there was little AA fire. Pre-defined defensive positions in the

Famagosta landing area – those that had not been seized by the FNS combat teams – were subjected to Ju88 and Ju87 dive-bomb attack. The Stukas were also active supporting the commandos at Kalafrana and Birzebbuga, engaging strong points. Two aircraft were lost to ground fire, and at the Kalafrana seaplane base the bombers hit buildings that had already been occupied by the Italian commandos, causing several casualties. The weight of attack, supported by Re2001s making strafing runs from the sea at very low level, enabled the second wave of assault craft to land, and the Marine Light Infantry were ashore, albeit with significant losses to machine-gun fire. The defenders gave ground slowly and were able to establish a new defence line on the northern edge of Birzebbuga, albeit this was to prove temporary and they were ordered to withdraw to a line Marsaxlokk to Zejtun, where 2nd Royal Irish Fusiliers had been positioned in a stop line that joined the line that went from Tarxien to Qormi. This new defence line would cede all of the airfields to the attackers and the strategy was hotly debated. The strategy also called for holding the high ground to the north of Rabat and then a line through Mosta to Qormi; this would enable a re-organization of the defensive forces and the ability to recapture Ta Kali, which was clearly the most exposed of the Axis footholds.

X-Day+1 saw the invasion fleet off the coast of Malta, the men of the Friuli Division of XXX Corps making their final preparations. The convoy had arrived in good order having lost only two ships to enemy action. The coastal guns of Malta had no chance to intervene; those that were in the right area – and one reason for the assault location was its perceived unsuitability – were out of action. The shore bombardment squadron, which included three battleships from the 5th Division at Taranto, was positioned to engage Fort Benghaisa if this had not already been taken, or to engage other strongpoints as directed. Nevertheless, the landing was not a simple operation as the ships involved were in many cases a "make do" selection and, despite the exercises that most units had undergone, this was still a new experience and the landing site was a difficult one. The first wave consisted of 2,000 amphibious troops plus the two infantry regiments of the Friuli Division and artillery and support units, and 1,000 tons of supplies. Two distinct locations were used, with similar efforts at each one, with the landing phase expected to last from 0600 to 1000. With the troops disembarked, the landing ships were to head back to Sicily as quickly as possible to collect the follow-up Assieta Division, although some of the supply ships would remain, as it would take longer for them to unload. The second wave, carrying the Livorno Division, was due to arrive in the afternoon, and its ships would head back to pick up the second wave Divisions, who were expected to land by X+3. Once ashore the 87th Regiment moved west to link up with and support the Italian commandos and German paratroopers and move north to join up with the forces at Luqa. The Regiment was supported by half of the 35th Artillery Regiment. The 88th Regiment, along with the 88th CCNN Legion (Blackshirts) and the other half of the Artillery Regiment, had the line Safi to Hal Far as their objective, linking up with the existing ground forces and, depending on resistance, to hold a line just beyond the airfields or to push on to Tarxien. Both combat units faced little opposition, and quickly linked up with the airborne troops; by early afternoon the attackers held an area that encompassed Krendi, Luqa and Hal Far, and had moved beyond Birzebbuga towards Marsaxlokk. This was important as it meant that the next seaborne wave could enter the Marsa Scirocco with its better landing areas.

The situation at Ta Kali was somewhat better for the defenders, as they achieved local superiority over the stretched airborne forces and were able to retake parts of the airfield. Once again this was temporary as German dive-bombers and fighters were on hand to break up significant threats. A final wave of air assault forces was also flown in, bringing with them a number of armoured cars and field guns. By early afternoon the initiative was once more with the attackers, although for now all their aim was to seize and hold the airfield. With Krendi airfield secured, the first German aircraft arrived to make use of the airfield, with the 109s and Ju87s taking up residence, ground-crew and supplies being flown in by Ju52s pending arrival of the main ground echelon with the second seaborne wave. The ability to operate close to the front-line enabled sorties to be mounted more effectively although a few 109s were written-off in landing accidents colliding with obstructions.

The second wave, having been delayed waiting for the new landing area, the Marsa Scirocco, began to send troops ashore in the later afternoon. The 33rd Regiment went in first followed by the 34th and the 28th Artillery Regiment, with support units interspersed in the landing order. They relieved the Friuli Division troops of their positions and the latter re-organized to push on Zebbug and Ta Kali, and then to swing down on Dingli. The Livorno Division was supported by a number of German Mk.IV tanks and its first objective was the Zejtun-Tarxien line and clearing the areas south and east of Zejtun.

The 2nd Irish Fusiliers had received some reinforcements from the 3rd KOMR but their position was still vulnerable, and they were short of heavy weapons, especially anti-tank guns. Advancing along the road from Marsaxlokk, the Italians were engaged by artillery and machine-gun fire from the village and called up an air attack; scrambled from Krendi, the Stukas were soon diving down on their targets. The tanks were of limited value as they had to stay on the roads, but the infantry deployed into the fields and advanced on the village, whilst sending a strong force to circle south and approach the village from the east. It was clear the position could not be held, and the Irish Fusiliers retreated towards Zabbar. The Italians occupied the village and deployed for the advance on Zabbar. They were told to hold position as an air attack was scheduled; Kesselring had decided to destroy Zabbar as an example of what could happen to Valetta; he was already considering a possible Allied surrender and this demonstration was to ensure that those who might want to fight to the last house would see what would happen. A strong force of Ju88s and Ju87s pounded the village and it disappeared under clouds of dust and smoke. This attack shattered the defence line and enabled the Italians to take the line from Luqa to Zabbar; one more drive and they could take the heights overlooking Grand Harbour. To the west the situation was equally promising, with surprisingly light opposition on the drive north-west to Hal Far, although by the end of the day they had only reached Zebbug despite patrols linking up with the troops at Hal Far.

The Axis forces spent the next day consolidating the areas they held, ensuring that they were secure from any counter-attack and mopping up areas such as Rabat, where strongpoints had continued to trouble the forces at Hal Far. The decision was taken not to drive towards Dingli, as the isolation of its defenders meant that it presented no threat unless it was reinforced by units moved from beyond the Victoria Lines. The total German air dominance made any such major troop movement unlikely, other than under cover of darkness. The landing of the Superga Division on Gozo, thus presenting a threat from that direction, made it increasingly unlikely that such troop movements would be made. Lord Gort and his commanders had few options; it was clear that the enemy was firmly established in superior numbers and had total control of the air and was using at least one of Malta's airfields. With no possibility of reinforcements, it was only a case of how long to keep on fighting, and what to do about Malta's port facilities and stores. The people of Malta had suffered a great deal since

1940, and the near total destruction of Zabbar demonstrated Kesselring's capability and intent. Destruction of the port facilities would have little effect, as the Axis did not need Malta as an operational base, they just needed the British NOT to have it as a base. After a tense conference the decision was taken to destroy vital stores and information, and for this to take place at least one more day of resistance was needed, after which an armistice would be requested.

X+2 (22nd August): no new ground forces were expected by the Axis until the next day, although additional air units arrived, taking up residence at Hal Far. In the morning Kesselring flew in to Krendi to confer with the senior commanders and review the plan for the next operational phase – the advance towards Valetta. It was agreed that positions would be established around Valetta but that no assault would take place, although selective bombing against defensive locations, especially gun positions, would continue throughout the day. On the eastern sector the pressure was maintained along the front, with two primary objectives, the Corradino Heights overlooking the inner part of Grand Harbour and Fort Ricasoli overlooking the entrance to Grand Harbour. Both objectives were subjected to dive-bombing throughout the morning, although at the cost of a number of aircraft, the AA defences around the Harbour still being substantially intact. Infantry assaults on the Fort suffered heavy casualties from well-sited machine guns, supported by artillery, and by early afternoon little progress had been made and the attack was halted. The attack on the Corradino Heights was more successful; the bombing had stunned the defenders and destroyed several key strongpoints. After overcoming some initial resistance on the outskirts of Paola, the attack, supported by an artillery barrage, was able to take control of most of the area, except for the old military prison. From this position, the Axis forces could establish artillery to dominate the areas on both sides of Grand Harbour. The front line was also advancing from Luqa towards Hamrun and from Ta Kali towards Birkirkara, the latter having Sliema as its ultimate objective to seal the line around Valetta. However, with the British decision not to contest the north of Malta, additional units moved south of the Victoria Lines to take up positions from Fort Madalena to Birkirkara. Three British battalions with supporting forces, including artillery and six tanks, had taken up the new positions the previous night. The German and Italian advance was held up at Birkirkara and it would take much of the day in house to house fighting to clear the area. The task was assigned to the paratroopers of 1st Parachute Regiment, supported by the Italian 125th Regiment. To the north of the town, progress was better, and the Tal Balal Cross-roads was soon taken; two miles down the main road lay the coast at Sliema. On the left flank the Italians made slow progress towards Fort Madalena, being held up at Gharghur, which would take them nearly two days to clear.

In the Lascaris War Room Gort was being urged to depart Malta in a submarine that had arrived that evening and was hiding on the seabed near its old base at Manoel Island. It was clear that the end was near, but as Governor, Gort saw it as his duty to remain on Malta to stand with its people. He was not to be swayed, but a few senior officers, along with critical documents and equipment were sent out of Malta that night. The following day (X+3) the final sea wave arrived, bringing the Assieta Division to Marsa bay in the morning and Napoli Division in the afternoon. Both Divisions joined the lines around Valetta. During the morning, the Axis forces had moved artillery into position on the Corradino Heights and had started to shell Floriana, being joined by the dive-bombers in pounding the buildings. The dive-bombers were also active again over Fort Ricasoli, and attacks on the other defensive sites around Valetta, but there was no further attempt at an assault on Ricasoli. With the planned arrival of the Assieta Division to take up positions on the left side of the front, the existing units moved forward from Luqa and Ta Kali, the objective being to complete the encirclement of Sliema-Valetta by reaching the coast at Dragunara Point and taking the coastal strip to Irqiqa Point, whilst avoiding Fort Madalena. In the now familiar pattern of ops, the attack was held up by a number of strong points, each of which was system-atically blasted by air attack and direct fire from support weapons. An attempted counter-stroke by three tanks near St Julian's was quickly destroyed by anti-tank fire, after which the paratroopers reached the coast at Spinola, overlooking St Julian's Bay. The follow-on troops reinforced the position and moved north towards Fort Madalena.

The situation map in the Lascaris War Room now showed that the Sliema-Valetta area was surrounded, and the Axis forces held domi-nant positions from which they could shell the city, in addition to free-dom in the air to bomb as they pleased. There were no military options left; the remaining forces outside of the beleaguered area, primarily those in the Dingli area, were not strong enough to influence the over-all situation, and it was known that another wave of seaborne troops was soon to arrive. German aircraft had been dropping leaflets high-lighting the situation and the option of an honourable surrender to preserve life and the historic heart of Malta. At 1400 hours, the British signalled that they wished to negotiate. Kesselring had remained on Malta with this in mind, and he proposed the Empire Sports Ground (Empire Stadium) as the meeting location. All units on both sides were ordered to cease fire at 1430 and to hold their current positions.

At 1500 hours, Gort and his senior land commanders arrived at the Sports Ground and were met by the German and Italian deputation, led by Kesselring. Having praised the brave defence in the face of overwhelming odds, Kesselring made clear that Gort had to surrender Malta immediately or risk a concerted bombing and bombardment of Valetta and Sliema. The negotiations were quickly concluded, as Gort had expected this and had already decided that the preservation of Malta's people and heritage required such an action. At 1800 hours the defenders were to surrender to the nearest Axis units, they would be disarmed and moved to holding camps at Ta Kali, Luqa and Hal Far. The surrender included all troops on Malta, much to the annoyance of the forces at Dingli.

After more than two years of resistance to the Axis bombing offensive and having taken the fight to the enemy with some success, Malta had fallen. This cornerstone of Allied Mediterranean strategy was now in enemy hands.

Chapter Four

Alam Halfa:
August–September 1942

"Since the beginning of August, the desert had been fairly quiet. The two
armies faced each other on the line south from El Alamein; the two air forces
flew as little as possible to build up their strength. The desert fighter force was
indeed stronger. Not only had it increased to 21 squadrons but the standard of
serviceability within the squadrons had been improved."
A nice piece of Spitfire mythology in *RAF Middle East*
(HMSO 1943)

As part of the Allied plan for securing the El Alamein line and disrupting German preparations, in July 1942 the Australian 9th Division
launched an offensive on the northern flank to take the high ground at
Tel El Eisa. The Australians spent the next few days fighting off heavy
counterattacks as Rommel redirected much of his forces against them.
The 9th Division infantry owed much to Australian, British and South
African artillery, as well as the Desert Air Force (DAF), in repelling
these counterattacks. Australians were also present in the DAF, flying
with Nos. 3 and 450 Squadrons, RAAF. Allied infantrymen had varying opinions regarding armoured support, feeling that sometimes
the tanks provided welcome support and protection, but also that
sometimes they failed them completely. Tanks and motor vehicles provided the punch and mobility of the ground forces – and so petrol
supplies were critical – increasingly in the mobile nature of the back
and forth conflict with Rommel. Whilst the air forces also needed petrol
this was small in comparison to the thirsty ground vehicles, especially
tanks, although it was to impact Luftwaffe sortie rates later in the North
Africa campaign. Whilst fuel was the key logistic element, all military
supplies also had to be conveyed to the theatre – for the Axis forces this
meant convoys, primarily from Italy. The Mediterranean was therefore

very much part of the North African War. The effect of all this effort and endeavour is seen in the diary of the German *Afrika Korps*, where difficulties of supply and damage and loss caused by Allied air attacks receive repeated mention. On 21st July, Rommel himself reported that "The enemy air force by its continual day and night operations has caused considerable loss among our troops, delayed and, at times, cut off our supplies ... the supply situation is tense owing to continual attacks on German supplies at Tobruk and Matruh.

"After the fighting of the 22nd July, I had the following signal transmitted to all troops: 'I send all ranks my special appreciation of their gallant action during our victorious defence of 22nd July. I am positive that any further enemy attacks will meet with the same reception.' Meanwhile, replacement infantry units had been slowly trickling into our lines for several weeks past and the very large gaps in the ranks of our formations were being gradually filled – not all, unfortunately, by 'fit for tropical service' troops. Elements of the 164th Infantry Division had been flown across from Crete but had brought neither heavy weapons nor vehicles. Several units of an Italian parachute Division – excellent troops by their appearance – also arrived at the front. All this while the army was working at feverish speed to strengthen its line." (*Rommel Papers.*) The Allies, primarily Australian troops, continued to make probing attacks in late July, seeking weak spots held by infantry, especially Italians, but each time they were repulsed by German armour, losing prisoners and tanks. Rommel concluded: "The German-Italian front had shown itself to be no longer penetrable by forces of the size they were committing. It was now certain that we could continue to hold our front, and that, after the crises we had been through, at least is something." But he also said, "Thus after immense victories, the great summer campaign had ended in a dangerous lull."

In mid-August 1942 General Alexander took over command in the Middle East and General Montgomery was appointed to lead the Eighth Army. Monty had been appointed following the death of Gott, who was killed when JG27 shot-down and then strafed the Bombay in which he was travelling. Churchill's directive to Alexander was "to take or destroy at the earliest opportunity the German Italian Army ..." With these changes of command and the arrival of strong reinforcements, a new spirit infused Allied forces in Egypt and the way was paved for a major offensive. The Allies had strengthened several key positions and intended to blunt and bleed any German advance. Montgomery was to prove an ardent supporter of air power: "I hold that it is quite wrong for the soldier to want to exercise command over the air striking forces. The handling of an air force is a life study and therefore the air part must be kept under air force command ... Eighth Army and the Desert Air Force have to be so knitted so that the two together form one entity. The resultant military effort will be so great that nothing will be able to stand up against it." And, very tellingly: "If you do not win the air battle first you will probably lose the land battle."

However, in typical Rommel fashion he gambled and attacked. Fierce clashes took place, especially around Alam el Halfa. With a new Allied commander, a massive build-up of strength in the ground forces – Montgomery had very firm views in the need for superiority in firepower and numbers – the race was on to:

- Deny Rommel supplies (material and fuel) and prevent him renewing his assault
- Build-up Allied strength, achieve air superiority and deny the Axis the ability to disrupt the Allied build-up, which including denying air reconnaissance

These twin aims dictated Allied air strategy in the weeks leading up to the El Alamein offensive. With Rommel's push now over, the RAF maintained and even increased its bombing offensive, with Tobruk and Benghazi still top of the strategic list, along with the battle area as tactical targets, and of course the anti-shipping war to deny further supplies. Benghazi was heavily hit on 16 August in the first of three heavy and effective attacks. This daylight raid by the RAF and USAAF hit the target just after midday and the B-24s pattern bombed the port, where several ships were being unloaded.

Such was the desperate nature of the supply shortage that the Axis was trying to get supplies to the El Alamein area using convoys of F-boats from Tobruk to Mersa Matruh. These 300-ton barges were no easy target, as they were armed with one 75mm and two 20mm cannon, and when in convoy could mount a formidable defence. The Australians of 459 Squadron started their offensive operations in June, having arrived in theatre in February and equipped with Hudsons the following month. Plt Off Beaton flew the first mission, but over the next few weeks the Squadron flew numerous low-level dawn attacks on this type of target, claiming 17 destroyed but losing three aircraft and crews, and with two others badly damaged. Losses continued to be high, with five aircraft lost in the period of intensive ops 28th July to 17th August. The most effective aircraft for hunting was the Beau-fighter. "Supplies were split up into small lots and carried forward either in trucks along the coast road or in barges, lighters and small vessels just off shore. The Beaufighters chose the shipping traffic for the first weight of their attack. Day after day they roamed in small formations up and down the coast seeking targets, always at risk of concentrated attack from the Messerschmitts and Macchis which were so readily available on the coastal airfields. During the first days of August the Beaufighters were sinking barges or setting them on fire one after the other. Some of them exploded when the cannon shells touched off their cargoes of ammunition or petrol. On 7th August they sank five barges within 12 hours. During the three weeks ended 9th August more than 20 barges and lighters were destroyed, a cargo load that was equivalent to 1,500 trucks." ("RAF in Middle East".) Two of the Beau units involved in this work were 227 and 272 with a DFC to the CO, Wg Cdr Donald Shore, 227 Squadron, September: "This officer has led his squadron on a number of successful attacks against enemy shipping in the Mediterranean. His squadron has also shot down numerous enemy aircraft, one of which Wing Commander Shore destroyed. Much of the success achieved can be attributed to this officer's great skill and courageous leadership."

However, the loss of Malta in mid-August was now to have a dramatic impact on the campaign. With the loss of coastal airfields and the loss of Malta, Allied air power relied on heavy bombers in the fight against Rommel's supply lines, with anti-shipping sweeps and, more importantly, heavy bomber attacks on installations. The "heavies" were now increasing in number, both with RAF and USAAF units. However, this also raised some politics between the air commanders "in as much as the 98th and First Provisional Groups made up four-fifths of the heavy bomber force in the Middle East, and American combat commanders were more experienced in the handling of these heavy bombers than were the British, it seemed fitting that the opera-tional control of all heavy-bombardment aircraft in the theater should be placed under the commanding general of the American air force. A suggestion to this effect, and subsequent negotiations with the RAF, resulted in the activation of the Bomber Command, USAMEAF, in Cairo, on 12th October." (*USAAF in the Middle East Campaign.*)

"Since the end of July, the R.A.F. had shifted the main weight of its activity to our lines of communication between the African ports and the front, where they were shooting up our transport columns and sinking one barge and coastal vessel after the other. No ship lying in the harbours at Bardia and Mersa Matruh, and frequently even at Tobruk, was safe from the attentions of the British bombers. Our Luftwaffe had its hands full at the front, where British air-power was also steadily increasing, and could only supply very meagre forces for the protection of the coast road and coastal waters. Thus, at the beginning of August, the R.A.F. sank three coastal vessels in Bardia harbour on one day alone." (*Rommel Papers*.) Air Commodore Alan Ritchie commanded the bomber force of No.205 Group and in addition to the battlefield targets and airfields, his major efforts in the Western Desert were focused on the ports of Benghazi and Tobruk. His force comprised the various medium bombers and an increasing number of heavy bombers. One of his challenges was that the retreat had meant the loss of many airfields and so increased the range to the main targets such as Tobruk. The medium bombers, Wellingtons, were now primarily based at the Canal Zone airfields, but making use of some refuelling locations on the Alexandria road, whilst the heavies, the Liberators and Halifaxes, were based in Palestine. During August the bombers flew 31 major raids against Tobruk, some 1,600 sorties. This pounding essentially closed Tobruk as a major supply route for Rommel, "closing the front door" as one account called it (with Benghazi as the back door). This meant that all supplies had to go to Benghazi and then make the long road journey to the front, which itself consumed fuel and wore out vehicles, as well as exposing road convoys to attack. As Benghazi was harder to hit – fewer bombers could reach this target – it became increasingly important to sink those supplies at sea.

Rommel had already proved that he did not need much in the way of supplies to take the offensive, so every ship that docked with tanks or guns was critical, but more so were the tankers. The Italians had promised to deliver. The first of Rommel's promised supply ships left Naples on 16th August. Escorted by destroyers and six aircraft, the *Rosalina Pilot*, an 8,300-ton MV carrying a mixed load of fuel, ammunition and general cargo, elected to use the shorter route round North Sicily and thence to the North African ports. With no Allied air effort from Malta, the convoy had an easy run, although it had been spotted by a Sunderland and a Wellington strike force had set out from Egypt on an abortive search. After the losses of recent months this was considered a major victory, and the Italians were already planning major convoys of supplies for late August.

The Italians, true to their word, were mounting another convoy to relieve Rommel. This was the 7,800-ton tanker *Pozarica* escorted by destroyers, a flak ship and seven aircraft. Although the convoy was spotted and attacked by a Dutch submarine, the tanker was undamaged and made its way to Tobruk. It was followed a few days later by the 1,500-ton tanker *Dielpi*. A fourth tanker, the 5,400-ton *Istria*, sailed by night and fell victim to a Wellington torpedo strike. This highly successful August fuel supply ended with a fifth tanker, the 5,000-ton *San Andrea*, also reaching port safely. Rommel had received a massive boost to his fuel supplies, albeit at some distance from his front-line positions. The old British railway line from Tobruk was not yet back in full operation, and there was also a shortage of locomotives, which Rommel had added to his urgent equipment requirement and were scheduled as part of a major convoy for the first week of September, which was also due to deliver tank, armoured car, artillery and truck replacements, along with ammunition and general stores. The success of the August convoys, with the loss of only one tanker, had encouraged the Italians to plan three major convoys for the period 1st to 10th September.

In the meantime, Rommel was also expecting one of the German parachute Divisions that had been used in the Malta assault, and 1st Parachute Division had already been brought up to strength by moving troops and equipment from the 4th Parachute Division. The latter was to remain on Malta where it too would be brought up to strength prior to moving to Egypt, with an expected deployment date of the end of September. The Italian 185th Folgore Division (paratroop) had started to arrive in August, and the Friuli Division was also slated to regroup and move to Egypt from Malta "as soon as possible". These reinforcements, along with the 164th Division from Crete, would give Rommel five additional Divisions, all combat experienced. One major challenge remained: the lack of motor transport, an issue that particularly affected his Italian Divisions and that had caused severe problems. To counter this, the Axis made extensive use of captured British trucks, but this too brought problems, and "Our endeavour now was to have all captured vehicles gradually withdrawn from the transport units and replaced by new or repaired vehicles of our own manufacture." (*Rommel Papers.*)

No fewer than 4,000 trucks were waiting to be moved from Italy to North Africa, but despite the convoy conditions now being better, there was still a lack of the large ships that were required. This was in part resolved by repurposing some of the ships which were used in the Malta operation, which, at the instigation of General von Rintelen, the German Military Attaché in Rome, were then included in the September convoy plan. He was also instrumental in ensuring the balance of cargo between Italian and German needs, which had up to this point generally favoured the Italian supply, much to Rommel's annoyance. The fall of Malta and the easing of pressure that this brought about seemed to instill a new mood of optimism amongst the Italians. At this point there was no intention of increasing the number of panzer Divisions, although it was intended to build-up a reserve of tanks and vehicles in North Africa to enable losses to be replaced as speedily as possible. To this end, a tank park was formed at Tobruk for both maintenance and training.

Tobruk was the key port as it was closest to the front; although smaller port facilities were available at places such as Bardia they had low capacity and were more vulnerable to air attack. Benghazi and Tripoli were secure and effective ports, but they were far back from the front. The logistics of managing the ports and depots had fallen to the Italians, and Rommel commented: "The unloading of shipping in Africa was also a terribly leisurely affair. It was only too often a triumph of antiquated ideas, lack of initiative and a total absence of any sort of technical ingenuity. Thus, we found it completely impossible to get the port capacity of Tobruk increased – 600 tons a day was all it could handle, with the result that ships were kept far too long in the harbour exposed to the danger of destruction by British bombers. We made repeated demands for increased port construction, the building of unloading facilities in neighbouring inlets by Italian labour, the provision of larger quantities of Italian dock equipment and stronger air defences for Tobruk. We had built tremendous hopes round the captured British military railway from Tobruk to El Daba and had supposed that large-scale railway traffic would soon be organised to the front, thus greatly relieving the pressure on our road transport. But here, too, nothing immediate was done. The cause of the trouble – as I have already said – lay in the over-organisation and muddle which characterised the Italian supply staffs." (*Rommel Papers.*)

Rommel pressed Kesselring to intervene to try to resolve this key issue, proposing a unified command, under Kesselring, of all sea traffic in Mediterranean and North African waters to ensure that the right supplies arrived at the right locations, and were handled efficiently. After some resistance, this was agreed, and with German planning

104 Disaster in the Desert

staffs working alongside the Italians improvements were soon in hand in terms of shipping manifests and loading and unloading. The importance of Tobruk as a port was at last recognized, and action taken to improve the unloading facility to speed up the process and move off-loaded material to camouflaged dumps to the east of Tobruk. The defence of the port against air attack was also important, and additional searchlights and guns were installed, whilst a Bf110 night fighter unit arrived, as the main threat was from night raids. An Italian day fighter unit with Re2001s provided the day cover. As well as offloading supplies and moving them to nearby dumps, it was crucial to move them to the front, and to establish dumps at key locations. With the railway repaired, the daily traffic of stores to the front greatly increased; however, this single rail, and the only good road, remained vulnerable to Allied air attack.

The fall of Malta had also enabled Kesselring to review the distribution of his air assets. Hitler was now convinced that Rommel could continue to drive forward and seize the Suez Canal, and then sweep north through the Levant, northern Iraq and Iran, seizing oil fields and strategic assets, and eventually meet up with the German forces that were heading for the oil fields in the Baku area. This broad strategic intent was fraught with challenges, but it was clear that the Allied hold on much of this area was tenuous and the local population in some areas was pro-German, or at least anti-British. There also remained the possibility of bringing Turkey into the war if the Germans were dominant and thus able to assist the Turks in the dream of restoration of the Ottoman Empire. As Rommel was aware, the additional land forces and supplies would only be of value if supplies could be maintained and if the Axis achieved air superiority over the Eastern Mediterranean and its coastal areas, and he discussed the issue with Kesselring when the latter visited Afrika Korps HQ on 9th August.

The overall strategic aims for Rommel were:

- To seize the British naval base at Alexandria, which with the loss of Malta would mean the fleet having to sail to Gibraltar, a risky proposition in the face of Axis air power, or retreat through the Suez Canal
- Close the Suez Canal and then seize it prior to the Levant operation. The decisive point for this would be Ismailia and with his thrusts on Alexandria and Ismailia he could then isolate Cairo and secure its capitulation

- Cross the Canal and drive through Palestine to secure ports and airfields to support the push to seize the oilfields of Iraq
- If conditions permitted and operations in Russia were progressing, drive north to link with the German forces in the Baku area

It was an ambitious plan and one that relied on ensuring the Allies could be brought to a decisive land battle in which their armour was destroyed, and then driving on before any reinforcement could stabilize the situation. In previous offensives, Rommel had achieved the battlefield victory but had been unable, through lack of supplies, to capitalize and achieve strategic victory. The new situation whereby supplies were arriving in quantity, and additional Divisions had been assigned, provided him with his best chance yet of reaching the Suez Canal. The Luftwaffe's role would be critical in direct support of the assault and in attacking RAF bases in Egypt, especially the Canal Zone, and Palestine. Units that had taken part in the Malta assault were re-assigned to Crete and to Egypt, with bomber elements comprising Ju87s, Ju88s and He111s, along with additional Bf109 fighter units. This build-up would take some time, as it was important for the logistic support for a sustained air campaign to be in place. The target date for the offensive was early December, but in the meantime Rommel had to prepare for an expected Allied attack.

There was one more added complication. Intelligence had revealed the Allies were planning a major amphibious assault in North Africa, which would involve American and British troops, and which was in part aimed to deflect Russian anger at the lack of an Allied Second Front in Europe. In his memoirs, Kesselring wrote: "The Allied invasion of North Africa was preceded by an intensive war of nerves. For weeks contradictory rumours and reports had been pouring into my headquarters. The landing objective, the strength of the invasion force and its constituents were varied with consummate artistry. Naval movements off the West African coast indicated a possible landing there and a march straight across the continent. The overcrowding of troops and ships into Gibraltar, on the other hand, pointed to an objective in the Mediterranean, the sudden appearance of aircraft carriers and large transports confirming the probability that the main landing would be attempted beyond striking distance from Gibraltar, Alexandria and Syria." He went on to discuss the various landing options and concluded that Corsica/Sardinia would be the bold move as a step towards Italy, but that Algeria or Tunis was most likely.

"On the basis of these calculations I proceeded to take appropriate counter-measures. The C-in-C Luftwaffe had sanctioned the most urgent reinforcements for Air Fleet 2 which I had asked for. The air bases in Sicily and Sardinia were overhauled, strengthened and provisioned. Air and ground reconnaissance activity was stepped up. German U-boats were disposed so they could attack large convoys entering the Mediterranean, and plans were discussed with the Supermarina in case the Allied fleet should after all make a surprise appearance off the Italian coast. I further asked OKW to order at least one Division to Sicily, where it could be held in readiness either to be moved forward to Tunis or to oppose a possible landing in Sicily itself." Back in Germany, however, this assessment was being disputed, with Goering and Hitler of the opinion that the Allied attack would be on Southern France, and for this reason several land and air formations that would have been earmarked for North Africa were held back in France. As Kesselring argued, such a plan by the Allies was not viable, as it would expose the invaders to overwhelming Axis air superiority from land bases, especially with Malta having been lost; it would also be out of character with the cautious strategic mindset of the Allied commanders. Concern over the proposed Allied landing enabled Kesselring to use the fall of Malta and the improved situation in Russia to persuade Hitler to assign additional forces to the North Africa theatre.

"All efforts of the Panzer Army were directed towards an early resumption of the offensive, for its success during the summer had, as expected, struck fear and dismay into the Allied camps in New York and London. It was therefore obvious that the Anglo-Americans would spare no effort to prevent a further advance by the Panzer Army to Alexandria. But their shipping from Britain or America required two to three months for the journey round the Cape to North Africa and therefore we had a few weeks' grace before the immense reinforcements which they had no doubt planned for the Eighth Army after the fall of Tobruk, could reach African soil. We reckoned on mid-September as the arrival date of the Eighth Army's reinforcements (other than normal routine replacements) from Britain and America." (*Rommel Papers*.) The race was on.

Whilst the Axis commanders were planning their strategy and the build-up was underway, the Allies were also active. Montgomery had assumed command on 13th August; in his account *El Alamein to the River Sangro* he stated: "The reverses suffered during the summer of

1942 had left the Eighth Army, in the words of Mr Churchill, 'brave but baffled'. The troops knew they were worthy of greater things, and indeed the Divisions comprised some very fine fighting material. But they had lost confidence in their higher leadership, they lacked a sound battle technique, and they were deficient of equipment and weapons comparable to those of the Germans. It was clear that Rommel was preparing further attacks, and the morale and determination of our troops was undermined by plans for further withdrawals. The 'atmosphere' was wrong." He had inherited an Empire force of Australians (9th Division), New Zealanders (2nd Division), South Africans (1st Division), Indians (5th Division) and British (7th Armoured Division and 50th Infantry Division), as well as Greek and French contingents. This disparate nature of men and equipment, as well as leadership styles, was without doubt a challenge, and he instituted a period of reorganization, re-equipment and training. He was also aware that Rommel was unlikely to give him the luxury of time, and so his defensive arrangements needed to be able to resist any German attack, whilst he built up his own offensive capability, a crucial element of which would be his reserve corps (X Corps), comprising 1st, 8th and 10th Armoured Divisions, which was intended as an armoured fist that would lead the offensive when it came. On his tour of the defensive zone he noted two main things: the importance of the Alam Halfa ridge, and the lack of fighting stocks in the forward area. Furthermore, he made it clear to all levels of the army that there would be no retreat from El Alamein; in part this was intended to boost morale and fix his commanders to the idea that they must fight. At the same time, he made demands for more and more men and materials. Churchill supported his requests wherever possible and supplies of armour, including the new Sherman tank from the US, flowed into the rear areas, as did large stocks of fuel and ammunition. Although the Sherman, with its effective 75mm main armament, had started to arrive, most of the tank units were still equipped with the Crusader, although some also had the Grant, neither of which had proved effective in the recent tank battles, although in part this was due to poor tactics. Montgomery was also an advocate of air power: "When I took over command, the Army and Air HQ were widely separated, and lacked that close personal relationship which is so essential. I therefore moved my Headquarters to a site adjacent to Air Headquarters, where commanders and staffs could plan and work together as a team." To some extent this was already in place at Corps level, and the concept had been proven during the CRUSADER offensive, albeit this was very much a learning exercise and the DAF was not always impressed with the Army's methods or viewpoints.

On 29th August Rommel had announced to his troops that within days they would be in Alexandria and that the forthcoming attack would be the final annihilation of the enemy. His overall plan was for the motorized main strength comprising Afrika Korps, the two panzer Divisions, plus Italian XX Motorized Corps and the 90th Light Division to move into positions on the southern part of the front. It was stressed that they would take all "possible precautions against observation. The armour was to move to its new positions a quarter at a time and there deploy under camouflage, the movement extending over a period of several days. With the armour in position, the wheeled vehicles were to be shifted to the assembly area in one bound, being replaced in their old positions by supply vehicles. No effort was to be spared to keep our intentions concealed."

The British forces were assessed as weak in this area and the plan was for a night attack by infantry, followed up by the panzers to throw the defenders back, disrupt any attempt at reinforcement and reach the initial objectives at El Hammam (25–30 miles from the start point) in the early morning. The northern flank of the thrust would be protected by 90th Light and elements of the Italian Corps, leaving the armoured spearhead to continue the advance. The other parts of the front were to be engaged with light thrusts, to keep the British uncertain as to the direction of the main assault. Following the initial breakthrough, the armour was to swing north to reach the coast just beyond El Hammam, behind the main British positions, and then move east into the supply areas, which would also force the British to commit their armour in an open battle, which historically had always led to decisive victory for Rommel. "Things were then to move fast. The decisive battle was on no account to become static. With large British forces pinned down by repeated minor attacks by the German-Italian infantry left in the Alamein line, the decisive battle was to be fought out behind the British front in a form in which the greater aptitude of our troops for mobile warfare and the high tactical skill of our commanders could compensate for our lack of material strength. Separated from their supply depots, the British would be left with the option of either fighting it out to the end in their line or breaking out and falling back to the west, thus relinquishing their hold on Egypt." (*Rommel Papers.*)

For once, Rommel's supply situation was favourable and he had built-up stocks of fuel, ammunition and vehicles, plus he had the expectation of seizing Allied supply depots during his offensive. There had been some debate with Kesselring as to delaying until the new Divisions were in place, but Rommel had determined that he needed to attack in order, at the very least, to disrupt any Allied plans for an offensive, and to prevent Montgomery from continuing to build his strength. If the attack stalled, then he was confident that he could retire to his start point and quickly rebuild from his stocks and feed the new Divisions into the line. Air power was expected to play an important role in the battle, and after the relatively quiet August, the first days of September saw maximum effort by the RAF squadrons – and the arrival of American bomber and fighter squadrons, including more P-40s – with the 57th Fighter Group. General American air strength continued to grow, with the 98th BG and 12th BG. The 98th, under the command of Col Hugo Rush, was a heavy bomber group that arrived in Palestine in early August, with its four squadrons based at St Jean D'Acre (345th and 415th BS) and Ramat David (343rd and 344th BS). The 12th BG, under the command of Col Charles Goodrich, was a medium bomber B-25 unit, and squadrons were initially deployed to Deversoir (81st and 82nd BS) and Ismailia (83rd and 434th BS). During August, the latter Group, like the FG, was under the tutelage of RAF and SAAF Wing, the Group was given a month of intensive training. This proved an experience of great value, for location of the target in the desert was a most difficult task, and one which often could not be mastered until the battle area had become fairly well known. During this period, five missions were flown to acquaint crews with the vari-ous aids to navigation available in the Middle East. The first raids were night attacks upon harbour installations at Mersa Matruh and enemy aerodromes at El Daba and Fuka. The American presence, and the promise of more units, especially heavy bombers with the range to reach strategic targets, would threaten Rommel's supply situation once more, by bringing ports and concentration areas under intense air attack. The tactical air power situation had also moved in the Allied favour in recent months, both in terms of numbers of aircraft and in tactical capability. However, the arrival of German and Italian units freed up by the capture of Malta was expected to have a significant impact on the air war. Additional units of Luftflotte 2 moved to North Africa and Crete, with I/KG26 and II/KG26 taking their He111s to Crete, whilst III/KG26's Ju88s went to El Daba, along with the similarly-equipped I/KG54. The whole of JG27 and JG53 were now on airfields behind the front line, along with over 200 Ju87s of LG1 and StG3. The rapid redeployment of these units had stretched the air transport force, which also had to move urgent fuel stocks to some air-fields, but most units were at least partially in place by the end of the last week of August.

The increase in German fighter units had made it increasingly diffi-cult for the Allied reconnaissance pilots to provide their usual high level of intelligence data, added to which the Axis forces had been very adept at hiding their movements and positions. Nevertheless, the fact that an assault was imminent was well-known to the Allied com-manders, with Montgomery stating, "It became clear that Rommel intended to attack during the coming full moon." As Alexander said in his memoirs, "Eighth Army's own preparations for an offensive were still in the organizational stage. Montgomery therefore planned a purely defensive battle." On the eve of the enemy attack, Coningham told his men: "The battle is on. Good luck in your usual brilliant work. This defensive land fight for Egypt will be followed later by an offen-sive and then away we go. Meanwhile go for him in the air whenever you can." At the end of August, the AOC-in-C sent an urgent message to his units: "Everyone must do his utmost and more than his utmost. The enemy this time can and must be finally crushed." Whilst some combats took place over the front lines, the more intense air activity in late August was an Axis bombing campaign against airfields and installations, including supply areas. There was also an intensification of the mining of the Suez Canal and Alexandria harbour.

Rommel's infantry moved forward in the early hours of 31st August but soon came up against an unexpectedly dense and complex mine-field, which was defended by infantry and artillery; as usual, Allied artillery in this type of fire support role proved effective, costing the attackers casualties and, more importantly, time. They were also harassed from the air: "Before long, relay bombing attacks by the R.A.F. began on the area occupied by our attacking force. With para-chute flares turning night into day, large formations of aircraft un-loosed sticks of H.E. bombs among my troops." (*Rommel Papers.*) The "holding attacks" in the north and south had also started in the early hours; the Italians of Trento Division along with elements of 164th Divi-sion in the north were held by 9th Australian Division and pushed back. In the centre the Italian Bologna Division struck the southern part of 5th Indian Division and reached Ruweisat ridge holding on the extreme west end of the ridge despite fierce counter-attacks by the Indians, supported by 2nd New Zealand Division. The main attack was still moving forward but there was some confusion and time had been lost; General von Bismarck, commander of 21st Panzer, had been killed by a mine, and the Afrika Korps commander, General Nehring, had been wounded in an air attack. The defenders had been more stubborn than expected but progress was still being made; in part this was because British armour had been ordered to only make harassing attacks and not to become fully engaged, but to retire to the area in which British armour would concentrate for the main battle. Such attacks were made by 4 Light Armoured Brigade and 7 Motor Brigade. "My plan for the motorised forces – to advance 30 miles east by moonlight and then strike north at dawn – had not worked. The assault force had been held up far too long by the strong and hitherto unsuspected mine barriers, and the element of surprise, which had formed the basis of the whole plan, had been lost. In these circumstances, we were now in two minds whether or not to break off the action." (*Rommel Papers.*)

Montgomery wrote: "My main preoccupation during 31st August was to determine exactly the direction of the enemy thrust line. I hoped he would move in a tight wheel to the north towards Alam Halfa, and not wide towards El Hammam. Our deception measures had been directed towards that end. During the early afternoon, the enemy armour began to move north-east, in fact directly towards the area for which the Eighth Army layout was designed." (*El Alamein to the River Sangro.*) Rommel's original plan had indeed been for a sweep to El Hammam, but he noted: "With the British armour now assembled for immediate action, it was impossible for us to continue with our wide sweep to the east, as our flanks would have been under a constant threat from the 7th Armoured Division in the south and the 1st and 10th Armoured Divisions in the north. This compelled us to decide on an earlier turn to the north than we had intended. The objectives of the attack were now set as Hill 132 for the Afrika Korps and Alam Bueit-Alam Haifa for XX Italian Corps." (*Rommel Papers.*)

Although not mentioned in his memoirs, it is likely Montgomery had the advantage of ULTRA intercepts to provide him with information on Rommel's plans, whereas the previous signals security weaknesses on the British side had been closed some months before. Allied deception plans, starting with Cascade, earlier in 1942, had been creating dummy formations and locations to also encourage the

Germans to base their offensive on areas of benefit to the Allies. However, such a sweep south to encircle the Allied position would likely have been Rommel's preferred action anyway. One difference now was that Montgomery planned to concentrate his armour and not fritter it away, pulling the German offensive into an area where flank attacks by concentrated armour could be made.

Alam Halfa was strongly defended; 44th Division was dug in and to the south of the ridge 22nd Armoured Brigade was in place, with 10th Armoured Division to the east, whilst 7th Armoured Division was well positioned to make flank attacks. General Bayerlein, having taken command of the Afrika Korps, was confident the attack could be pushed forward, and at 1300 hours, after replenishing fuel and ammunition, the panzers rolled on again. A heavy sandstorm continued to ground the RAF and progress was good, despite the Ariete and Trieste Divisions being held up for a few hours as they continued to clear paths in the minefields. The advanced elements of 15th Panzer came up against 22nd Armoured commanded by Brigadier George 'Pip' Roberts, an experienced Royal Tank Regiment officer, the main armour components being the 1st and 5th Royal Tank Regiments. The British tanks, supported by artillery positions on the ridge, proved impossible to dislodge, and Rommel called a halt in the early evening. The situation was still balanced, with the panzers positioned to continue their advance once the Italian Divisions caught up and the panzers had been replenished. Throwing a gun screen to the east and west as part of his flank protection, Rommel discussed options with his commanders. The weather having improved, the RAF was back in action: "After nightfall our forces became the target for heavy RAF attacks, mainly on the reconnaissance group, but also – though less severe – on other units. With one aircraft flying circles and dropping a continuous succession of flares, bombs from the other machines, some of which dived low for the attack, crashed down among the flare-lit vehicles of the reconnaissance units. All movement was instantly pinned down by low-flying attacks. Soon many of our vehicles were alight and burning furiously. The reconnaissance group suffered heavy casualties." (*Rommel Papers.*)

Major H. Woods of the KRRC was on Alam Halfa and was impressed by the bomber attack: "At 1230 a.m. our bombers ... found his whole strength had moved eastwards and located him with flares in the valley below us. It was one of the most awe-inspiring sights I shall ever see, I think – there were seldom less than 20 flares in the air at any one time and the whole valley with its mass of the Afrika Korps stationary was lit up like a huge orange fairyland. All the time, red, orange, white-green tracer was darting hither and thither like 100mph coloured fairies. The huge flash of bombs, which include two of 4,000lbs, also inspired the whole thoroughly warlike scene, with little figures silhouetted against their vehicles as they tried to find cover from our bombs." (*Bombers over Sand and Snow.*)

The Luftwaffe was also airborne, the He111s bombing Alexandria harbour and its installations, losing three bombers to anti-aircraft fire and fighters, but causing heavy damage to harbour facilities and setting fire to one major oil installation. The Heinkels were also active against the Allied bomber airfields being used by No.205 Group and the Americans. In August the Allied bombers had flown nearly 2,000 sorties, with three-quarters being by the Wellington squadrons, and 70% of the total being against ports, Tobruk heading the list and being attacked on 28 nights in the month. Although the port area was now strongly defended, the Germans had to ensure that it could operate on a 24-hour basis, as it was in reality the only practical port, Tripoli and Benghazi being too far back, albeit safer as they could only be reached by the longer-range Allied bombers. The Luftwaffe attacks caused damage at Kabrit and Shallufa, and four aircraft were destroyed on the ground. The Wellingtons of 40 Squadron had just left Kabrit to attack battlefield targets when the Luftwaffe arrived.

The following day, 1st September, opened with 15th Panzer attempting to move left of Alam Halfa to flank 22nd Armoured, whilst 21st Panzer and Ariete renewed the frontal attack; the east flank was left to a gun line and a screen of reconnaissance troops. As they moved forward, 15th Panzer was engaged on its left flank by elements of 7th Armoured Division, and a hot fight developed; at one point the panzers were driven back but when the British followed up they ran into a concealed line of 88s, and the battle area was soon littered with destroyed or damaged tanks. Elements of 10th Armoured Division had been ordered to move towards the area but before they left their positions they were attacked by a formation of Ju87s. The Stukas had been heading for gun positions on Alam Halfa ridge but had seen the tank concentration and peeled in to attack. Several tanks were immobilized during the attack and the formation was thrown into confusion. A second formation of Stukas was bounced by South African Kittyhawks, quickly losing five aircraft. It was the most intensive period of air activity for many weeks; for every formation that made it to their target areas at least one was intercepted, and losses on both sides mounted as the day wore on. For the Luftwaffe, the priority became the defenders on Alam Halfa, with artillery positions in particular attracting attention. For the Allies it was any formation of vehicles, although in most instances aircraft had to target individual vehicles.

By the end of the day there had been little material change in the ground position, although the Germans had secured a foothold on Alam Halfa ridge and had pushed the Allied armour back to the west, towards the Ruweisat ridge. On the east flank it had remained relatively quiet, although most of 10th Armoured Division had concentrated to the south-east of Alam Halfa. Nevertheless, the mass of British armour was now split in two, and much would depend on what happened the following day. Meanwhile, in the centre, Rommel had ordered a renewed attack on the Ruweisat ridge, in part to maintain a level of uncertainty amongst the Allies. In view of the previous attack the 2nd New Zealand Division, under the command of the tenacious and experienced General Bernard Freyberg, had extended its position to support the 5th Indian Division to its north and provide a stronger defence of this important ridge. The Italian attack supported by elements of the German 164th Division was almost immediately held up when it ran up against a number of heavily-defended boxes. By midday it had ground to a halt. Montgomery wrote about the situation on the evening of 1st September: "I am now confident of holding the enemy's attacks, and of preventing infiltration behind the main defensive position. I began to consider re-grouping in order to form reserves and to seize the initiative." With the northern sector quiet, he pulled troops out of XXX Corps to form this reserve and ordered his armoured units to consolidate. The latter would prove difficult because of the position of Afrika Korps between the two British units unless they could be forced to retire. The defence of Alam Halfa ridge remained the key.

Overnight, reconnaissance elements of 90th Light had pressed the flanks of 2nd New Zealand Division and had cleared a way through a minefield providing a route to the left flank of 15th Panzer and towards a weakly-held position to the west of Deir el Hima. Rommel immediately ordered Ariete Division to follow 90th Light, and to leave only Littorio as the flank guard. This was a risk, but with the New Zealanders now exposed on three sides it seemed unlikely they would leave their boxes. These boxes were also subject to air attack overnight, as were the positions on the ridge. As on previous nights the Allied bombing was even more intense and effective, leaving Rommel to comment: "In the evening I conferred with Field Marshal Kesselring and gave him a detailed account of the effect of the British air attacks, in particular of their 'bomb-carpets' in an area covered with tanks, guns and vehicles. He promised to do all he could to help us. But that night again (2–3 September), the Afrika Korps, part of the Italian armoured Divisions and the 90th Light Division, were once more subjected to non-stop pounding by powerful British bomber formations. A steady succession of parachute flares kept the whole of the desert bathed in a brilliant light – Magnesium incendiaries, impossible to extinguish, many flaring on the ground, lighting up the whole neighbourhood. Meanwhile, vast quantities of HE and fragmentation bombs, even some land-mines, dropped into the territory occupied by my troops. Many of the 88-mm AA guns, which had previously scored an occasional hit, were now picked out by the British, attacked from a great height and destroyed. Hundreds of our vehicles were destroyed or damaged." (*Rommel Papers.*)

The fourth day of the battle once again brought mixed fortunes, but without the intervention of Allied air power it would likely have seen a more decisive outcome for Rommel. The weather was better on the 3rd and the light bombers were out in force, flying over 200 sorties: "Early in the day air reconnaissance disclosed the enemy had broken off contact and was moving back through gaps in the minefields. The ground troops intensified their effort against the retreating Axis columns while the air effort was stepped up to 200 sorties on the southern sector alone: 92 by Baltimores, 90 by Bostons, and 18 by Mitchells. These attacks were carried out against Axis columns wherever suitable concentrations were found. The bombers were escorted by Kittyhawks, Tomahawks and P-40s, which made 156, 21 and 60 sorties respectively." (*The Ninth Air Force in the Western Desert*, USAF Historical Study #30.) Coningham sent a message to the US commanders: "Many thanks for your assistance in the current day's bombing. We are full of admiration for the grand work of your crews and I know our squadrons are delighted. Well done and good luck."

The move of the 90th Light and Ariete caught the Allies by surprise, and also led to the capture of Brigadier Clifton, Commander of 6 New Zealand Brigade, when his troops made a night attack on the Italians and suffered heavy losses. More importantly, these formations, along with 15th Panzer, were now in a position to strike 10th Armoured Division and move towards Ruweisat ridge and around the north of

Alam Halfa, whilst 21st Panzer maintained pressure on the Alam Halfa defenders. The Stukas were back in force and now that the fixed positions of 22nd Armoured Brigade were known, this unit suffered mounting losses. Artillery positions on Alam Halfa continued to cause problems and losses, but the balance of the battle in this area was starting to move in favour of the Germans. In the tank battle developing between 15th Panzer and 10th Armoured Division, the losses were fairly even until the Sherwood Rangers Yeomanry were lured onto a concealed gun line and suffered heavy loss; the panzers followed up, overrunning a British anti-tank gun line, but were hit in the flank by the 3rd RTR, which brought the advance to a halt. As units of Ariete and 90th Light moved up, the British retired down the back of Alam Halfa. This effectively left the route to Ruweisat ridge open. Allied air power once again came into play with very heavy attacks overnight, during one of which the HQ of 15th Panzer was hit, causing casualties amongst the staff officers and wounding General von Vaerst. The air attacks also caused losses in 90th Light and Ariete, effectively disrupting any attempt at an early advance the next day. It also provided an opportunity for the elements of 7th and 10th Armoured Division to link up and take up positions on the north-west edge of Alam Halfa, positioned to flank attack any push on Ruweisat. The New Zealanders were now under pressure from the west and south and had the panzers to their east. Rommel's plan was to use the Italian Divisions and 90th Light to roll-up the New Zealand boxes one by one. This was no easy task as each box had been carefully sited and constructed, with deep minefields and interlocking fields of fire, all well covered by artillery, and with confidence of support from the air.

Montgomery's centre was now at risk and there was discussion as to the viability of the New Zealanders being exposed; Alexander's "no retreat" order was still in place, and for now Montgomery was content to see how the battle would develop. He hastened the move of 50th Division to positions south of Alam Halfa, and linked to the 44th Division, and brought 4th Light Brigade and elements of 7th Armoured Division together as the armoured element of this part of the front. The reserve that had been drawn from XXX Corps was moved to the Ruweisat ridge, and also occupied previously prepared positions between there and Alam Halfa. Rommel now considered his options; his armoured strength had been depleted, not so much through combat losses but because the difficult terrain had been hard on the vehicles and had also consumed more fuel than expected. So far, no

British dumps had been captured and despite the efforts of the Luft-waffe, Allied air remained dominant. He decided that 4th September would be the decision day; he would try one more armoured push to capture Ruweisat ridge, adding elements of 21st Panzer on the right flank and pressure would be maintained on the New Zealand Division. However, he first needed the overnight resupply of fuel and ammunition for the panzers. Infantry attacks on the New Zealand boxes suffered heavy losses but managed to take two key positions, capturing their garrisons and equipment. However, the resupply operation was a failure; one convoy was virtually destroyed in an air attack, one lost its way, and only one managed to arrive at its planned location on time. Despite this, he determined to press ahead with those vehicles that could be brought to readiness, although this was less than half of his available armour. This reduced force pushed north-east and almost immediately came under heavy artillery fire. Racing forwards they were then engaged by hull-down tanks and were attacked by fighter-bombers. The attack was quickly brought to a halt and the panzers retired to their start point.

It was clear to Rommel that he did not have the strength to force a decisive conclusion in the face of supply problems and Allied air dominance. His offensive had gained some territory, including the western end of the Ruweisat ridge, but it had not achieved its objectives. By the 5th the battle was over; Rommel had made progress but had exhausted his forward supplies. "The continuous and very heavy attacks of the RAF," Rommel stated, "absolutely pinned my troops to the ground and made impossible any safe deployment or advance according to schedule." General Bayerlein, Chief of Staff of the Afrika Korps, afterwards declared: "Your air superiority was most important, perhaps decisive ... We had very heavy losses, more than from any other cause." Tedder was quick to recognize the contribution of the night bombers: "There is no doubt that these continuous night attacks were one of the decisive factors in crushing the enemy attack."

As the front settled down in Egypt, a new front was opened in North Africa with the Allied landings under Operation TORCH. The final conquest of Egypt would have to wait until this new threat had been countered. For Montgomery it was a period of frustration; he was determined to renew his offensive, but only when he had the men and material to do so with assurance of victory. With resources now assigned to Operation TORCH, his flow of such men and material was slowed and his timeline for a renewed offensive pushed back.

Chapter Five

Operation TORCH and Tunisia: October 1942–February 1943

Allied commanders considered that the fall of Malta would lead to an inevitable increase in strength of the Axis forces in North Africa, with the easing of the shipping routes and the release of units no longer required to be held back in Italy. Churchill was increasingly concerned over the possible loss of Egypt, which would have major political and military repercussions, and pressed the Chiefs of Staff for options to ease the pressure on General Alexander. Increasing the flow of men and materials to Egypt was not considered viable; the Suez Canal was now an increasingly vulnerable point and yet was the only route for shipping. The air reinforcement routes were already at capacity, although it was agreed that additional American heavy bomber units should move to the Middle East. At a meeting of the Combined Chiefs of Staff it was agreed that the planned invasion of North Africa, Operation TORCH, must be accelerated, as opening this second front in Africa would require the Axis command to send reinforcements to counter this new threat rather than build-up forces for a decisive blow against Egypt.

This was to be the first Anglo-American operation and it would highlight political and military differences between the Allies, some of which would have a direct impact on the campaign. Invasion of North Africa was very much a British idea, indeed a Churchill idea; in part this was to provide a second front for the Desert War that would help secure victory, which some Americans saw as a British desire to shore up a key geographic location. It also made some sense as a second front to drain German resources, as demanded by Stalin, at far less risk than jumping into northern Europe. In part to smooth American concern, an American Supreme Commander was chosen, with Dwight D. Eisenhower being put forward by General George Marshall. It was an inspired choice in that Eisenhower proved adept, though not

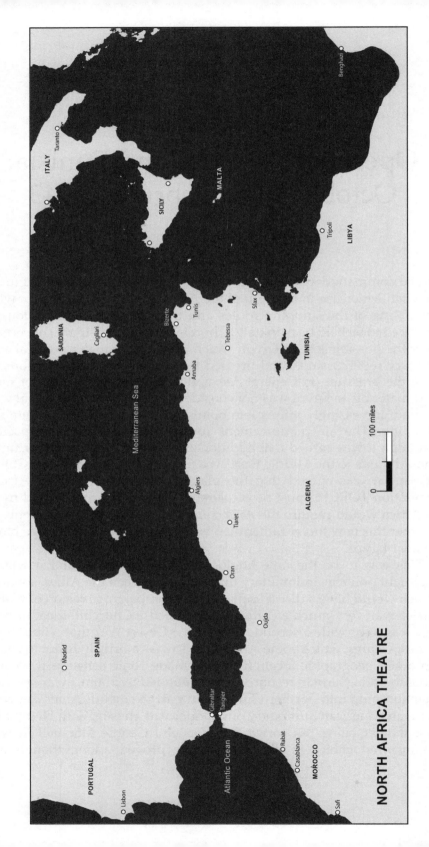

NORTH AFRICA THEATRE

Benghazi

Taranto

ITALY

MALTA

SICILY

Tripoli

LIBYA

Bizerte

Tunis

Sfax

Cagliari

SARDINIA

Tebessa

TUNISIA

Annaba

Mediterranean Sea

Algiers

Tiaret

ALGERIA

Oran

Oujda

Madrid

SPAIN

Gibraltar
Tangier

PORTUGAL

Rabat

Atlantic Ocean

Casablanca

MOROCCO

Lisbon

Safi

0   100 miles

always successful, at juggling politics and the egos of some of his commanders, British, American and French. Once committed to the venture, the American planning and their contribution of men and material was impressive, albeit that with the exception of some air units, all the American forces were inexperienced.

The failure of the Germans to neutralize Gibraltar had already had an impact on the Mediterranean and Malta campaigns, and Gibraltar was to be a key point in the invasion of North Africa. The overall landing plan was for the American Western Task Force, direct from the US, to assault Morocco's Atlantic coast (Safi, Fedala, Mehdia-Port Lyautey) and the Anglo-American landings on Algeria's Mediterranean cost (the Centre and Eastern Task Forces – Oran, Algiers), plus a battalion-sized airborne assault near Oran to seize two important airfields. The Anglo-America force sailed from the UK and elements staged via Gibraltar. It was estimated that the French had 60,000 troops in Morocco and 50,000 in Algeria, the majority being native troops with French officers, plus air and naval assets. Pétain and his Vichy French government had made it clear that any Allied attack would be resisted; in part this was based on concern that failure to do so would give the Germans reason to move into the two-thirds of France that was currently not occupied. However, it was by no means certain how individual commanders in North Africa would react, and the Allies spent a great deal of effort trying to persuade these commanders to either stand aside or join the Allies. American General Mark Clark undertook a covert mission to Algeria, landing from the submarine *Seraph* to hold talks with Vichy authorities. The Allies also made it clear what would happen if the French resisted.

The Allies realised that air power would be a key element in successful assault landings and rapid exploitation of the landings, and that much of that air power would have to come from American sources. "The 12th USAAF was to form a Western Command, with headquarters at Oran. Similarly, the RAF squadrons that were assigned to the operation were to form an Eastern Command, with headquarters at Algiers. With a view to the achievement of a maximum in flexibility in air power, to the reinforcement on occasion of each command from the other, and to necessary concentrations in strength in certain parts of the theater of operations, truly, all units in our operations were to be subject to my centralized direction and control. Though the initial assaults were to be supported by seaborne aircraft, it was essential that the maximum possible strength of fighter aircraft should be available as soon as landing grounds had been seized. It was therefore planned to fly from Gibraltar 160 fighters to each of the Oran and Casablanca areas, and 90 to the Algiers area within three days of the attack. Thereafter, the build-up was to reach, at the end of seven weeks, a total, in all types of aircraft, of 1,244 in the Western Command, and 454 in the Eastern Command. These aircraft were to be responsible in providing air cover to shipping and to ground forces, and in protecting bases and communications against air attack; also, in conjunction with the naval forces, they were to protect convoys against attack by submarines or surface raiders; and, finally, they were to provide air cooperation and support for land operations after the assault phase. Once adequate bases had been secured, strategic air forces for the bombing of possible Axis installations in Spain, and, ultimately, in the rest of the Mediterranean area were to be built up. The rate at which this could be done was to be limited by the number of squadrons of suitable types which could be made available in the United States and in the United Kingdom. The R.A.F. was already heavily committed in other theaters of war, both in fighter and bomber strength, and it was clear from the outset, that United States air forces would have to be provided on a considerably larger scale than British." (Eisenhower: "Report by C-in-C on Operations on North Africa".)

German agents and U-boats reported that the fleet had left Gibraltar and was heading east. Attacks were mounted from bases in Sicily and Sardinia, but the inability to use the excellent French airfields in Algeria and Tunisia meant the attacks were limited. The fleets were also well defended by anti-aircraft fire and carrier-based aircraft. The landings took place on 8th October, a massive Anglo-American operation under the command of General Eisenhower, and with major naval and air assets to ensure the beachhead and initial advance was successful. The overall Allied Naval Commander Expeditionary Force was Admiral Sir Andrew Cunningham, the most experienced Mediterranean commander and an ideal choice. In addition to the three assault fleets, the British Force H, reinforced from the Home Fleet, was positioned to intercept any action by the Italian Main Battle Fleet.

The Western Task Force, under the command of General Patton, bracketed Casablanca with landings at Safi, Fedala and Port Lyautey; the main landing at Fedala met the most resistance and suffered some losses but nevertheless was soon established ashore. A French naval force moved out to engage, but was intercepted by US carrier aircraft, who were soon joined by naval escorts, with the French losing heavily.

The USS *Ranger* led the Air Group and in a copy of its newsletter reported: "The French battleship *Jean Bart*, immobilized in Casablanca harbor, turned its 15-inch guns on the American landing force. The battleship USS *Massachusetts* sent a 16-inch shell into *Jean Bart*, jamming its one working turret. As the battle progressed, French resolve strengthened, and several Vichy destroyers and submarines sortied against the Allied forces outside the harbor. *Ranger's* Wildcats and Dauntlesses bombed and strafed the French ships and targets ashore. They also engaged in unexpectedly intense aerial encounters with their French opponents. In the first battles, 16 Vichy fighters were shot down for the loss of 4 Wildcats. Even biplane Curtiss SOC liaison float-planes contributed by breaking up a French tank column with depth charges using impact fuses. The SOCs flew from cruisers and battle-ships and usually carried messages and spotted for artillery." The convoy was also attacked by German U-boats from the north, losing four ships before the escorts drove the attackers away.

The Central Task Force at Oran met more resistance, with an initial coup de main on the port failing, although the landings on beaches east and west were successful. Meanwhile, the 2nd Battalion of the 509th Parachute Infantry Regiment (PIR) had flown from the UK for its assault on the airfields at La Seina and Tafaraoui. Despite unexpected high winds scattering the paratroops, they were still able to secure their objectives. The landings by the Eastern Task Force at Algiers were made easier by a French Resistance coup that seized key facilities and disabled shore batteries, although attempts to land troops in the docks met resistance. The cruiser *Aurora* and a number of destroyers fought off an attack by French destroyers, driving one ashore and disabling two, whilst the destroyers *Achates* and *Westcott* sank two French submarines (*Acteon* and *Argonaute*). Nevertheless, Algiers was in Allied hands by the early evening. Eisenhower summarised the day in his report: "During the day of October 8th, our forces moved to their objectives, though not without opposition. In the course of the morning, Combat Command 'B' took Tafaraoui airfield and advanced on La Senia. Early that afternoon, 26 United States Spitfires flew into Tafaraoui from Gibraltar; one Spitfire was shot down by a French pursuit plane just as the former was about to land. The Cap Matifou Battery which resisted obstinately during the morning was finally silenced by gunfire from HMS *Bermuda*, and by bombing by aircraft from the Fleet Air Arm. The latter force rendered excellent service that day in bombing and fighter protection to aid the ground forces and the fleet. Fort Dupere held out until it was bombed. For a while in the afternoon, the 39th Regimental Combat Team met strong resistance at Fort de l'Eau, but the latter eventually was taken. At the chief airfield at Maison Blanche, there was a slight brush with French tanks, but we had possession of the field and its defenses by 0830 hours. Not long after that time we were able to use this field for 19 Hurricanes and 35 Spitfires of the RAF, which flew in from Gibraltar." (Eisenhower, ibid.)

Politics also played a role in preventing the Germans making use of any French territory on North Africa; "Neither the Germans nor the Italians had many preparations in Tunisia, and in view of the mutual hatred of the French and Italians it was certain that whatever measures were taken would be met with obstinate resistance. For C-in-C South [Kesselring] the French colonies were taboo. It was forbidden to put in at any of the ports, supplies must not be routed via Tunis and Bizerte, and of course no German garrison could be moved to Tunis to guard against surprise attack. The limited strengthening of the German striking forces in the air could neither prevent a landing where their range of action ended nor halt or annihilate the troops once landed without the aid of parachute forces or army support." (*Kesselring Memoirs.*) He also called into question "what amount of opposition the French would offer." This indeed was a key question; it was impossible for the French forces to influence the overall outcome of any invasion, they were simply too weak, but there was the political aspect to be considered – heavy French losses and invasion of French territory – plus any delay in the Allied progress would enable a potential German counter-stroke.

On the 9th, Hitler authorized Kesselring to provide assistance to the French in Tunisia. German reinforcements had been arriving since early October and Allied reconnaissance showed 115 aircraft at Tunis airfield, whilst Bizerte was receiving over 50 transports a day as the Germans took the risk of flying in men and equipment. "The occupation of the country was begun with an understrength parachute regiment and my HQ battalion. It was hoped that negotiations with the French would result in the French military and naval forces joining us or at least remaining neutral." (*Kesselring Memoirs.*) Marshal Pétain ordered French colonial forces to march with the Germans, and initially cooperation was good, with German troops using French vehicles. The local commanders, especially General Georges Barré, GOC Tunisia, seemed less happy to cooperate.

	Casablanca (Morocco) 35,000 US	Oran (Algeria) 39,000 US	Algiers (Algeria) 33,000 US & British
Departure from	United States	Britain	Britain
Naval Commanders			
Western Rear-Adm H. K. Hewitt			
Centre Cdre T. H. Troubridge			
Eastern Vice-Adm Sir H. Burrough			
Battleships	3	–	–
Carriers	5	2	2
Cruisers	7	2	3
Destroyers	38	13	13
Other warship	16	41	40
Others	36	47	33
Total Ships	**105 USN**	**105 RN**	**91 RN**

The RAF was soon established ashore, with Maison Blanche and Blida as the main airfields, although temporary strips were soon to be the order of the day. The first RAF fighter Wing to arrive was No.324 Fighter Wing, which had formed in September 1942 under Gp Capt R. Lees and, according to its history, "after a very intensive programme of training, including some unpleasant items such as a battle and general toughening-up courses, embarked for North Africa in September." The toughening up had been a recognition that such advanced units would have to operate in difficult conditions right up with the front.

Casablanca was an important objective for the Western Task Force, and there was a brief naval engagement at the harbour approaches before the city was surrendered ahead of an all-out attack. Casablanca and Oran soon fell and on 10th October the French commander, Admiral Darlan, ordered a cessation of resistance. The "Darlan Deal" was not popular with the Free French or with some Allied politicians, because of his collaboration with Germany, but it made sense in that it stopped French resistance. Pétain was furious and ordered "resistance to the end" in North Africa, although this call from a discredited leader was ignored. Hitler had other ideas and now decided that Tunisia was to be saved and would become the platform for Axis victory in North Africa. The Luftwaffe was also concentrating assets in Sicily and Sardinia to support operations. Kesselring commented: "Eisenhower's

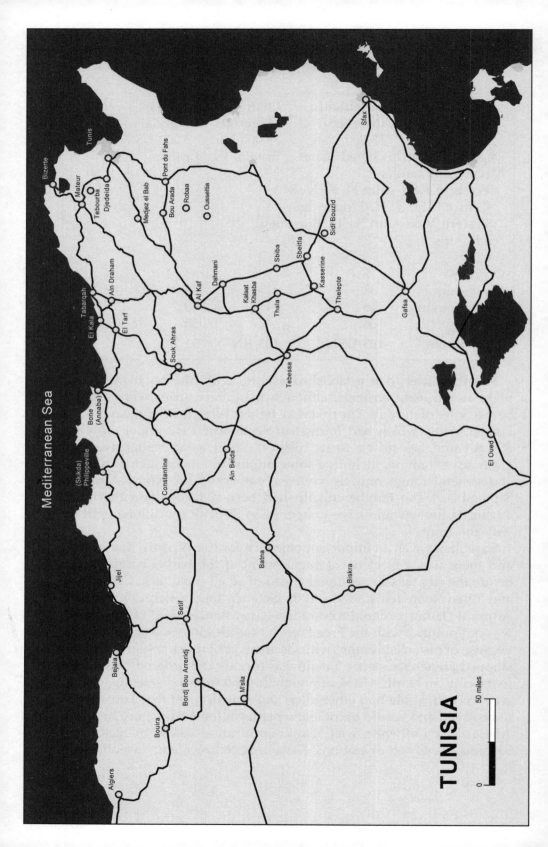

Mediterranean Sea

TUNISIA

0   50 miles

Algiers
Bouira
Bejaia
Bordj Bou Arreridj
Setif
Jijel
M'sila
Bone (Annaba)
(Skikda) Philippeville
Constantine
Ain Beida
Batna
Biskra
El Oued
Souk Ahras
El Kala
El Tarf
Tabarqah
Ain Draham
Bizerte
Mateur
Tunis
Tebourba
Djedeida
Medjez el Bab
Bou Arada
Pont du Fahs
Robaa
Ousseltia
Al Kaf
Dahmani
Kalaat Khasba
Thala
Sbiba
Sbeitla
Kasserine
Thelepte
Sidi Bouzid
Gafsa
Tebessa
Sfax

invasion troops certainly had the best possible equipment; they were eager to go into action, but they had no combat experience. Even an unfledged German army, unacclimatised to Africa, could deal with this enemy in a difficult, mountainous and desert terrain, but it must be sent quickly and in sufficient strength." On 15th October General Walther Nehring took command of German forces in Tunisia, and promptly set about organizing the defence of Tunisia, taking full advantage of the terrain in the west of the country, where a limited number of mountain passes led through the Atlas Mountains. To the north there was a narrow strip between the mountains and the sea, and new defences were constructed in this area, while to the south the French Mareth Line defences were improved. The build-up by air and sea was effective and by the end of the month the Germans had over 15,000 troops, over 150 tanks and supporting artillery in place. This was an initial force of five Divisions, three German, including 10th Panzer, and two Italian.

Meanwhile, with the collapse of French resistance, the Allies knew they had to move into Tunisia as quickly as possible to prevent the Germans building up a sizeable force that could defend Tunisia and potentially use Tunisia as a base from which to retake Algeria. To speed this up, General Anderson was ordered to use 1st Army's 36th Infantry Brigade to jump ahead. This Brigade was still afloat as it was the floating reserve for the initial landings. It was now ordered to land at ports closer to Tunisia – Bougie, Philippeville and Bone – and to seize the airfield at Djedjelli. The 36 Brigade landings at Bougie on 11th October were unopposed but they were slow to bring up supplies and did not reach Djedjelli until the 13th, by which time a parachute assault by 3rd Parachute Battalion had taken the airfield at Bone and 6 Commando had taken the port. Advanced elements of 36 Brigade reached Tebarka on the 15th, only 60 miles from Tunis, and Djebel Abiod three days later, where they at last came into contact with Axis forces. Meanwhile, the Americans were also on the move in the south, with a parachute assault taking the airfield at Youks-les-Bains on the 15th and the airfield at Gafsa two days later.

Air strength had increased with the arrival on 13th October of the B-17s of the 97th Bomb Group at Maison Blanche, assigned to 12th Air Force as its first heavy bomber unit. The 13th also saw the arrival at Tafaraoui of the first P-38s of the 1st Fighter Group. The same day, five C-47s of the 64th Troop Carrier Group flew urgent supplies, primarily fuel and anti-aircraft ammunition, to the British troops at Duzerville airfield. A second flight was made later the same day and proved the importance of this type of air supply in areas where the logistics and transport system were still, at best, unreliable. By 15th October more USAAF units had arrived, having staged via Gibraltar, once again proving the value of this airfield. By the end of the day the P-38s of the 1st and 14th Fighter Groups were in the Oran-Tagaraoui area, as was the 62nd Troup Carrier Group (TCG) and the 15th Light Bombardment Squadron, the latter with A-20s for tactical support. The same day saw two small paratroop operations, with the 60th TCG dropping 350 American paratroops at Youks-les-Bains, and the 64th TCG taking British paratroops to Souk-el-Arba, although the latter was recalled because of bad weather. This gave the Allies the ability to hit the more distant targets, although the first target, on the 16th, was the airfield at Sidi Ahmed near Bizerte.

The French XIX Corps under General Koeltz reported contact with German motorcycle troops between Beja and Djebel Abiod on the 16th, and Eisenhower noted that cooperation with the French "had started to appear" and "not more than 20 miles from Bizerte drove off German patrols. Our plans for offensive action were now able to count on at least some measure of French assistance. Although General Barré, as Commander of all French Forces in Tunis, had negotiated with General Nehring ever since the arrival of German forces, he now agreed that his forces would cover the concentration of our 78th Division in the Tebarka-Souk el Arba-Ghardimaou area and that they would likewise cover, to the best of their ability, our right flank during our subsequent advance on Tunis. As quickly as the first signs of French tactical cooperation began to appear I proposed to Giraud that the whole Eastern front be placed under General Anderson's command. I met the most bitter opposition to the idea. Giraud even said that any such attempt, at that time, would result in open French rebellion. Instead, he proposed that he take command of the front; manifestly, I could not agree." (Eisenhower, ibid.) Inter-allied politics were to have a significant impact on the campaign. On the 17th, the leading elements of the 36th Brigade advancing along the northern road clashed with an Axis force of 400 paratroops with 17 tanks, plus artillery support – and with the Luftwaffe dominant overhead. The British lost 11 tanks and were brought to a halt. This was the first indication that the easy days of the advance were over, although the situation still seemed favourable overall. But, "it was the enemy who seized the initiative by attacking the French at Medjez el Bab on the 18th and 19th. Von Arnim sent two separate ultimata, demanding French surrender, which was not conceded by General Barre; and the ill-equipped French, assailed three times by infantry supported by tanks, artillery and dive-bombers, suffered 25 per cent casualties. They sent us urgent pleas for air support, which we could not supply." (Eisenhower, ibid.) Kesselring recalled the incident as well: "I had to do something about the Divisions under the command of Barre. This gentleman's intentions and dealings were so inscrutable that I could not afford to waste any further time. I had to end an intolerable situation by sending in the Stukas against the French Divisions." (*Kesselring Memoirs.*) The initial German attacks were repulsed, but at heavy loss to the French, who subsequently withdrew. By the 20th, Blade Force was established in the Souk el Arba area and 11th Brigade Group of 78th Division was concentrated in the Beja area. "Though we were able thus to hold the enemy in check, it was clear, however that our 78th Division was not as yet strong enough to press the advance. Hence, they were ordered to delay temporarily any move forward until the build-up of forces and supplies was sufficient to give the assault on Tunis a reasonable chance of success. We had also to straighten out the considerable intermixture of French and British units which had occurred as a result of rapid improvisation following the French decision to act with us." (Eisenhower, ibid.) This was true, but the moment for victory had been missed.

On the 22nd the American paratroops at Gafsa were forced to retreat when attacked by tanks of the Italian 50th Brigade. The Allies now concentrated in the Djebel Abiod-Beja area to prepare for a two-pronged attack, the 36 Brigade towards Mateur and the 11 Brigade down the River Medjerda valley to Medjez al Bab and then Tebourba. A third unit, Blade Force, an armoured regimental group with 17th/21st Lancers, moved across country between the two main prongs, to make flanking attacks on Tebourba and Djedeida, on the north-west outskirts of Tunis. The stage was set for a fierce contest, one that would bloody the enthusiastic but inexperienced American ground and air forces. There was also to be a significant amount of politics between the British and American commanders and between air and land commanders. By the 24th Lt-Gen Anderson had concentrated for the push to Tunis, to be led by 78th Division and Blade Force, with follow-up forces from 6th Armored Division and US 1st Armored Division. The attack was delayed 24 hours by heavy rain, and when it did start, with 36 Brigade in the north, Blade Force in the centre and 11 Brigade in the south, progress was initially good. After advancing 10 miles towards Mateur,

36 Brigade ran into concentrations of mines and booby traps and came to a virtual halt. In the centre, Blade Force progressed well but was running ahead of its supply line and was also subject to intense air attack. On the right flank, 11 Brigade captured Medjez el Bab after a fierce fight, taking Tebourba in the early hours of the 27th, and reaching the outskirts of Djedeida, only 16 miles from Tunis, the following day. It was to prove the high point of the Allied advance and the symbol of a missed opportunity. According to Eisenhower's report: "In every sector the enemy's dive-bombing was an important factor in finally stopping our advance, because our own airfields were too far away to provide us with the necessary cover. With our long lines of communications, with insufficient landing grounds, and with an inadequate number of planes for the missions they had to perform, it became increasingly difficult to cope with the airpower that was aligned against us." The Germans put in a strong attack on the 27th, tumbling the Americans back. A planned counter-attack, including Combat Command B of US 1st Armored and Blade Force, was under preparation when the Germans struck again, led by the newly-arrived 10th Panzer Division. This was a major shock to the Americans, but in desperate fighting they prevented a breakthrough and were able to retire to a new line east of Medjez el Bab.

The Allied race to Tunis was over, as the delays in moving forward had enabled the Axis to put sizeable reinforcements into Tunisia; indeed, an assessment around this time suggested that the Allies had around 134,00 men (54,000 British, 73,000 American and 7,000 French), excluding French colonial troops, whilst the Axis had around 125,000 plus 70,000 service troops. With their shorter and protected reinforcement lines from Italy, the Axis forces were in a position to build-up more rapidly than the Allies, who still relied on naval convoys, and a lengthy overland route from their ports. Allied strength had been building in the rear area, and additional units now moved forward. British 1st Army received 1st, 4th and 46th Infantry to add to 6th Armoured Division and 78th Infantry; US II Corps, 1st Armored and 1st and 34th Infantry. The French XIX Corps remained – Giraud refused to serve under British 1st Army. With the arrival of Combat Command B (CCB), Anderson planned to renew his offensive in early November by this unit and Blade Force. Before it could be launched the Germans attacked on the first day of the month, inflicting heavy losses, including 40 tanks, on Blade Force, which had to withdraw, leaving 11 Brigade and armoured infantry of CCB to hold the line. A further German push on the 3rd broke through and cut-off 11 Brigade, although they managed to extricate themselves overnight, albeit with heavy losses, especially of equipment.

"By November 4th it was clear that our offensive against Tunis would have to be postponed, to give time for the refitting of badly battered troops, and for a build-up of adequate resources. Several battalions of the 78th Division were under 350 strong, and the strain of persistent dive-bombing was beginning to tell. On November 8th I approved General Anderson's proposal to withdraw his forces to more defensible ground. This I considered advisable, but I was resolved that no vital areas were to be given up, and the important center of Medjez el Bab was to be held at all costs." (Eisenhower.) The ambitious Allied plan that had put forces across the area Morocco-Algeria-Tunisia was now at breaking point having failed to secure Tunis. The poor communication network, terrain, long distances and bad weather all counted against the Allies' current situation, whereas the Axis had short and secure supply lines – as long as they held Tunis. German forces were still weak overall, and the Allied retreat was generally able to proceed without major attacks, although the weather that restricted the Luftwaffe also meant that roads became mired. Combat Command B had to abandon most of its equipment, managing to save only three of its eighteen 105mm howitzers, 12 of its 62 medium tanks, and 38 of its 122 light tanks, thus greatly reducing its combat capability. The British too had suffered heavy losses, but Eisenhower remained convinced that if he could move forces from the rear area and re-equip his units then he could still make a decisive strike towards Tunis later in the month.

"More and more in time the weather appeared to be our worst enemy, crippling both our offense and defense, and making it increasingly difficult either to advance or to withdraw. Rains saturated the valleys of Northern Tunisia and made a quagmire of the airfields. While enemy aircraft continued to use their all-weather airports, our bombers were glued in the mud; and, when they could take off, it was frequently only to discover that their primary targets were shrouded in heavy clouds. Two thirds of the aircraft at Souk el Arba were inoperative because of the mud. Air operations were virtually closed-down because of the appalling conditions on the ground and in the skies. The broken stone which we laid down to give solidity to the air fields merely sank in the mud, and to surface adequately a single runway, we required 2,000 tons of steel matting. Such a quantity as this would absorb for at least two days the entire capacity of the [text obscured] in the forward area, for their usable daily capacity at that time was only 950 tons. Since our only real hope of victory lay in the use of air power, and in the skilful maneuver of artillery to blast the enemy's armor, our operations had again to be postponed, and finally abandoned." (Eisenhower, ibid.) Indeed, he was now of the opinion that no major offensive would be possible before February or March 1943; "and we had to set about the slow business of building up for an attack at the end of that period. The logistic marathon, which I had desperately tried to avoid, had begun." The Allies left a screen of French troops and American paratroops covering the Tebessa-Thelepte region, and Eisenhower planned to move the US II Corps, centred on the US 1st Armored Division, as a striking force behind this screen, his aim still being to renew the offensive. The Corps was commanded by General Fredendall and he was also assigned XII Air Support Command as his tactical air asset. The 33rd Fighter Group had moved into Thelepte on 11th November with its P-40s: "The next day, without benefit of communications or planned strategy, the officers of the 33rd, forming their own on-the-cuff manoeuvres, strike for what they can find." The Group was still short of everything and was close to the front, so the mechanics had to work on the aircraft during the day and stand guard at night. "Thelepte is nothing like the secure, comfortable, well-supplied training bases back in the United States. It is cold, uncomfortable, isolated and close to the front with a shortage of mechanics, pilots, planes, replacement parts, tools, warm clothes and many other things, but the 33rd will continue to operate here and provide valuable support to the front-line forces." (33rd FG history.) This was yet another example of the Allied dash forward that was bold but ill-considered regarding logistics back-up. They were also "running into larger forces of German planes and paying the price"; one reconnaissance mission of six aircraft met a superior force of Ju87s and 109s, and only one P-40 returned to base.

Meanwhile, the German build-up continued, and Kesselring had visited the front and then flew to meet Hitler: "We have succeeded in the improbable task of building up a bridgehead and pushing forward a front which, though it will not be able to stop a major offensive, can be consolidated. To do so fresh reinforcements are needed. It is hopeless to think of pushing forward to the line we have to occupy with the available force of three and a half German Divisions, including only one Panzer Division, and with a total of only 100 guns, on a front over

250 miles long. There is still time, but the sands are running out." (*Kesselring Memoirs.*) He also highlighted the poor performance of the American commanders whose indecision and poor deployments were open for exploitation. The establishment of 5th Panzer Army on 5th November enabled more coordinated activity of the Axis forces that had been built-up; it also brought a new commander, with Hans-Jürgen von Arnim replacing the out of favour Nehring. His initial command comprised 10th Panzer Division, the main armoured element, the von Broich Division, which had been made up from the various units that had been rushed to Tunisia in early October, and the Italian 1st Mountain Division Superga and 18th Infantry Messina. He had also been promised six more Divisions. The Italians were initially assigned as a security garrison in the central sector, with the German forces being concentrated in the northern sector.

During early December both sides undertook probing assaults, with mixed results and no real change of the overall situation. To ease his supply line situation, Eisenhower attempted to route more shipping to the ports at Oran, Algiers and Bône and to build up advanced depots at Bône (on the coast), Constantine and Tebessa. The role of the C-47s in air-lifting supplies from the rear areas was also important. Meanwhile, in an attempt to interdict Axis shipping routes, RAF and Royal Navy torpedo bombers operated from Reghaia and Bône, whilst aircraft also mined the approaches to Bizerte and Tunis. Allied submarines were also active, and on 2nd November a cruiser-destroyer force intercepted and sank or damaged four supply ships and three of their escorts. Despite this one-off success, and the night patrols by the ships of Force Q, there was little overall impact on the flow of supplies. Axis submarines were also active, as were Italian torpedo-bombers, and several Allied ships were sunk in early December. Bône, as the main depot for Anderson's command, was subject to intense air attack, with almost daily raids, and several merchant ships were sunk in the harbour, and the cruiser *Ajax* was damaged, after which use of the port was restricted. Additional anti-aircraft guns were moved into the area, as were Beaufighters of 600 Squadron for night defence.

Throughout early December both sides built up their forces and most activity was confined to air attacks on ground positions and supply areas; the Luftwaffe seemed, to the Allied ground troops, to be ever present. Eisenhower was concerned over the capabilities of the French XIX Corps, which was occupying a central position, but which was very poorly equipped. "My most serious concern in mid-January was the French, General Giraud had proposed early in December that the French XIX Corps take over the defense of the critical high ridge which forms the western barrier of the coastal plain of Eastern Tunisia. The most dangerous aspect of the French situation was their appalling lack of equipment which seriously affected both efficiency and morale. They were completely lacking in the types of weapon needed to cope with German armor, and there was little we could do to supply their needs, because of the pressing urgency of our own. Many of the French were poorly trained, and some, who had families resident in the areas of Tunisia under German control, were of very doubtful reliability." Eisenhower was stuck with the French, even though they added a difficult political dimension. Although a plan was put in place to re-equip the French, this would take many months and, in the meantime, this central sector between the British and Americans was very vulnerable.

Then on 18th December von Arnim launched his Operation COURIER I (Unternehmen Eilbote I). Elements of 10th Panzer and 334th Infantry Division attacked from Pont du Fahs. The thrust against the right wing of the British V Corps at Bou Arada was repulsed. Further south the attack which struck the French positions in the critical hinge between the Eastern and Western Dorsales was almost immediately successful, breaking into the French positions and causing the French to fall back. By early the following day the thrust had reached Ousseltia, an advance of 35 miles, and Robaa, an advance of 25 miles. The French were poorly equipped and despite pockets of resistance, there was little to hold up the attackers. General Anderson immediately sent a squadron of tanks and some artillery from 6th Armoured Division to support the French, and a battalion of 1st Guards Brigade who were already in the area. Elements of 36 Brigade were sent to Robaa to prevent a break-out in that direction and Fredendall was ordered to move Combat Command B to Ousseltia. Despite these moves, the Germans pushed on down the valley and linked up at Robaa. Gen Alphonse Juin of XIX Corps withdrew his French troops westward to a line Djebel Halfa-Siliana, forcing the British V Corps to the north to conform by withdrawing its right flank.

The advance continued on the 20th, with the French positions in the Eastern Dorsale isolated; by evening the Germans had taken Ousseltia. In confused fighting the next day, a counter-stroke by 6th Armoured Division caused heavy losses and restored the situation, enabling the French to extricate themselves. By 23rd December the situation had stabilized, but it had been a close-run thing and it flagged to Eisenhower a number of deficiencies in the command arrangements, and to help address this he appointed Anderson to coordinate all Allied troops at the front; a front that was now some 200 miles long and across which communication was limited. This was the first intensive encounter between American and German forces and it revealed several deficiencies in both ground and air operations. "The use of light and medium bombers for low-level close air support missions proved disastrous because of effective German light antiaircraft artillery. Arnold's fears about the new bombers were justified. The A-20, B-25, and B-26 crews were forced to high altitude operations while in the middle of combat operations. While flying at a new altitude of 10,000 feet was not difficult, trying to hit targets using crude bomb sights and flying in formation proved impossible without intense training." ("A pattern for Joint Operations: WWII Close Air Support, North Africa", Daniel Mortensen, CMH 2005.)

Additional Allied forces were moving up, including the US 9th and 34th Divisions and the British 25th Armoured Brigade, whilst other key units were supplied with better equipment, such as 6th Armoured Division receiving Shermans. On 27th December, Portal (CAS) proposed that Coningham be appointed to command of "Air Support Tunisia", a suggestion supported by all the RAF commanders and key USAAF figures. "He was the logical person to head the tactical air command. There was just no doubt about it. We didn't have anybody that could even come close to him ... his was the easiest of all the selections that had to be made." (Lt-Gen Quesada.) Other Command changes also took effect across the Allied command structure; Eisenhower remained C-in-C, with Alexander moving from Cairo to become his Deputy C-in-C and commander of 18 Army Group (British 1st and 8th Armies, French XIX Corps, and the American II Corps). Most command organizations had a mixture of British/Commonwealth and American commanders, and at times it seemed more about balancing egos and numbers than effective appointments. There remained a distinct difference of opinion in "ownership" of air assets and how much credit/recognition/understanding should be given to the British experience to date. The good, bad and ugly of the politics is beyond the scope of this book, but it was there, and was to remain to the end of the war. "Any operation is complicated by the competing demands of individual commanders on a far-flung battle front, each of whom would naturally like to have at his disposal some segment of the air forces for his own exclusive use. To a large extent in our experience the creation of separate Strategic and Tactical forces resolved the conflict between the immediate needs of the commander for direct air support, and the equally compelling necessity of knocking out the enemy's war potential far behind the lines; but, perhaps, the greatest advantage of our new organization was its flexibility. Aircraft of the different combat formations could be fused in a single mission as the need arose, and as a result the local commander had for direct support the combined weight of the Strategic and Tactical forces when he most needed it." (Eisenhower, ibid.)

The Germans had also made command changes. Having had a period of rest in Germany, Rommel was summoned to a conference with Hitler and Kesselring. In view of the position in Tunisia it was proposed that Rommel would take command in Tunisia, forming a second Panzer Army with the new units that had been assembled in Italy. As the situation on the Egypt front appeared stable, and the prediction was that Montgomery would make no aggressive moves until Spring 1943, it was also agreed that elements of 21st Panzer and 90th Light would join the new Panzer Army in Tunisia, providing a core of very experienced commanders and men; these would be shipped along the Mediterranean coast. The Allied forces, especially the Americans, had shown themselves to be vulnerable and a decisive offensive could lead to a total victory. It was agreed that a deception plan to convince the Allies of a new offensive in Egypt would keep them from launching an attack; additional bomber assets were to be assigned to the east to increase the pressure on the British. For the Tunisian campaign the critical elements would be the prevention of major Allied reinforcements, and an intensive U-boat campaign would be mounted to destroy Allied troop and supply shipments. Political attempts would be made to bring Spain into the war, thus threatening Gibraltar and, through Spanish Morocco, the Allied bases in Morocco and Algeria. Rommel requested two armoured and three infantry Divisions; he also expected the Italians to offer two to three infantry Divisions. Kesselring promised a significant increase in Luftwaffe strength.

The decisions made, Rommel immediately flew to Tunis to confer with von Arnim, who would retain command of 5th Panzer Army but under Rommel's overall direction. On his arrival he was pleased to discover that three Divisions, one armoured (Hermann Goering) and two infantry (one German and one Italian), had already arrived in

Tunis and had been moved south to the Sidi Bouzid area, from where they could support a thrust via Kasserine or a southerly sweep via El Oued and up to Biskra and Batna, to cut-off the Allied forces in the central area. However, before this more complex and riskier move Rommel planned to test the Americans in the centre and the British in the north. His initial strategic aim was the destruction of the Allied forces in the area of the front, dragging reinforcements from the rear area that could then be engaged and destroyed, thus weakening over- all Allied strength. Unlike the situation in the Western Desert there were few options for flanking manoeuvres, and much of the fighting would be in constrained terrain. The weather was also a factor, as this would be a winter campaign. With the Allied forces destroyed or disrupted, he would move on Algiers to deny this logistics hub to the Allies and enable his own use of this port. Once Algiers had been secured, the next phase of the offensive would be Oran, thus depriving the Allies of any significant Mediterranean port and completing the seizure of Algeria. Morocco was a more difficult prospect, as its Atlantic ports made it easier for Allied reinforcements, although it was hoped that losses to U-boats and the loss of Algeria would persuade the Allies to abandon the campaign. The timeline was tight; Rommel wanted to be back in Egypt ready for the spring campaign.

The French sector was attacked again on 30th December and was pushed back to the road junction at Sidi Bouzid, so elements of 1st Armored Division were ordered forward in support. During early January confused fighting continued east and southeast of Sbeitla, and Combat Command "A" suffered further heavy personnel casualties from dive-bombing. By this time the United States II Corps had suf- fered serious losses in equipment: 98 medium tanks, 57 half-tracks, 12 155mm guns and 17 105mm guns. "Such losses ruled out the possi- bility of further counterattacks to hold the enemy, much less to restore our strategic position. During the early phases of the engagement we had been much hampered by weather conditions which prevented continuous air operations, but during the decisive period of the struggle we were able to strike telling blows with our air power. The brunt of the air defense fell on XII Air Support Command, but other elements of our air forces gave a coordinated support which demon- strated the effectiveness of two newly created organizations, North- west Africa Air Force, and Mediterranean Air Command. Air Force's diversionary attacks in the South pinned down the German Air Force in that area." (Eisenhower, ibid.)

Following the success against the French, Rommel decided to launch an attack on the American sector, his rationale being that these inexperienced troops would be pushed aside and then the whole Allied line could be rolled-up. The offensive was spearheaded by the 21st and 10th Panzer Divisions via the Kasserine Pass and started on 14th January. The Pass was a 2-mile-wide gap in the Dorsale mountain chain and his plan was to concentrate on the inexperienced US II Corps, drive through and capture the major supply bases on the Algerian side and disrupt Allied operations along the coastal corridor.

The panzers of the 21st Division caught the Americans of the 1st Armored Division around Sidi Bouzid by surprise, Gen Omar Bradley later commenting that the German attack had been expected further north. The US 34th Infantry was established just west of Sidi Bouzid and was also caught up in the confusion, with poor weather contributing to the initial problems: "a strong westerly wind picked up, and by 0400 hours started a sandstorm. The German staff weatherman had accurately predicted these conditions, and when combined with the normal early morning haze, observation of the Faid Pass exit had become impossible from the American positions. Primarily due to the difficult weather conditions the screening elements forward of the American positions, the attached 1st Derbyshire Yeomanry and the 81st Reconnaissance Battalion, failed to intercept attacking German forces and the carefully prepared artillery concentrations on the pass exits went unfired. Visibility limitations hindered surveillance and target acquisition to such an extent that the American artillery was overrun around the rear of Lessouda. Additionally, a clear picture of the size and composition of German forces was not relayed to the Commanding General of the 1st Armored Division." (*The Battle of Sidi Bouzid*, Combat Studies Institute.)

The Germans also took advantage of the Americans' inexperience by pinning them down with one assault, and sending an armoured group around the northern sector into their flank, whilst another swung round to take them in the rear. Rommel wrote: "A violent tank battle developed in which the inexperienced Americans were steadily battered down by my tankmen – veterans of hundreds of desert battles – and soon large numbers of Grants, Lees and Shermans were blazing on the battlefield. The bulk of the American force was destroyed, and the remainder fled to the west." (*Rommel Papers.*) With the Americans in confusion, the pursuit was pushed but was met with a stout defence at Sbeitla. This was overcome by the evening of the second day, by which time the Germans estimated that they had destroyed over 150 tanks and taken 1,600 prisoners. "The Americans had as yet no practical battle experience, and it was now up to us to instil in them from the outset an inferiority complex of no mean order." (*Rommel Papers.*) The overall position compromised, the Americans withdraw from Gafsa on the morning of the 15th, which was promptly occupied by Italians of the 131st Centauro Division. "During the night of January 15th–16th, our infantry withdrew from Djebel Lessouda, in the North. It was necessary for them to withdraw to escape complete encircle-ment, and they were obliged to leave the bulk of their transport behind. The 168th Infantry Regiment remained completely isolated on Djebel Ksaira." (Eisenhower.)

Fighting continued next day east and southeast of Sbeitla, with Combat Command A suffering heavy losses; by the end of the day II Corps had lost much of its fighting equipment, including 98 medium tanks. The German drive threatened the integrity of the Allied line and a withdrawal was ordered. Driving north-west, one combat group captured Feriana on the 17th after a hard fight with the American defenders, who also had time to destroy important stores. The offen-sive continued to the key centre and airfield at Thelepte, which was quickly taken, the defenders hastily destroying aircraft on the airfield. "From the two Thelepte (air)fields a total of 3,496 individuals were evacuated and very little organizational equipment was left behind. Fifty thousand gallons of gasoline were burned, as well as four P-40s, three A-20s, three Spitfires and eight P-51s; of these, five were non-repairable. Intensive air operations continued. On the 17th the Spitfires and P-39s performed their reconnaissance missions over the fluid front, strafed where targets presented themselves, and furnished cover for Command A stubbornly defending Sbeitla. A Spitfire squadron up at 1115 hours reported one of the Thelepte fields being shelled and Feriana swarming with Axis transport. Late in the afternoon six A-20s struck the road below Feriana claiming 35 vehicles destroyed after a low-altitude attack with 100-lb bombs fuzed for delayed action. A road and a highway bridge were also declared out." (12th AF North Africa Ops.) But there were problems: "As the fighting continued, the XII ASC suffered serious losses while attempting to provide cover over a wide front ... The technical superiority of German aircraft was demon-strated beyond any doubt during these engagements ... technical superiority alone did not give the Germans an edge over the Americans in the air. Pilot fatigue caused by long patrol and cover missions reduced crew effectiveness in combat. There were simply not enough pilots and aircraft in the XII ASC alone to meet adequately every demand." (*Tunisia Air Power: The Evolution of US Tactical Air Doctrine, Tunisia*, Mark Conversino.)

The Combat Studies Institute analysis of the battle of Sidi Bouzid concluded: "This battle at Sidi Bou Zid went to the Axis forces because of their technological advantage in the Part 11-1 9 main weapon system employed, the tank, and because of their skilful ability to employ combined arms forces. The Germans knew the capabilities of their weapons systems and had learned how to maximize those capabilities. The Allied forces, especially the Americans who were the Allied combatants in this battle, had not yet learned how to differentiate 'parade ground' and 'map bound' tactics from actual 'battle ground' tactics. In the final analysis, this weakness had a far greater impact on their defeat than did their shortcomings in the technological arena." This was an apt assessment and a key element in the Allied failures in the campaign.

The Americans now seemed to be focused on a retreat to Tebessa, a critical road junction that if lost would give the Germans multiple options. "The Americans seemed to be pulling back to Tebessa. Their command appeared to be getting jittery and they were showing the lack of decision typical of men commanding for the first time in a difficult situation. Now that the operation had gone successfully for four days, I wanted to push forward with all our strength to Tebessa, take possession of this important airbase, supply and transport centre, and strike on deep into the Allied rear." (*Rommel Papers*.) Rommel now proposed a main thrust to seize Tebessa and then strike into the Allied rear areas, whilst a combat group would also head through the Kasserine Pass via Thala to seize the road junction at Kalaat Khasba and then swing north; this latter was under the command of von Arnim, but at a conference with Rommel he expressed concern over the dual attack and his own lack of armour, with Rommel having taken half of 10th Panzer to join his strike force. Nevertheless, the plan was agreed.

The initial attack by Panzer Grenadier Regiment Menton had initial success, and moved up the pass, its StugIII self-propelled guns proving effective in supporting the advance. However, the attack was soon under heavy artillery fire, as the Americans held the high ground on either side, enabling artillery observers to direct accurate and concentrated fire. The attack stalled until Ju87 formations appeared and engaged the Allied positions, whilst the mountain infantry unit assaulted the high ground. "At about 1300 hours on the 19th January, I drove to the headquarters of the Afrika Korps group to obtain an exact picture of the situation. At intervals along the road we passed American vehicles, their drivers dead at the wheel – obviously victims of our air attacks. Numerous small groups of scattered Americans were still being brought in. I dispatched General Bülowius with a combat group to make an outflanking attack on the Kasserine Pass." (*Rommel Papers.*)

The Sbiba thrust was led by 21st Panzer but they made slow progress, having been held up by the condition of the roads, which were waterlogged after heavy rain. They also ran into a dense minefield which was defended by 1 Guards Brigade. Heavy fighting continued for much of the day, with no real progress being made, and tank losses mounting. Once again, the failure to consider how to take the surrounding hills had subjected the Germans to a stagnating battle in which Allied artillery could play a major role. The main offensive on the Tebessa route was led by 10th Panzer, with Rommel accompanying what he had always planned as the key thrust. The advance was rapid as the Americans had withdrawn to the ridge line near Darnayah, some 8 miles north-west of Thelepte. The road climbed up the ridge and through a one-mile pass, with the ridge itself providing excellent observation and gun positions. Rommel sent a combat group to sweep around the western end of the ridge, threatening to cut-off and isolate the defenders. Operating from Thelepte, Stukas and Bf109s provided air cover and close air support, whilst Allied air was proving less effective, and a source of tension between the Allied commanders. The Anglo-American and land-air politics and "debate" about how to apply air power increased in intensity in February, with Patton and Bradley in particular pushing the US doctrine that the American soldier expects (demands even) a constant air umbrella and that anything else was not the correct use of "close support". This remained anathema to the likes of Tedder, Coningham and Broadhurst. This was born out of the American lack of experience in modern air-land warfare and their lack of resilience under air attack, despite the fact that to date they had not suffered significant attacks. In part to waylay at least some of the issues, on 20th January Coningham placed his British and American bombers (the tactical ones) under a new Tactical Bomber Force (TBF) under Air Commodore Laurence Sinclair. "By mid-January the U.S. Ground Forces around us were hard pressed by the Germans and we had to evacuate Thelepte and move back to Youks-les-Bains behind the mountains. About five days later deserted by our Army as well as our own Headquarters and Service Squadron, we had one of our biggest days of fighting. The last time we were to use low-level attack. Beneath low cloud in the valleys northwest of Kasserine Pass we pounded the Germans all day." (47th BG history.)

These air attacks were having an impact on the central thrust and Rommel was furious that the attack had stalled and there seemed no sense of urgency in pushing forward, demanding renewed effort to break the stalemate. He sent a Nebelwerfer unit in support, the first use of this highly-effective barrage system in this campaign. "Finally, at about 1700 hours, the pass was at last in our hands. The Americans had fought extremely well and Menton's losses had been considerable. During the evening we discovered an enemy armoured formation on the other side of the pass. It was partially formed up in a side valley and was apparently intended to come to the aid of the Kasserine defenders. I immediately passed an armoured group forward through the pass. This advance made over the quickly rebuilt bridge across the Hatab river took the enemy completely by surprise; they were pressed back against the mountains and soon destroyed by the veteran tank-men of the 8th Panzer Regiment. The action took place at point-blank range, and the enemy soon abandoned his tanks and vehicles and tried to escape on foot over the hills. We captured some 20 tanks and 30 armoured troop-carriers, most of which were trailing a 75-mm anti-tank gun." (*Rommel Papers.*)

By early evening the Germans had entered Thala, overrunning a British battalion: "During our entry a British battalion allowed itself to be overrun by the tank spearheads before opening fire. Our tanks wheeled about, attacked the enemy in the rear and drove them out of their positions, 700 prisoners falling into our hands." The eastern thrust to Sbiba had also made progress, again due to excellent support by the Luftwaffe and the absence of Allied tactical aircraft. By the evening of the 20th the advanced units were approaching Dahmani, a key crossroads, but the Allied units that had been pushed back by the initial offensive were joined in the new positions by reinforcements rushed in from the north, with the British 6th Armoured Division and the US 34th Infantry Division moving forwards. Meanwhile, the Americans had been warned by Allied reconnaissance aircraft of the enemy forces sweeping west around the Darnahya ridge and had begun to pull back to a defence line on the high ground south and east of Tebessa. Rommel urged his panzers forward and changed the axis of the western sweep to the road that headed directly for Tebessa, as the need to come in behind the defended ridge had gone. Heavy rain in the afternoon delayed the pursuit and grounded tactical aircraft on both sides. The 501st and 504th Heavy Panzer Battalions went into action as part of the southern thrust, although only 50% of the tanks were serviceable, with mechanical issues continuing to plague the units. They proved their superiority to any of the Allied tanks, both in fire-power and survivability (88mm gun and 102mm frontal armour).

The next day, the 21st, was one of mixed fortunes, with a temporary setback in the centre, when the advancing Germans were ambushed. "The American defence had been very skilfully executed. After allow-ing the attacking column to move peacefully on up the valley, they suddenly had fire poured on it from three sides, quickly bringing the column to a halt. Our men had been astounded at the flexibility and accuracy of the American artillery, which had put a great number of our tanks out of action. When they were later forced to withdraw, the American infantry followed up closely and turned the withdrawal into a costly retreat." (*Rommel Papers*.) It was only a temporary set-back and, reinforced by three Tigers from the 501st, the Germans renewed the attack, joined by Italian mountain troops who did an excellent job of clearing the wooded hillsides, opening the way for the advance to continue through the valley.

Kesselring visited Rommel's HQ on the morning of 22nd January and discussed the overall situation. Although the central and eastern thrust had been slower than expected, and with heavier losses, especi-ally in tanks, the western thrust was progressing well and was likely to result in the Allies having to make a general withdrawal that would also open-up the stalled thrusts. Rommel stated that it was vital that supplies and reinforcements continued to flow, so that he had the resources to make the break-out into the Allied rear area effective. He also stressed the importance of the Luftwaffe's tactical support.

Following integration into the new TBF, the 47th BG history recorded: "With few aircraft and all of our people we moved further back to the well-stocked base at Canrobert. Here in the true spirit of the Casablanca Conference for 'Allied Cooperation' we added several members of the Royal Air Force (RAF) to our group; veterans all and really great guys. Until now our bombardiers were self-trained volun-teers from within the group using home-made bomb sights. Now Lead Bombardiers joined each squadron from RAF flying officer ranks and brought along the Mark IX-E bombsights. Between widely-spaced combat missions we put in several weeks of intensive medium altitude formation flying with many newly received replacement aircraft and some new aircrews."

"On the 24th January, I [Rommel] held a conference with the 1a [chief staff officer] of Fifth Army to discuss their plans. Von Arnim was planning an outflanking attack to destroy the enemy forces which had assembled in the area round Medjez el Bab [40 miles west of Tunis], I agreed the scheme, but could not accept their further plan to evacuate the plain of Medjez el Bab after the operation and return to their starting point." (*Rommel Papers.*) With the operation further south now looking favourable and the centre and southern columns linked at Tebessa, Rommel was keen to exploit this area but also to push on the British in the north, to probe for weakness as they had sent units south to reinforce the central front, and to prevent further reinforcements being sent. From Tebessa he proposed to make two main thrusts, one towards Setif, and ultimately Algiers, and one to Constantine and the coast, to trap the British. This task was assigned to von Arnim and 5th Panzer Army. Rommel had met with von Arnim to discuss the operation, and to stress the importance of rapid movement and exploitation of the breakthrough, as he had previously believed that von Arnim had not been aggressive enough in previous thrusts. The enemy on this front were the British, he argued, a different proposition to the Americans and although many of the troops were inexperienced they would be a tougher opponent, and once broken had to be followed-up quickly. Having been reinforced by two recently arrived Divisions, one German and one Italian, as well as a detachment of Tiger tanks, and with significant air support assigned, Rommel had assigned a tight schedule for the offensive, with the line Annaba to Souk Ahras as the first objective, and then a drive to Constantine coordinated with operations further south.

"The Fifth Panzer Army's offensive opened on the 26th January. The attack appeared to take the enemy completely by surprise and was thus able to achieve a comparatively easy break-through. But soon the enemy was launching heavy counter-attacks. The wet weather in which the attack was made was in some ways a disadvantage, as it provided our attacking forces with great difficulty in getting up their heavy weapons." (*Rommel Papers.*) When the panzers rolled forward in the early hours of the 26th they met little initial resistance, as Allied commanders had their attention focused on the various operations in the centre and south of the front, and indeed the line had been weakened in the north when armour was despatched to shore up the collapsing American front. The main thrust along the coast road towards Tabarka was led by a Tiger detachment supported by Panzer Grenadiers; there was no minefield and the overlapping anti-tank and machine-gun positions were no match for the Tigers, which quickly overran the front positions. Meanwhile, a combat group had made good progress along the route to Ain Draham, 10 miles south of the main thrust. By midday the main thrust had reached Tabarka, although it had left three of its Tigers behind because of breakdowns and the support combat group had reached Ain Draham. The latter sent a reconnaissance group down the road south to Jundubah as a flank guard, with orders to seize and hold that road junction; the rest of the combat group moved forward towards El Tarf. Low cloud and rain kept the aircraft of both sides grounded, although the rain also made heavy going for vehicles and restricted movement of heavy vehicles to the main roads and tracks. The difficult conditions also meant that it was hard for the retreating British to extricate their heavy equipment, and in Tabarka the Germans found several abandoned tanks and artillery pieces.

It was now clear that a major offensive was underway in the British sector, and a defence line was established on the line El Kala to El Tarf, with an armoured counter-punch being prepared at El Kala. The Allies had also assembled strong artillery in the area and the Germans on the road from Tabarka were soon being subjected to accurate barrage fire, which slowed the advance. Nevertheless, progress was being made and in the late afternoon the weather had cleared enough for the Luftwaffe to appear over the battlefield, its all-weather airfields being usable and close. In addition to supporting the battle area, fighter-bomber sweeps were also made over the Allied airfields at Constantine, Canrobert and Youks les Bains. By early evening the advance was near-ing El Kala, having swung forces to north and south of Lake Tonga. The Allied tank attack was disjointed and was quickly broken up by the Tigers and the supporting 88s, with the Allies losing 15 tanks before they withdrew, heading back to Bône. Having cleared the area of lakes and low ridges west of El Kala, the advance was able to fan out and make better use of the coastal terrain in the race to Constantine, von Arnim having changed the objective from the Bône-Souk Ahras line. There was something of a race between von Arnim's forces and

Rommel's forces to reach this key point, which would then open the main road to Setif and Algiers.

By the morning of the 27th, the German columns were subject to air attack by American fighter-bombers, P-39s of the 350th FG, and light-bombers. "The P-39 with its (deck) speed and tremendous fire power, proved the most effective aircraft for strafing. Its sturdy construction enabled it to complete its mission even though often hit badly by Anti-Aircraft fire. Strafing missions-were normally effective against moving columns. P-51s performed approximately 90% of our strafing missions and accounted for about that percentage of damage." (USAAF Report on Operations NWAAF.) Despite the increased appearance of Allied air power, the overall advance progressed on all fronts; although there were a few hold-ups on the 27th the panzers continued to roll forward and the Allies were unable to establish a defensive line. On the central axis, the advance from Tebessa had started slowly, the Americans making excellent use of the terrain to lay ambushes and disrupt the advance. As the infantry units gained experience they became increasingly tenacious in holding ground, relying on artillery support to help break up German assaults. But as the weather improved and the Luftwaffe appeared in greater numbers they began to suffer heavy casualties. Patton was furious at what he considered the failure of Allied aircraft to protect his troops and berated the Allied air commanders. "Much of the difficulty was due to inexperience from which the ground forces suffered as severely as the air forces. Fear of a Stuka attack was out of all proportion to the material damage inflicted. This resulted in demands for local fighter cover over all movements and local operations. This cover, in addition to being inefficient, prohibited the offensive use of aviation to attain air superiority. When ground troops become seasoned to air attacks, it is anticipated that demands for local cover will decrease. However, as long as the US Air Forces are part of the Army, these demands are extremely difficult to resist." (USAAF-NATAF study "Organization of American Air Forces", May 1943.)

By midday on the 27th the Allied commanders had decided that the twin-thrust in the north and centre could not be held and that a planned defence line was needed, where they could feed troops and supplies from Morocco into the battle in a decisive way. The lessons of the desert war showed that the commander with the shortest re-supply route held the advantage, and as the Germans advanced from their Tunis supply base this would make them vulnerable. Eisenhower met with Alexander and the Corps commanders and it was agreed that this defence line would be in the key road junction in the Bouira area to the south-east of Algiers – some 150 miles west of Constantine – but that the forces engaged should withdraw slowly to enable the new line to be established. Churchill was furious and demanded the stand be made at Constantine, to deny the Germans the initiative, or at the very worse at Setif. The argument was presented to the Joint Chiefs of Staff, which decided in favour of Eisenhower's plan, in part to prevent a major disaster to American troops in this their first major campaign. However, it was important that some defence of Constantine was put in place, if only to keep its airfields active for as long as possible, and to prevent the British units on the northern flank being cut-off. Alexander proposed to Eisenhower that elements of 6th Armoured Division along with 4th British Division be moved to Constantine to hold up the German advance as long as possible. The first elements of these units took up positions south-east of the town, covering the expected line of German advance, with 4th Infantry Division in the advanced positions, and armour provided by US 1st Division, as 6th Armoured Division was too thinly spread to provide support. This weakened the proposed defence line, which now relied on infantry positions with minimal anti-tank and artillery support.

Meanwhile, as resistance to his advance weakened, Rommel sensed the opportunity for a breakthrough and the potential to cause confusion and panic, as well as capture what he knew were extensive Allied supply depots in the Setif area. He sent motorized columns along every road and track towards Constantine and Setif, gambling that if he kept up the pressure the inexperienced Americans would continue to stumble backwards. He maintained the strongest thrust on the main road and ordered von Arnim to keep pushing on the British in the north to prevent them moving to help the Americans; he also hoped that by a rapid advance in the centre he could cut-off the retreating British by closing the coast road and striking north from Setif. Whilst one of his columns was striking directly towards Constantine, the other was heading due west, intending to sweep 50 miles south of Constantine and then direct to Setif; this thrust was so far meeting little opposition and was progressing well. Signals intercepts picked up messages from American units saying, "there are Germans everywhere", although in some areas the infantry simply dug in and fought it out; one German combat group was ambushed near Ain Djasser, a key point south of Constantine, the entire group being killed or taken prisoner. When this bag of prisoners arrived in Setif they were put into a holding camp to the east of the town, along with other German and Italian prisoners. It was clear that Setif was in chaos, there were plumes of smoke from supply depots being destroyed, and columns of vehicles and infantry were heading west, crippled vehicles being left behind in the streets. The hold-up at Ain Djasser was short-lived: "Having taken one load of Germans prisoner we thought that we could hold our position, but a strong force of German tanks appeared, and our position was literally blown away; it was every man for himself." Rommel's combat group was in a position to move the 60 miles north-west to Setif, at which point he could cut-off any retreat from Constantine and strike north to the coast road. Meanwhile, 5th Panzer Army had been making slow progress along the coast road, supported by probes along any suitable tracks. However, it was the Italian mountain troops that proved invaluable as they infiltrated across the north-south ridges that dominated the area and came almost down to the sea. Rommel ordered von Arnim to keep up maximum pressure on the northern flank to ensure the British could not just slip away; he also requested the Luftwaffe to focus attention on the coast road, as well as the airfields around Algiers. Those airfields were the last all-weather fields within easy reach of the battle area, and so were subjected to intense air attack. In the air battles the defending fighters held their own, with combat losses roughly even. Nevertheless, the bombers were inflicting damage, especially at Blida. Attacks were also made on the main airfields in the Oran area. The British had been slowly pushed back in the north, but losses had been steadily mounting and the combat capability, especially of the tanks of 6th Armoured Division, had been reduced, as there had been no time for maintenance. The two infantry Divisions, 46th British and 4th Indian, had fought hard, but they were becoming exhausted. With the loss of Bône and its port and airfield facilities, the British had little choice but to move back through Constantine before it fell to the Germans. As more intelligence reports and air reconnaissance reached Allied HQ it became clear that the Constantine position could not be held, and if the defenders became locked in combat then to disengage and retire would be difficult. With this in mind, the position was abandoned. The road to Setif was now crowded and became a prime target for the Luftwaffe; Ju87s and Ju88s attacked the columns, whilst 109s provided air cover, and strafed targets. All of this slowed down the retreat and led to an ever-increasing amount of damaged and burnt-out

equipment littering the sides of the road. The Allied forces were fortunate that the Luftwaffe was now suffering logistics problems and so
was able to mount only a limited number of sorties.

When news reached him that Constantine had been captured,
Rommel was already on the road from Ain Djasser to Setif and was
only 25 miles from that key town. There was still little resistance
and he pushed recce forces forward as fast as they could go, but
when they reached the outskirts of Setif they ran into tanks from US
1st Armored and had to make a hasty retreat. Rommel's panzers
soon appeared and in a short but sharp tank battle they were able to
drive the American tanks back. Setif fell after a short fight on
1st February and although some supplies had been destroyed, the
Germans found a large quantity of petrol and ammunition. Having cut
the road from Setif to Constantine, Rommel had trapped a mix of
British and American forces to his east; his dilemma now was should
he push on to Algiers or should he mop-up the trapped enemy. "On
the evening of the 1st February we had a major tactical victory and
large parts of the Anglo-American forces had effectively ceased to
exist. I ordered von Arnim to mop up these forces, and I pushed on
towards Algiers, leaving a blocking force at Setif to ensure the Anglo-
Americans could not escape." Rommel had learned his lessons in the
desert campaign and resupply convoys followed the advance at regular intervals, with Setif now destined to be the main supply depot for
the next phase. The first Luftwaffe units were soon established at the
airfield and flying support for the continued advance, as Rommel was
not pausing and pushed his main thrust on towards Algiers but with a
strong combat group taking the north road to the coast.

Algiers was now only 80 miles away and its capture would give the
Germans an excellent port and access to important airfields, as well
as denying those assets to the Anglo-American forces. Rommel once
again gambled that the confusion of the Allied forces would enable
him to take risks by sending multiple thrusts along a number of routes,
including a sweep south from Setif via Tiaret and towards the coast at
Oran, thus threatening to cut-off Allied forces in the Algiers area. This
combat group would be prone to flank attack from the north, but his
intent was that the speed of advance would keep the Allies off-balance
and the threat would make them abandon Algiers. He would lead
this thrust, with 21st Panzer as the main armoured element. Meanwhile, von Arnim would head straight to Algiers. Whilst pressure was
maintained on the forces in contact during the 29th, the day was

mainly used for resupply and re-organizing the two strike forces, whilst the Luftwaffe attacked airfields and front-line positions. The Allied air forces were also very active, the American medium-bombers of the 47th BG attacking the staging area near Setif and the airfields around Constantine. At Allied HQ there was debate as to where to stand and fight, with some commanders in favour of a withdrawal to Oran and others supporting a stand at Algiers. Patton proposed an armoured counter-attack to the south through the Great Western and Great Eastern Erg to threaten the rear of the Axis position and even Tunis itself. This bold move was rejected on the grounds that the area was unknown, the distance too great to impact the immediate battle, and there were simply not enough armoured forces to spare. Under pressure from Churchill and continuing to juggle his Anglo-American military and political inputs and egos, Eisenhower decided that Algiers should be defended but that a new defence line be established at Oran, manned by the Divisions recently arrived in Morocco. Alexander considered this a mistake and that every effort and resource should be assigned to a decisive battle in the Algiers area. The British were established on the northern part of the front, from the coast at Bejaia along the main road to Tazmalt, with the Americans holding the line from there to M'Sila, and the French on the southern flank.

In the early hours of 4th February Rommel renewed the offensive, von Arnim in the north, 10th Panzer on the road west from Setif, and with himself at the head of the southern strike force, 21st Panzer and supporting troops heading south from Setif and then to M'Sila. In typical Rommel fashion he had given his orders but was then effectively placing himself out of overall control, as communication would be difficult in the mountainous terrain. With fighter-bombers sweeping ahead and Stukas attacking fixed positions the panzers on the northern thrust soon broke through at Bejaia, pushing aside the British tanks, which still had no answer to the German Tigers. Heavy artillery barrage fire once again saved the British as they disengaged and pulled back along the road to Algiers. In the centre initial progress was good but the advance was held up when a number of tanks were destroyed by an American tank-destroyer unit, whose 76mm gun on the M10 TD was effective against most armour. The unit had set up an ambush point where they could use their "shoot and scoot" tactic and knocked out four tanks. As they pulled back they were attacked by Stukas, losing two vehicles. By midday the German lead elements had reached the outskirts of Bordj Bou Arreridj where they were engaged once more by the tank destroyers and dug-in infantry of Maj-Gen Charles W. Ryder's 34th Infantry Division, supported by tanks of 1st Armored Division. The 34th had already taken part in some hard fighting and was becoming combat experienced and more inured to air attack. From well-sited positions and supported by artillery and tanks they put up stiff resistance, and at one point drove the Germans back five miles.

Rommel's combat group made rapid progress and by midday the reconnaissance group had entered M'Sila without facing any opposition. Racing on westwards they were strafed by fighter-bombers and Rommel's vehicle was hit, injuring his driver; he transferred to his tank and the advance continued. Allied aircraft were active all day, many squadrons flying multiple sorties: "When the target is located, attack from the sun immediately, always leaving a top cover. If your first run up on the target is bad, carry on and let the Hun think you are going on to another job and that you have not spotted his position. Return a few minutes later, making sure of your position, and make a quick dart down before he realises that he has been spotted. He will not give his position away by AA fire unless he thinks that he has been spotted, i.e. if he sees Spitfire circling round overhead and he is pretty certain they are going to attack and will open up. Never attack the same target twice on one patrol. Open fire at maximum range and closing to zero feet and carrying on at ground level, weaving frantically." The Allied squadrons were also aware of the increasing Luftwaffe threat "To escape superior odds it was found that by flying at ground level and making use of the mountainous country one could invariably shake-off one's adversary who would lose you due to the good camouflage of the Spitfire. While carrying out standing patrols over the Army it was found that the German fighters knew exactly where you were and how long you could maintain your patrol, and invariably came into attack the squadron as it was on its way back short of fuel, or to attack the Army when our fighter cover had returned to its base."

The continued dominance of German air power and the fact that Allied air seemed unable to stem the enemy air attacks over the battlefield caused commanders to raise concerns. General Robinett (1st Armored Division Combat Command B) stated: "Men cannot stand the mental and physical strain of constant aerial bombing without feeling that all possible is being done to beat enemy air efforts." General Anderson suggested that unless enemy air attacks could be reduced,

Allied forces would have to withdraw to a position where they could get cover. The ground commanders and their troops wanted constant air cover; the air leaders held to their doctrine of air superiority and the strategic use of air power.

Kesselring was summoned to meet Hitler to discuss the campaign and the situation in Egypt. Hitler saw an opportunity to turn the French colonial forces on their masters, but only if the Italians could be kept away, and potentially to offer Morocco to Franco if he brought Spain into the war. Mussolini was already eyeing Algeria and Morocco as extensions of the Italian Empire. It certainly seemed possible to turn the Algerians against the French, as their colonial control was very unpopular, but only if they were not replaced by another colonial power. Kesselring expressed that the colonial troops had not been particularly effective in the Allied army, so he saw little military value, although he understood the political gain, which could stir up anti-British feeling in Egypt and the Middle East. Of more concern to Kesselring was the Allied build-up in Egypt and the likelihood that Montgomery would launch an offensive within weeks. The North Africa campaign would need to be concluded soon to enable additional forces to be assigned to the Egyptian zone. Hitler waved this aside, offering additional Divisions from France. Following the meeting, Kesselring flew to meet Rommel. It was decided that Rommel would hand the North African campaign to von Arnim no later than 1st March, or following the capture of Oran, whichever came first, and would then go to Egypt, with a view to launching an offensive by 20th March. They discussed the allocation of resources, and Rommel was promised two additional German Divisions, including a Tiger detachment, and two Italian Divisions, plus additional air assets, for the Egypt campaign. These units were to be in place by mid-February. They also discussed the supply situation and with the Mediterranean now effectively controlled by the Axis the continued build-up of supplies in accordance with the previously agreed schedule was confirmed. Kesselring also outlined a plan put forward by Student for an airborne assault on Cyprus, as the Allies had increased the number of aircraft based on the island. Rommel saw little value in this and counter-proposed paratrooper use in the Egypt campaign.

Rommel's offensive remained well-placed; although the central column had stalled he was happy to keep the Americans there engaged and feeding more troops in, whilst his two flank attacks pressed on. He might even be able to trap the Americans by pinching off the front at Bouira. Having cleared Bejaia, the northern thrust was now on two main axes, one direct to Algiers and one down the main route to Bouira, whilst reconnaissance forces probed minor routes. The Allies held the high ground overlooking the southern of these axes and observation directed accurate artillery fire, causing losses and making the advance slower than expected. The northern arm, with more open terrain, made better progress, and at midday on 7th February defeated a counter-attack by the 142nd Regiment Royal Armoured, which was supporting the 1st Infantry Division. The British Churchill tanks had some initial success against the panzers but then ran up against the Tigers and lost 29 of their 52 tanks. The British withdrew down the Algiers road, covered by an artillery barrage. Rommel was also making progress and having brushed aside a French counter-attack, was soon astride the crossroads at Ain el Hadjel, which to his surprise was undefended. His original plan had involved a move north towards Bouira to link up with the other combat groups, but he was now tempted to press on westwards towards Oran. With virtually no radio contact with the other combat groups this was risky, so he sent a strong reconnaissance force in that direction, with orders to cause chaos and disruption but to retire if heavily engaged, whilst he turned north with the main force.

At Allied HQ Alexander was unclear as to the situation in the south; he had tasked air reconnaissance but had yet to receive formal news of the situation, as the French were out of contact and the Americans in the centre and those supporting the French were passing positive messages that the Germans had been held. It was clear that his line had pulled back in the north, although he hoped that a new counter-stroke planned for the morning of the 2nd and involving the 51st RTR and 1st Infantry Division might restore the situation. Around mid-afternoon he received the news that Rommel had broken through in the south, air reconnaissance showing strong motorized forces heading north towards Bouira and a second force on the road west towards Oran. This dramatically changed his situation; he ordered Anderson to retire to the outskirts of Algiers, but to hold a defensive position at Bouira until the Americans could withdraw from Boudj Bou Arreridj. The rest of Patton's II Corps was ordered to assemble in the Tiaret area ready to make a counterstroke or to cover a further retreat. Alexander consulted Eisenhower as to the overall strategy and the fall-back plan if Algeria could not be held. If the Allies were driven back as far as Oujda they would risk losing the whole of North Africa as they would be relying on the Atlantic supply route to Rabat and Casablanca, and losses to U-boats had been increasing in recent weeks. The Germans would almost certainly put additional pressure on this long and vulnerable link. There were also rumours of possible uprisings amongst the native population, which would increase the security requirements for troop movements. There were already rumblings in Washington as to the viability of putting more troops into this theatre and support for building up strength in the UK for the eventual invasion of Europe.

Patton had thrown out a strong reconnaissance force east from Tiaret as the rest of his troops moved into defensive positions around the town and along the main routes, whilst XII ASC was sending roving fighter-bombers along the main lines of communication and "immediately threw itself into the battle. Its fighters carried out repeated reconnaissance and strafing missions, and the A-20s bruised a tank column with demolition and frags. During this attack, the escort became involved with an unreported number of Fw190s, which engaged the close cover P-39s and P-40s. Spitfires, flying top cover, dived to attack but found their guns had been jammed by a sand storm. On another mission the A-20s caught a convoy of perhaps 100 tanks at an undispersed halt. Moreover, on the way to the target the escort broke up a fighter-bomber raid of 109s and 190s." (*Twelfth Air Force in the North African Winter Campaign.*)

The American recce force bumped into their German counterparts some 80 miles east of Tiaret, the Shermans driving off a group of German Panzer Grenadiers but then running into two concealed 88s, which quickly claimed three tanks. As the infantry deployed in support, a sharp fight ensued. By nightfall on the 3rd both groups had dug-in to await further support. The same day, Rommel's main force was engaged with the British blocking positions south-west of Bouira, which held firm as the Americans withdrew from the east. In the early afternoon von Arnim's forces at last pushed their opponents aside at Tazmalt; the first the retreating Americans knew was when the panzers appeared from the north-east and caused havoc amongst the column of trucks. The retreat was blocked and faced with strong forces on both sides of them the Americans had little choice but to surrender. Further north the German advance was also going well, overrunning a British tactical HQ. Allied aircraft were active from all the airfields in the Algiers area, but the battle front was confused and on more than one occasion casualties were caused by friendly fire, which led ground troops to engage any aircraft they saw.

As it now seemed likely that Algiers would fall, those supply depots that could not be moved were ordered destroyed, vulnerable shipping left the port and some air assets were moved back to the Oran area. The defensive positions around Algiers and Bouira came under intense air attack, Ju87 and Ju88 dive-bombers flying relay sorties from their bases around Setif and Constantine. Now that he had linked with his central column and with von Arnim, Rommel sent a strong force west from Bouira to cut the road 80 miles to the west near Khemis Miliana. He also ordered the combat group in contact with Patton to withdraw and pull the Americans eastwards, where a combat group would cut-off and destroy them. Eisenhower and Alexander were now convinced that Algiers could not be held and ordered the retreat to Oran. With the limited road structure over which the large number of Allied troops had to pass, and the threat of air attack on congested roads, the decision was taken to abandon large amounts of heavy equipment. British and American fighter squadrons were tasked with maintaining air cover over the retreating convoys to help minimize air attacks. As the first troops headed west, the defenders around Bouira were under intense attack, the Germans having brought up Nebel-werfer batteries to pound the enemy positions. British armour had already been withdrawn. The battle lasted all day and for much of the time it was German infantry trying to infiltrate and coming up against determined British and American infantry. By the evening of the 4th the Allies had disengaged all but a strong rear-guard, and the columns passed through an eerily quiet Algiers, but one littered with aban-doned equipment.

Algiers was captured on 9th February. Even though his lead troops were fatigued, and equipment breakdown was increasing Rommel maintained the pressure on the retreating Allies, the main advance keeping to the road to Oran whilst a combat group headed towards Tiaret to link up with the southern thrust, Patton having not fallen into the trap that had been set. With the capture of the airfields around Algiers, Gibraltar and the remaining Allied ports and depots were within easy range of the Luftwaffe's Ju88s and He111s, and units moved in from Sardinia immediately, taking up residence at Blida, whilst Italian torpedo bombers moved into Reghaia and fighters occu-pied some of the other airfields. The bomber forces were now well-placed to attack Allied positions and infrastructure, including key ports and even Gibraltar, whilst the presence of the Italian torpedo bombers added even more risk to Allied shipping.

Whilst the pursuit force kept up pressure on the retreating Allies, at Algiers Rommel reorganized the bulk of his forces. The port was open and Italian supply ships began to arrive, easing his fuel and ammunition concerns, and enabling units to be brought up to strength. Kesselring flew in on the 10th to consult with Rommel and it was agreed that von Arnim's 5th Panzer Army would take over the pursuit and Rommel would return to Egypt, taking with him 21st Panzer. With the threat from the west nullified, it was time to finish affairs in the east.

Chapter Six

The Conquest of Egypt – Rommel Victorious

During the winter period both sides had been building their strength, receiving reinforcements and conducting training ready for the expected spring operations. Rommel was active on the North Africa front and Montgomery was under pressure to launch an early attack to draw Axis forces away from that front and thus relieve pressure on the Anglo-American forces. There was also a new overall commander in Egypt, with General Wavell replacing Alexander. This was an interesting choice; Wavell had already commanded the desert army as C-in-C Middle East in 1940–41, defeating the Italians but then being defeated by Rommel; he was replaced and sent as C-in-C to India. His return to the desert was based on his experience, and a lack of other senior commanders with such experience. Having learnt first-hand the challenges of logistics and fighting power he supported Montgomery's rationale for building-up overwhelming strength and for training. Montgomery wrote: "There must be no more failures. Officers and men of the Eighth Army had a hard life and few pleasures; they put up with it. All they asked for was success, and I was determined to see they got it this time in full measure. The British people also wanted real success; for too long they had seen disaster or at best only partial success. But to gain complete success we must have time; we had to receive a quantity of new equipment, and we had to get the army trained to use it, and also rehearsed in the tasks which lay ahead." (Montgomery, *Memoirs*.) So, he continued to build his strength and put in place training to improve the combat capability of his units. Churchill had visited Egypt shortly after the Battle of Alam Halfa and Montgomery had taken him on a tour of the Allied positions and explained his strategy. However, with the pressures on the North Africa front he continued to urge an early offensive. There was discussion of removing Montgomery, but Alexander insisted that another

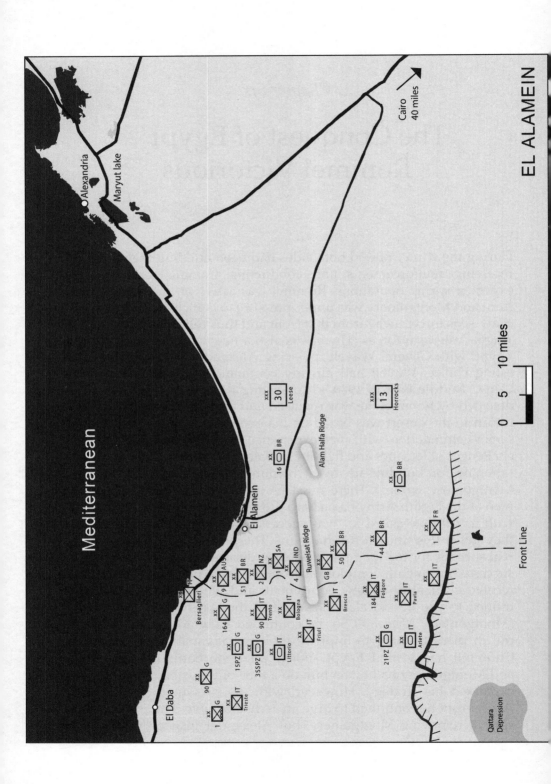

Mediterranean

Alexandria

Maryut lake

El Daba

El Alamein

Cairo
40 miles

EL ALAMEIN

XXX 30 Leese

XXX 13 Horrocks

XX 16 BR

Alam Halfa Ridge

XX 7 BR

Ruweisat Ridge

XX HT Bersaglieri

XX 9 G AUS

XX 51 BR

XX 2 NZ

XX 1 SA

XX 4 IND

XX GB

XX 50 BR

XX 44 BR

XX 1 FR

Front Line

XX 164 G

XX 90 IT Trento

XX IT Bologna

XX IT Friuli

XX IT Brescia

XX 184 IT Folgore

XX IT Pavia

XX 90 G

XX 1SPZ G

XX 3SSPZ G

XX Littorio IT

XX 21PZ G

XX Ariete IT

XX 1 G

XX Trieste IT

Qattara Depression

0   5   10 miles

change of commander would not be good for morale. Instead, it was agreed that 8th Army should be ready to attack by early March.

The Alamein line was well established by late 1942, although it was not so much a continuous defended line as more a series of defended boxes from the coast to the northern edge of the Qattara Depression. XXX Corps, under General Leese, held the northern sector, with the reliable 9th Australian Division on the right, and 51st Infantry, 2nd New Zealand, 1st South African and 4th Indian along the line to the south of the Aussies. The southern sector was held by XIII Corps (Horrocks) and comprised 50th and 44th Divisions, plus on the extreme south of the line, the 1 Brigade Free French. The main armoured force, X Corps under General Lumsden and comprising 1st and 10th Armoured Divisions, was in the north, whilst 7th Armoured Division was in the south. Although there was little ground activity, the RAF and USAAF units were, however, still waging a daily war, both around the front and to more distant strategic targets. The "heavies" were now increasing in number but this also raised some politics between the air commanders "in as much as the 98th and First Provisional Groups made up four-fifths of the heavy bomber force in the Middle East, and American combat commanders were more experienced in the handling of these heavy bombers than were the British, it seemed fitting that the operational control of all heavy-bombardment aircraft in the theater should be placed under the commanding general of the American air force. A suggestion to this effect, and subsequent negotiations with the RAF, resulted in the activation of the Bomber Command, USAMEAF, in Cairo, on 12th October." (*The AAF in the Middle East*, USAF Historical Study #108.) The 57th FG had moved to the Middle East under the command of Lt-Col Frank Mears in summer 1942, initially to Palestine but then to Egypt to work with RAF squadrons. The Group comprised three fighter squadrons, the 64th, 65th and 66th. Kesselring also sent additional Luftwaffe units to North Africa, which included II/JG.51 from Russia with 109Gs and II/JG.2 from France, bringing with them the first Fw190s to operate in this theatre. Other units also arrived, including II/JG53 and I/JG77 (which gave Major Müncheberg the whole of JG77 in Libya).

For most of the British units it was a mixture of time in the line, and the boredom and hardship of desert life, and periods of training: "The Regiment was ordered out of the line for a few days to mark out the course and run through the card that we should have to play in Montgomery's hand. For three consecutive nights the Regiment rehearsed finding its way through our own minefields and those of the enemy. During these long, carefully planned exercises the guns and vehicles were guided through narrow lanes marked with white tape and lit by storm lanterns burning inside masked, empty four-gallon petrol cans. There were three main channels through the minefield and they were named 'Boat', 'Bottle' and 'Hat'. Each petrol can had the symbol of the particular lane cut out of the tin and the lighted shape shone through towards us. The Regiment was attached as artillery support to the 10th Armoured Division, which had a core of experienced, battle hardened, desert worthy fighting men. From the realistic rehearsals it was easy to work out that our role in the forthcoming battle would be to pass through our own minefields and those of the enemy with our guns as soon as a lane had been cleared and a bridgehead established. From the bridgehead we should lay more barrages for the army break-out to the west." (*The Fusing of the Ploughshare*, Henry Ritchie.)

"The Corps Commander, Lieutenant General H. Lumsden DSO MC, had a sand-model exercise at Divisional Headquarters, some 30 miles east of Gebl Ruzza, at which all formation commanders attended. In great detail they explained the forming up of a Division, the march to the assembly area, the passage of the Division through our own and the enemy minefields, and then into the forming-up position beyond ready for the attack. It must be mentioned that our advance party was to be preceded by an infantry Division plus a few Valentine tanks to establish a bridgehead into which the 8th Armoured Division would move. The Division actually carried out this exercise in every detail and it was successfully done. The sand was very soft, tanks had to pull out guns and lorries, and many had to be left behind and some days passed before all were recovered. Our tanks, Shermans, and transport have had a gruelling time since we received them new in early September and all ranks long for the day of battle, feeling that both 'A' and 'B' vehicles are being worked too hard with little time for maintenance. The Regiment moved slowly by bounds in a north-westerly direction across the desert and long journeys had to be done daily for water and rations." (47th RTR.)

Air power remained active, from reconnaissance to fighter and fighter-bomber ops, and strategic bombing. The medium bomber pace remained hectic. Reg Thackery joined 40 Squadron at Kabrit as a second pilot: "By the time I reached the squadron a regular pattern of long-range ops to Tobruk had been established under Wg Cdr Ridgway. My first trip as a second pilot was, inevitably, to Tobruk and the skipper, a New Zealander, Flt Lt Morton, was on his second tour. This first trip lasted eight hours and I had not previously been in the air for more than five hours and so had recourse to the caffeine tablets provided and managed to keep awake to handle the aircraft on the long flight to and from the target. The skipper, of course, did the take-off and landing and the time over the target. Our target was the dock area at Tobruk but there was a great deal of cloud and eventually Morton ordered an attack on a heavy gun position north of the harbour. During the bombing run we lost height from 13,000 to 6,000ft to avoid the Flak but saw the bursts, smelt the cordite and felt the bumps. The bomb load of 250lb and 500lb bombs were released by our observer at 9,000ft. The flight back was uneventful, and we landed back at Kabrit in daylight having been airborne since 2240. I slept for about twenty-four hours after that initiation and it was a week before I was again on the order of battle – to Tobruk again." The Wellingtons could only reach Tobruk and so they took the major load on this target, whilst the heavies took on Benghazi.

On 6th January 1943, very heavy rain began to fall, and three days later reconnaissance photographs showed the enemy landing grounds at Daba under water and those at Fuka usable only with the greatest difficulty, which meant that the Axis aircraft on those fields were vulnerable. The rain had been far lighter at the Allied locations and "sufficient rain fell on our own airfields only to lay the dust". "Just before dawn on the 9th the desert airfields were vibrating with the noise of aircraft engines. At first light the biggest day striking force which had ever flown on the desert was bearing down on Daba. In the centre were the light bombers, several squadrons of them. Pressed close around them were the fighter bombers. Weaving and turning all over the surrounding sky were the fighters. Spitfires on top. All told more than 150 aircraft flew out of the rising sun over Daba airfield. The bombs were released in a pattern, all at the same time. This first attack was in fact an affair of three levels. In the middle was the bomber force, fanning out to bomb, closing in to move steadily in a broad circle. Below were the fighter bombers and cannon fighters sweeping through the dust at little more than the height of tent poles, shooting everything that came into their sights." This was also recalled by one of the pilots: "Over the landing ground itself there were dozens of fighters all close to the deck dodging among the tents and trucks, their guns firing streaks in all directions. Several of us came across aircraft parked in dispersals and shot them up thoroughly. The confusion among the Jerry troops must have been awful." ("RAF in Middle East".) More missions were flown the same day and the RAF reckoned that by the end of the day it had accounted for 50 or so enemy aircraft, including 10 in the air. The damage to ground facilities, loss of equipment and personnel, and an inevitable morale impact, made this a very successful day. It cost the attackers 12 aircraft, mostly amongst the ground strafers. The event became known as the "weather blitz".

News from the North Africa-Tunisia front remained grim for the Allies, although many still believed that the situation could be restored, especially if Rommel was forced to turn his attention back to the Egyptian front. By mid-January Montgomery had formulated his plan: "This plan was to attack the enemy simultaneously on both flanks. The main attack would be made by XXX Corps in the north and here I planned to punch two corridors through the enemy defences and minefields. X Corps would then pass through these corridors and would position itself on important ground aside enemy supply routes; Rommel's armour would have to attack it, and would, I hoped, be destroyed in the process. In the south XIII Corps was to break into the enemy positions and operate with 7th Armoured Division with a view to drawing enemy armour in that direction; this would make it easier for X Corps to get into the open in the north." (Montgomery, *Memoirs*.) He was still, however, planning for March, partly to ensure good weather for his air power, and he was expecting additional reinforcements, including more Shermans for his armoured units. His senior armoured commander, General Herbert Lumsden, was recently appointed from command of 1st Armoured to X Corps (1st and 10th Armoured Divisions), but he and Montgomery were soon having differences of opinion over the planned offensive. Lumsden considered the planned armoured thrusts too risky and likely to expose his armour. Montgomery had wanted Horrocks for this command, but the latter had turned it down and recommended Lumsden. In the meantime, those units that had not yet been engaged in desert fighting, such as the 51st Infantry, which had arrived in August, were undergoing intensive training, and learning from those with desert experience. Montgomery had expressed concern over the quality of training across his force and had directed a focus on this, as well on the qualities of leadership that he also considered lacking. He also directed that the forthcoming battle would be an "Army battle" directed by and in line with the Army Commander's (Montgomery's) plan. "Therefore, every commander, down to Lt-Col level must know the details of my plan, how I proposed to conduct the fight, and how his part fitted in to the master plan. Only in this way could perfect co-operation be assured." (Montgomery, *Memoirs*.)

General Wavell, British Commander-in-Chief, regarded the coming battle with confidence. "We had the advantage over the enemy in men, tanks and guns and we had a vigorous and enterprising field commander who knew well how to employ these advantages. The Eighth Army was certainly the finest and best equipped we had put in the field so far ... The RAF had established such complete air superiority that enemy aircraft were unable to interfere with our preparations, and Eighth Army was kept supplied with regular air photographs of the enemy disposition." However, the senior commanders were under no illusions that the fight was going to be easy; Coningham, told his Wing Commanders to inform Squadron Commanders that "it is likely to be a hard, gruelling and extended fight and that the Army will require every possible help that maximum and continuous air operations can give." (Elmhirst Papers.) In keeping with his hands-on approach, Coningham went on a tour of operational units. On 20th February, 6 Squadron noted he: "informed the pilots that our offensive would start very soon. A maximum effort would be required from the RAF for a period of about ten days at the end of which it was expected that the enemy would start to give way. All leave was stopped." (6 Sqn ORB.) The previous day he had confirmed that when the ground attack commenced there would be an all-out air offensive with three major objectives:

1. Knock out the enemy's air opposition and deny him air reconnaissance
2. Destroy supply and communication facilities in the Tobruk-Sollum area
3. Break the morale of the enemy troops by keeping them awake for three successive days

This was all part of "preparing the battlefield". From the time of contact after the offensive started, the missions would be in direct support of the ground forces, including "on call", and indirect beyond the immediate battle area. On 5th March "all pilots and officers attended a meeting in the Pilots' Mess to hear details of the coming offensive. A message was received from the AOC-in-C: 'for the defence of Egypt I called for a supreme effort. You gave and gave magnificently. We now pass to the offensive. Once again it is for each of us wherever our duty calls us, to do our utmost and more. Our duty is clear, to help our comrades in the Army in their battle and relentlessly to smash the enemy in the air, on land and at sea. With the inspiration of a great cause and cold determination to destroy an evil power, we now have a great opportunity to strike a decisive blow to end this war. On with the job.'"

On 10th March Rommel returned to his old HQ at El Daba and held a conference with his General Georg Stumme, who had taken his place whilst he was in Tunisia, and his land and air commanders. In Rommel's absence a number of new units had arrived, and the existing Divisions were brought up to strength in men and equipment. The new Divisions included the 3rd SS Panzer Division 'Totenkopf' that had been moved from Russia late in 1942; Rommel would have preferred not to have had an SS unit, but this move had been directed by Hitler. This was also an indication of how well the campaign was proceeding on the Eastern Front, with Hitler offering additional units to Rommel. Other arrivals included units released from the Malta campaign, including the German 1st Parachute Division, the Italian 184th Airborne Division and the Italian Friuli Division. The arrival of the new units and their positioning had been kept as secret as possible; the two airborne Division dispersed around the El Daba area, whilst 3rd SS Panzer was placed in the same area as 15th Panzer to confuse Allied reconnaissance, and Friuli moved in alongside Trieste. Equally importantly, Rommel now had significant supply dumps in place as his supply route from Italy was now delivering 90% of what was being shipped. Intelligence reports suggested that Montgomery would soon be ready to launch his own offensive, the expectation being that the blow would fall on the German left flank, closest to the sea and in the area held by the 164th Division and the Italian Bersaglieri and Trieste Divisions. Rommel's main armour strength, 3rd SS and 15th Panzer, were positioned a few miles behind. Contrary to his usual aggressive style, Rommel planned to await the British attack, destroy its armoured thrusts and then launch a counterstroke that would smash through the remaining British defences and roll on to Alexandria. He realized that he would never have a better opportunity than this to complete the conquest of Egypt. The Luftwaffe's primary task in early March was to prevent Allied reconnaissance of the deployment areas for his armour, and to stop the Allies gaining air superiority over the battle area.

The Battle of El Alamein was launched with Operation LIGHTFOOT on 15th March 1943 with massive air support provided by the Desert

Air Force, and a barrage by over 1,000 guns. The Luftwaffe responded, and major air battles ensued over the front lines. Four infantry Divisions of XXX Corps attacked north of the Miteiriya Ridge, between Ruweisat and the sea, their primary task being to punch two corridors through the Axis defence line, one for each of the Armoured Divisions of X Corps. The overnight attacks saw hard fighting, although on the right flank the Australian 9th Division made good progress against the Italians. Further south, 51st Infantry was held up by the 164th Division. The important action was that of the engineers tasked with clearing paths through the five mile or more depth of the "Devil's Gardens". The aim was to establish bridgeheads before dawn such that the tanks could then exploit the situation. However, it was much slower going than expected and by dawn the columns were strung out and vulnerable in their corridors. Daylight brought intense air activity on both sides.

The records for 80 Squadron are typical: "The Sqdn was scrambled E of Alamein in the morning, 1 SAAF was out there when we arrived and Sqdn was climbing to act as top cover when 8 ME109s attacked from above. They made diving attacks, six pilots fired but only three claimed, P/O Hill attacked a 109 which fired on him and he was forced to land at 435889. Sgt House who claims a destroyed and a damaged was separated from the rest of the Sqdn by 4 109s. In evading them he was forced out over the sea with enemy a/c on either side of him, he shot one into the sea and probably damaged another and was well W of the line before being able to evade the remaining a/c. His destroyed completed the score of 200 enemy a/c in the MR. Unfortunately, one of our best pilots was killed, Sgt Keeping, when he crash-landed, was taken to 18th Field Hospital, but did not recover ... Readiness from dawn. It has been exceedingly hot today, with no breeze, and it was very close. The Squadron carried out a cover patrol over LG224. There were several enemy aircraft over, and one was shot down in flames by a Beaufighter ... In the evening escorted a Tac/R aircraft over enemy lines. The job was carried through successfully, but unfortunately Sgt Thompson and Sgt Montgomery did not return. P/O Handyside damaged an ME109F. Squadron Leader Dennison was hit by cannon fire and force landed in the C track but returned to base in the evening ... It was a very bad day for bombing. There was a dust storm all day. The Squadron was scrambled for a Stuka party in the evening. There were about 20 Stukas with 15 ME109s above. Visibility was poor. Light was failing, and many aircraft had cannon stoppage, or at least

4 Stukas would have been destroyed. The 109s did not attempt to come down. Many of the Stukas were forced to drop their bombs out of the target area. There was a fairly heavy raid tonight, flares, bombs and spikes were dropped. 92 Squadron had 2 Spits slightly damaged." (80 Squadron ORB.)

To help keep the Germans uncertain of the Allied intention, infantry attacks were ordered along much of the front, although with orders not to become too heavily engaged. This appeared to work and whilst there was no real progress from any of the attacks, there was also no major focus by the Germans on the corridors. What Montgomery did not know was that Rommel was simply waiting for the Allied armour to break-out so that he could engage and destroy it; he could then use the corridors to thrust his own armour forward. Further south the deception attack by XIII Corps got off to a bad start when the 44th Infantry Division, supported by 4 Armoured Brigade, was repulsed by the Italian paratroops of the Folgore Division, the Italians taking over 300 prisoners. By dawn of day three the armour was almost clear of the minefields but was still moving cautiously. A formation of Stukas caught an Allied supply convoy, destroying at least 25 vehicles that were carrying vital fuel and ammunition. Lumsden wanted to call off the attack as it was behind schedule and the element of surprise had been lost. Montgomery was not impressed with progress: "I expected the armoured Divisions to fight their way out into the open. But there was some reluctance to do so and I gained the impression during the morning [of the 18th] that they were pursuing a policy of inactivity. There was not that eagerness on the part of senior commanders to push on and there was a fear of tank casualties. The X Corps Commander was not displaying the drive and determination so necessary when things begin to go wrong and there was a general lack of offensive eagerness in the armoured Divisions of the Corps. I therefore sent for Lumsden and told him he must drive his Divisional commanders, and if there was any more hanging back I would remove them from their commands and put in more energetic personalities." (Montgomery, *Memoirs.*)

Montgomery now determined that XIII Corps would convert to defensive-only operations, which would enable him to move 7th Armoured Division. He decided to create a reserve based on 2nd New Zealand Division, which was ordered to disengage, and two of his armoured units, 10th and 7th, neither of which had yet seen much action. This reserve was concentrated to the north of the Alam Halfa ridge, and able to intervene to the north or south. With the success of the Australians on the right flank – "the intention being to stage the final breakout operation on the axis of the coast road" – his intelligence reports suggested that the German armour had been concentrated in the north to deal with such a thrust and that the Italian Divisions were largely unsupported. He changed his plan to aim his main thrust at what appeared to be the weak point in the German-Italian position, just north of one his original corridors. The Australians were to push strongly to keep Rommel focused on that area, and Allied air was instructed to focus on this and to aid the impression of a major offensive, whilst signals deception would reinforce the idea. Meanwhile, the following night, he intended for the New Zealanders to "blow a deep hole in the enemy front just to the north of the original corridor. Through this gap I would pass X Corps with its armoured Divisions." (Montgomery, *Memoirs*.) He still had some concern over his senior armoured commanders in X Corps and in his directive for the battle made it clear that "Should XXX Corps not succeed in reaching the final objective [a 4,000-yard penetration and creation of a debouchment area] the armoured Divisions of X Corps will fight their way to the first objective." It was essential that the flanks were held and that, once through, the armoured units and armoured cars were to cause havoc and confusion behind the German lines. This was operation SUPERCHARGE and was intended as a knockout blow and for two days the battlefield was quiet, as the British moved into position. The plan had its detractors, including many in London, the concern being that if it failed then there would be nothing to prevent Rommel seizing Egypt, as there was no fallback defence line behind El Alamein. Montgomery agreed that there was no fallback, it was fight and win. "This operation if successful will result in the complete disintegration of the enemy and will lead to his final destruction. It will therefore be successful. Determined leadership will be vital; complete faith in the plan, and its success, will be vital. I call on every commander to carry through this operation with determination."

At 0100 on 24th March the attack was launched on a front of 4,000 yards, one of the most concentrated areas of military power ever assembled in the Desert War. Under the cover of an intense artillery barrage and heavy air attack, the infantry went forward, supported by 9 Armoured Brigade. By dusk the attack had netted 1,500 prisoners and had achieved its initial objectives. The Italian Trento Division was all but destroyed and the Bologna Division to their south was badly disrupted, although they fought well, in part bolstered by a German paratroop detachment that was embedded with them. The initial objectives secured, the 10th Armoured Division streamed through the corridor and was poised to break-out behind the Axis line, aiming to swing north. As the British armour pushed on they were followed-up by the New Zealand infantry, and on their left flank the South Africans of the 1st SA Division. The 1st Armoured Division also pushed forward, its line of advance being more or less due west, whilst infantry units were to roll-up the Italian Divisions on the southern flank.

Rommel commented on the day: "With our outposts pinned down by British artillery fire – their positions had been located long before by air reconnaissance – highly-trained British sappers, working under cover of smoke, cleared mines and cut broad lanes through our minefields. Then the tanks attacked, followed closely by infantry. With the tanks acting as artillery, British storming parties worked their way up to our defence posts, suddenly to force their way into our trenches and positions at the point of the bayonet. Everything went methodically and according to a drill. Each separate action was executed with a concentration of superior strength. The artillery followed up close behind the infantry to crush any last flickers of resistance. Success was not usually exploited in any depth but was confined to occupation of the conquered positions, into which reinforcements and artillery were then brought up and disposed for defence." (*The Rommel Papers.*)

Rommel had positioned his armoured forces for just such an eventuality. The tanks of 1st Armoured promptly fell into a German gun trap, losing a number of tanks to 88s, the very concern that some British commanders had expressed, and once again they had committed the same errors as in previous battles, although the "get on with it" messages from Montgomery and his threat to replace commanders may also have contributed to the error. Not all the British armour was drawn in: "They closed to about 1,800 yards and, with the sun behind them, commenced firing heavily on us; at the same time a screen of anti-tank guns revealed themselves in front of the enemy tanks. A number of our tanks were hit, but at this range, no damage whatsoever was done, and there was little doubt that had we attempted to mop-up this body in front, the mopping up would not have been done by us." (10th Hussars.) To the north, 10th Armoured Division had smashed the Friuli Division and were pushing on to the positions held by the Littorio Division, leaving the follow-up infantry to bag the Italian prisoners. As the day's operations ended, the British were advancing in the north, with 10th Armoured Division, and had held the German counter-attack in the south in the 1st Armoured area. However, this had opened a gap between the two armoured formations and Montgomery ordered his Army Reserve of 7th Armoured Division to close the gap. They moved forward overnight and by daylight had linked up with the rear of 1st Armoured. Montgomery ordered the offensive to be renewed, although Lumsden was concerned and in a heated call with Montgomery had recommended pulling the armour back, a suggestion supported by the commander of 10th Armoured Division, General Alexander Gatehouse. Montgomery decided to replace Lumsden with General Brian Horrocks from XIII Corps; he wanted to replace Gatehouse as well but with the 10th heavily engaged he decided to postpone this command change.

Rommel now had five armoured Divisions concentrated: three in the north (3rd SS Panzer, 15th Panzer and Littorio) and two in the south (21st Panzer and Ariete). His plan in the north was to use Littorio, supported by German anti-tank units and a regiment of Panzer Grenadiers, to draw the Allied armour into an engagement, whilst swinging 15th Panzer into a flank attack from the north and 3rd SS Panzer south to come up behind the British armour. Conscious of the threat from Allied aircraft, the move into position was to be completed before daylight on the 25th, and air cover was to be provided throughout the day. At the same time, 21st Panzer was to renew its attacks on 1st Armoured, with Ariete covering the right flank and aiming at the rear of the British armour. Overnight the British conducted bombing raids under the light of flares, causing comment that it was as bright as day. Most of this activity was on the southern flank and caused some disruption to 21st Panzer's positioning, with refuelling and re-arming delayed. The Luftwaffe had made its first sorties over Cairo, dropping leaflets and not bombs; the messages, in Arabic, encouraged the inhabitants of Cairo to drive out their British oppressors and look forward to the freedom that would be theirs once the British had been defeated. In the name of Allah, they were encouraged to attack the British. Although there were some incidents, most Arabs were waiting to see how the battle would develop. The Luftwaffe also attacked Alexandria, damaging shipping and port facilities.

As daylight dawned on the 26th, Gatehouse (10th Armoured Division) and Briggs (1st Armoured) received a message from their new commander; Horrocks made it clear that they were to continue to push

forward but to flow around any major hold-ups to keep the momentum going and the Germans confused. There was to be no retreat and
he expected his commanders to be at the point of the battle and not in a
rear HQ. He also said that he would be visiting them to see for himself
the progress of the battle. As Gatehouse was reading this, the first
reports were coming in of a major German attack on his right flank,
with a tank battle raging in the desert. The blow had fallen on 8 Armoured Brigade and 3 RTR soon lost 30 of its Crusaders and Shermans,
although they inflicted losses in return.

Gatehouse ordered the regiments of 24 Brigade to support 3 RTR,
and Brigadier Kenchington was quick to respond, deploying two or
his regiments (41 and 45 RTR) as a screen and sending 47 RTR on a
flank drive. The lead elements of 15th Panzer crashed into the screen
and were brought to a temporary halt with additional disruption being
caused by effective artillery fire and the appearance of Allied fighter-
bombers. The Allied tank-busters were roaming the battle area;
Wg Cdr Porteous led six cannon-armed Hurricanes of 6 Squadron and
two from 7 Squadron SAAF to "attack enemy tanks and armoured cars
in Southern Sector. Six Honeys being used by the enemy were hit." In
the afternoon a similar mission was led by Sqn Ldr Weston-Burt:
"another most successful operation for the Squadron, the score being
eight Honeys and two Crusaders hit." These references to destruction
of Allied armoured vehicles in use with the enemy flags three important points. Firstly, to recover equipment for re-use, you need to
control the battlefield, which is normally only possible in an advance;
secondly, the Germans made extensive use of captured vehicles –
including to them what were generally seen as inferior armour; and,
finally, the difficulty for pilots in ensuring that their targets were
indeed enemy and not friendly.

The flank drive by 47th RTR bumped into 3rd SS Panzer and was
overwhelmed, the survivors fighting a rearguard action as they withdrew east towards 133 Brigade, the Sussex battalions, the only element
of the Division not yet engaged. The infantry of 133 Brigade, along
with their anti-tank company, waited for the onslaught, tasked with
holding up the attack until 7th Armoured Division could come up.
As 3rd Panzer was inexperienced in desert warfare, Rommel had
attached elements of 90th Light Division (190th Panzer Battalion and
200th Light Infantry) operating with this combat group. He was also
concerned about the reputation this SS Division had from its time in

Russia and had issued strong orders concerning conduct and treatment of prisoners; he also assigned staff officers to keep him informed. Despite these concerns, there was no doubt as to the combat effectiveness of the Division. As they sped forward they were engaged by British anti-tank fire, which disabled a number of tanks; the advance faltered and was bracketed by an artillery barrage. The tanks of 190th Battalion flanked the guns and the infantry was sent in to clean out the British infantry positions. The men of 133 Brigade were not to be easily dislodged and they caused heavy losses whilst the guns continued to take on the tanks. A Stuka formation was hit by fighters from two South African squadrons just as they were diving to attack, losing half their number before German fighters intervened and drove off the P-40s. On the other flank of this battle, 15th Panzer had made progress and broken the two British tank regiments, which, having given a good account of themselves, were forced to withdraw. By early evening, 10th Armoured Division was heading backwards and away from the rest of the British armour.

Meanwhile, the battle further south was more balanced, with 7th Armoured Division having been fed into the battle. General Briggs started the day in a bullish mood, fanning his brigades out in the belief that he had overcome the German resistance and could exploit the rear area. However, by mid-morning he had reports of enemy tanks on both his flanks, whilst there appeared to be no major opposition to his front. He was in favour of moving forward and heading towards the important airfields of El Daba and cutting the coast road in that area. Having communicated this to Horrocks he was told to send an armoured group ahead, making use of his armoured car units to cause chaos in the German rear areas, and hunt supply depots and HQ units, but for his main armoured strength to move north-west to link up with 10th Armoured Division. This move meant they crossed the line of approach of 21st Panzer and just after midday the tank formations clashed, with the Germans initially being taken by surprise and suffering several tank losses. To add to the confusion 7th Armoured Division had taken the wrong route and had ended up too far east, which enabled Ariete to hit 1st Armoured in the rear left flank. The Italians were now operating a mix of Italian and German tanks and were one of the best fighting units, and one in which Rommel had confidence. With the British attention focused on the tank battle with 21st Panzer, the sudden appearance of this new threat caused confusion. The British turned to face the attack, but with poor signals communication,

Briggs was finding it difficult to get firm information. In an effort to see for himself, his command vehicle became exposed and he was captured when the position was over-run by the Italians. Engaged on two sides and losing tanks at an alarming rate, 1st Armoured began a fighting withdrawal through 7th Armoured Division and towards the positions held by 50th Division, who had opened a gap in their mine-field on their northern flank near the Ruweisat ridge, in preparation for a move forward by XIII Corps. As night fell on the 26th the battle area was lit by burning tanks, mainly British, although 7th Armoured Division had, with assistance from fighter-bombers and artillery, blocked the panzer advance.

Overnight on 26th March both sides prepared for the continuation of the battle, re-supplying their units. Montgomery knew that he had to consolidate his armour in order to mount a counter-offensive, and he ordered 1st and 10th Armoured to disengage and regroup: 10th Arm-oured Division to the north of Ruweisat ridge in the area held by 1st South African Division and 4th Indian Division, and 1st and 7th Armoured Division to the south of Ruweisat ridge, in the 50th Infantry Division sector. With the Australians still seemingly successful in the north, he ordered continued pressure there, with 51st Division to add its weight to the attack, in the expectation that this would draw off some of the German armour. Rommel determined to renew the arm-oured battle in the north, using 3rd SS and 15th Panzer to follow-up the British retreat, with the latter heading for the area held by 4th Indian Division and the former striking the New Zealanders. The Italian Littorio Division was given the task of following up the line of retreat of British 1st Armoured, with orders to pursue but not to become heavily engaged; Trieste Division was moved from El Daba to back up this thrust. This freed up his other two panzer units for a southern flanking movement just north of the Qattara Depression. These two units were to position overnight and then lie-up with the two Italian infantry Divisions on the southern flank and prepare for an assault in the early hours of 28th March. This was a risky manoeuvre but he believed that the British armour would not take any offensive action in the centre.

Poor weather in the morning of the 27th limited the amount of air activity and in limited visibility the defenders in the 4th Indian Divi-sion boxes could hear armour moving but could not see anything. A box barrage was put down on the expected line of approach but seemed to have little effect. The first contact was with the Greek Brigade on the southern side of the Ruweisat ridge, with German paratroops assigned to the Bologna Division infiltrating the forward positions. The Greeks put up stiff resistance and the Germans retired. The Italians of Bologna had spent the night hours clearing paths in the minefields in front of the Indian Division in preparation of the panzer assault. Work progressed well as the minefields here were less deep than in other sectors; one group of Italian sappers had the misfortune to bump into a patrol from the 2nd Battalion of the 7th Gurkha Rifles and all were taken prisoner. The first Indian boxes came under attack just after dawn, the attack falling on the area held by 11 Brigade. In fierce fighting the under-armed Indians were gradually rolled-up, but every box held out as long as possible, and German losses mounted. However, by early evening the Germans were in control of much of the area, the armour having been backed up by Italian infantry.

Further north, 3rd SS Panzer had found the minefield gap the British had created for their own advance; this put them in the New Zealand boxes rather than their planned line of approach, but with the attached units of 90th Light infiltrating the South African boxes, the revised line of approach made good progress. They were up against two of the toughest and most combat-experienced Divisions of 8th Army, both of which were used to marauding panzers and knew how to take advantage of terrain to create their own kill zones for anti-tank guns and artillery. The Germans were soon in difficulty, with tank casualties mounting and with not enough infantry in support. Across the coastal road the Australian 9th Division, supported by the 51st, had pushed on the positions held by the German 164th Division and the Italian 10th Bersaglieri Battalion. The latter were in danger of being overrun but even when surrounded fought on, delaying the Australian advance and enabling elements of 184th Division to move forward from El Daba in support.

As evening fell, the overall situation was relatively stable; the Axis forces had taken some areas held by the 4th Indian Division and the 2nd New Zealand Division, but the front was still holding and, significantly for Montgomery, his armour had not been engaged and had time to rest and refit. Meanwhile, Rommel had joined the southern sweep as the two armoured units there positioned for their offensive. The target area was held by 1st Free French Division, a very mixed unit commanded by General Edgard de Larminat and comprising three brigades, one of which included two Foreign Legion battalions. In general, their equipment was poor and their standard of training low, and they had been placed in this location as no attack had been expected here. To their south they were protected by the Qattara Depression but to their north they had the 44th Division, although this unit had a large area to cover and its boxes were thinly spread; it had also lost 133 Brigade to 10th Armoured Division a few weeks before.

Overnight on 27th March the Allied bombers were once more active over the front, although as there was no bombing of Rommel's assembly area it seemed as if his strategy had not yet been detected by the Allies. The Luftwaffe was ordered to concentrate on the positions around the Ruweisat ridge with nuisance bombing, and also to maintain pressure on Arab sentiment by further leaflet drops on Cairo and Alexandria. A number of He111s also laid mines in the Suez Canal. In the late hours of the 27th, Rommel's force moved into position, with 21st Panzer leading and Ariete as support, and the Italian Pavia Division engineers undertaking mine clearance. Rommel had planned a coordinated offensive along the front, to swamp the British signals network and keep them confused as to the strength of his southern thrust. At 0400 hours Axis forces rolled forward, with 15th Panzer and its support forces rolling over more defensive boxes held by 4th Indian Division, and 3rd SS Panzer making gains against 2nd New Zealand Division. By early afternoon a hole had been punched in the 4th Indian Division line and the panzers debouched into the desert, where they were immediately engaged by 10th Armoured Division. The tank battle was initially evenly matched and for some time the result looked in doubt; then came word that there were panzers to the north, 3rd SS Panzer had managed to break through the New Zealanders and were moving to engage the British armour. Knowing that there was nothing between them and Alexandria, the British tankers fought fiercely, whilst the Desert Air Force mounted numerous sorties in their support. The New Zealanders, with support from the South Africans, sealed the gap and the panzers were now exposed and cut-off from their supply routes. In the centre, Littorio and its supporting units had continued their probing of 50th Division, penetrating the defences in a few areas but never making significant progress. By late morning it was clear to Horrocks that this was little more than a feint, and by then first reports were coming in of 'significant German armour' on the southern flank. In consultation with Montgomery he ordered 1st Armoured to move south and 7th Armoured Division to move to the east of the Alam Halfa ridge, from where it could operate to support either flank as required.

The Stukas attacked the French positions at first light, by which time Rommel's advanced troops had penetrated the minefields and engaged the first defensive box. Under the concerted pounding the French defenders were unable to engage the advancing Germans, and the boxes held by 2 Brigade soon fell. The Foreign Legion boxes proved to be tougher nuts to crack, but they were only able to hold out until late morning; the panzers were through by early afternoon with 21st Panzer leading and Ariete on the right flank. Rommel's objective was to sweep east of the Alam Halfa ridge and on to the coast, cutting off any Allied withdrawal route, and engaging and destroying any British armour that attempted to intervene. The Allied position had been punctured in three places and Axis armoured forces were on the loose. Montgomery had few options left; he assembled a scratch armoured unit from the various depots and ordered it to move to Alam Halfa. He could not reach Horrocks but was confident that Horrocks would be pressing his commanders to engage the enemy at every opportunity.

News of Rommel's offensive towards Alam Halfa had caused alarm in Cairo and Alexandria. With the risk to his fleet increased, Admiral Sir Henry Harwood declared the time had come for him to move his warships to a safer location. The command stance of "no danger and business as usual" that had been in place since Rommel had launched his original Alam Halfa offensive was now crumbling. The Mediterranean Fleet was ordered to route via the Suez Canal, as with the Axis now dominating the Mediterranean it would not be safe to run for Gibraltar. Key port installations were set for demolition, although they were not to be blown until the enemy had reached the outskirts of Alexandria. In Cairo, HQ staff were destroying documents and those who could demonstrate that they were no longer needed joined convoys heading to the British bases in Palestine. A number of supply dumps were emptied, their contents being sent on that same route. However, there was far too much equipment in Egypt, where massive logistics depots and repair installations had been created, so demolition plans were put in place. None of these developments could be hidden from the Arab population and civil unrest started almost immediately, with attacks on Allied servicemen, theft from British depots, and even a few swastika flags appearing. In Cairo the civil police took no action, and there were rumours that the Egyptian Government was considering negotiations with the Germans. The military authorities in Alexandria took firmer action, declaring martial law and using troops to control the streets around the dock area.

Unless there was more positive news from the front, this situation was likely to deteriorate rapidly.

Churchill had been in frequent contact with General Wavell and stressed that the Allies had numerical superiority and plentiful equipment so demanded to know what had gone wrong. In a strongly worded message he wrote: "Under no circumstances must there be a surrender, we must fight and fight to win. If Egypt falls our entire position in the Middle East is at risk. All efforts must be made to hold Cairo, a symbolic location in the Arab world." The reality was that whilst there were tens of thousands of military personnel behind the El Alamein position the majority were support troops and not combat troops. The decisive battle was at El Alamein and unless that could be turned there would inevitably be an increase in civil unrest. For the Allies the day did not get any better, despite the improvement in the weather and a massive effort by Allied air power to influence the battle. The 20+ Landing Grounds south-west of Alexandria were a hive of activity all day, with fighter-bombers flying missions on a non-stop basis, whilst fighters provided cover for those missions and to protect the Allied ground forces. The medium bombers attacked troop concentrations and the British and American heavy bombers attacked German airfields in the Daba-Fuka areas. They were well-defended targets, as 55 Squadron's Baltimores found out at El Daba on one mission, losing three of the 12 Baltimores – all to intense flak that caused critical damage.

On the ground, the New Zealanders and South Africans were still holding 3rd SS Panzer; the problem for the New Zealanders was that they were unable to be resupplied, as German units had cut-off the supply line. Horrocks ordered Gatehouse to move forward to support the infantry, open the supply line and engage the German tanks; however, before any such move could take place, 15th Panzer had appeared and was engaging the left flank of 10th Armoured Division. Gatehouse was concerned that he would be caught between the two German panzer units but threw an anti-tank gun screen, along with 47th RTR, to his north whilst focusing most of his armour on the immediate threat.

According to the War Diary of the 47th RTR: "At approximately 1000 hours, a warning came from Brigade Headquarters that 25 tanks were attacking on a compass bearing of 120 degrees. The first signs of this attack were the appearance of a concentration of tanks and trucks on the ridge on our left in front of 41 RTR. They were well out of our range and we held our fire. Tanks then appeared in front of us and to our right, mostly at 3,000 yards, and several seemed to come close, down to about 2,000 yards, but withdrew when engaged. For the rest of the afternoon these tanks demonstrated in front of us, but Lieutenant Colonel Parkes held his position, and, when they came near enough, they were engaged, and a number hit." These were the first panzers from 3rd SS Panzer, elements of which had now cleared the rear area of the New Zealanders. Although they had been ordered to swing north to the coast, their commander had decided to join the tank battle so that his SS unit could gain some glory. Whilst 41 RTR engaged some targets, others fell victim to the British anti-tank guns, and for a while the German advance was stemmed. However, more tanks appeared, and it was clear that the battle could only end one way; under cover from the tanks, the gunners withdrew. As the British tanks moved back, an intense artillery barrage was called down, and the German formation disappeared in the smoke and thrown-up sand, enabling the British to disengage without further loss.

The rest of 10th Armoured Division was heavily engaged with 15th Panzer. Their War Diary later commented: "The high explosive shooting at this time was bad. Tanks were not registering on and sticking to targets, nor were they making sure before even engaging a target, that another tank was not already registering on it." For every German tank that was destroyed or disabled, three British tanks were put out of action. Many tanks were hit multiple times, but their crews fought on, the standing order being only to evacuate a tank if it was on fire. Outnumbered and outgunned, the British were fighting a losing battle and as they ran out of ammunition, tanks withdrew westwards towards their resupply and repair area, having left 30 tanks destroyed or disabled on the battlefield. As they withdrew they saw thick black smoke in the area of their resupply point; a German Armoured Car unit had found and destroyed the site. Gatehouse ordered his remaining tanks to pull back towards Alam Halfa, but as they did so they came under air attack, which caused further losses and confusion. "The rear-link tank was leading Regimental Headquarters with the navigator and soon became mixed up with 41 RTR. At this stage we did not know who was the leading regiment or where 41 RTR fitted in, or the whereabouts of 45 RTR, this was to lead to confusion later on."

On the southern flank Rommel's combat group was racing northeast towards the rear of the Alam Halfa ridge, his aim being to establish a gun line to catch the British armour as it raced to intercept him,

and then to engage and destroy the British armour. Ariete's Reconnaissance Battalion was ordered to scour the area to the north-east to
disrupt Allied supply convoys but also to locate and seize a major
supply dump that was believed to be 15 miles east of the Alam Halfa
ridge. The Italian armour and guns were to remain with 21st Panzer
until the tank battle developed. That battle was not long in coming.
A British reconnaissance unit from 7th Armoured Division bumped
into the advancing panzers and was able to communicate with its HQ
before it was destroyed. Rommel threw out a gun line of 88s, backed
up by the Italian 75mm and 100mm guns, and sent a weak tank force
in the direction of the British to draw them in. "The Regiment took
23 Sherman tanks and 8 Crusader tanks forward. Heavy anti-tank fire
and artillery shelling were encountered. 'C' Squadron on the right
had four tanks knocked-out and some burnt out. 'B' Squadron had a
troop knocked-out very early on and then moved over to the left of
'C' Squadron. The ground was very unfavourable for the Regiment to
fight on and littered with anti-tank guns – 50mm, 7.62cm and 88mm.
Heavy shelling made visibility difficult and our artillery was not able
to silence the enemy guns. The whole battlefield was strewn with
tanks – many on fire – some with tracks blown off and others damaged. Tank casualties were heavy." It was a similar story with the
other regiments of 7th Armoured Division and by midday the unit was
no longer combat effective.

The lead elements of 1st Armoured were drawn into the battle,
making some initial impression as they had stood off and engaged the
gun line, destroying a number of 88s and forcing gunners to go to
ground. German tanks soon appeared and in the long-range tank
gunnery neither side was making much impact; the panzers closed
and began to score hits, although the Shermans were proving far more
resilient than the Crusaders: "The Sherman tanks have behaved
grandly, not a single case of turrets being pierced. The Crusaders,
nothing more than armoured cars, could not be committed to the
attack and little can be said of their usefulness." Nevertheless, British
losses mounted and again exceeded those of the Germans. With the
loss of 7th Armoured Division and intelligence that enemy tanks had
been seen east of Alam Halfa, almost certainly the Italian armoured car
units, the decision was taken to retire all remaining armoured units
towards Alexandria. This was easier said than done, as the armoured
forces of both sides were now mixed up; in a confused battle a group
of tanks that appeared to be winning its part of the battle would

suddenly be hit in the flank, and then that flanking unit would itself be hit. At one point the group of tanks around Rommel's own position was almost overrun by Shermans and they were only saved at the last moment by the appearance of more German tanks. There was little command and control and every tank was pretty much fighting its own battle ... observe, range, fire, search, avoid, spot, range, fire. Almost every tank was hit by one or more shells, some surviving multiple hits, others being destroyed by a single hit. A large area of the desert was littered with burning or immobile tanks, whilst others sat and looked for targets or manouevred to escape unwanted attention or to get into a better firing position. The radio nets crackled with messages but any attempt at coordinated action was impossible. By mid-afternoon the frenetic battle was over, both sides having reached exhaustion of men and equipment. It was the Germans who held the battlefield and in the evening hours it was their recovery teams that took charge of repairing tanks ready for the next day.

In the late evening of 29th March, the German units gradually came together, albeit not always back to their original formation, but the impor-
tant thing was to refuel and re-arm, and undertake critical maintenance. Overnight the units were reformed and made ready; losses were not as great as expected, the 21st Panzer Division having lost only 20 tanks destroyed, although 15 more would not be ready to return to action for a few days. Ariete was still intact as a fighting unit, as it had missed the main tank battle. Rommel ordered it to proceed to the Alam Halfa position, establish a holding force of guns and tanks, but be ready to drive on to the coast or to swing west to support 3rd and 15th Panzer if required. He was woken from his usual upright nap by news that 15th Panzer was already nearing the east side of the Alam Halfa ridge and that the British armour, or what was left of it, was retiring eastwards. He immediately ordered Ariete and elements of 15th Panzer to race north-east to cut-off this retreating British armour, putting himself at the head of this force and ordering the remainder of 15th Panzer to move to Alam Halfa and await further orders. He received one final piece of good news: the Italians had found and captured a British supply base and reported that it had plentiful supplies of fuel, ammunition and other equipment, including a large number of lorries. This latter was welcome news as his motorized infantry had begun to suffer through lack of serviceable transport. He sent the 21st Panzer's 104th Rifle Regiment and 33rd Recce Battalion to take

over this key facility and to release the Italian armoured cars to raid further north and east.

Rommel's combat group set off just before dawn and was making good progress when three tanks in the lead formation struck mines and were disabled. The Germans had stumbled into a minefield protecting the approach to Alam Halfa. He sent recce forces east and west to find the extent of the minefield and was soon able to shift his axis to the right, as the edge of the minefield was only three miles from his present position. Once clear, the combat group headed due north, the Alam Halfa ridge clearly visible to their left. Shortly afterwards a group of armoured vehicles was spotted moving left to right. As the range closed they were identified as German, a link-up had been made with 15th Panzer. But where were the British?

Horrocks had spent the night trying to bring his armour together, but with continued poor communication and confused intelligence reports this was proving near impossible. By the early hours of the morning it was clear that little fighting cohesion remained amongst his units, although 41st RTR of 10th Armoured Division appeared to be almost intact and ready to renew the fight. Despite their losses, 1st and 7th Armoured Divisions were also eager to renew the battle; Horrocks was impressed with the morale of the Divisions but was conscious that one more battle in their current state could see them wiped out as a combat force. With German tank formations roaming the rear of the El Alamein line the main question for Montgomery was what to do about the infantry that were still in position, as less than 50% of the boxes had been attacked. If they were left where they were then they would eventually be rolled up. If the coast road was cut then the four Divisions in the northern sector, all of whom could use that road to withdraw, would be cut off and lost. He conferred with General Leese at XXX Corps HQ, who confirmed that 4th Indian Division was holding its northern boxes adjacent to 1st South African Division, whilst further north 51st Division and 9th Australian Division had retired from the positions taken in their advance and were back in their original locations, albeit having suffered significant casualties. They also reported constant heavy air attack. Montgomery and Leese decided to withdraw in as orderly a fashion as possible, with rearguards provided by the Australians and the New Zealanders to prevent the retirement turning into a rout. These forces were to withdraw as quickly as possible along the coast road and join a new defence line being established in the Amiriya area just west of Alexandria. The remnants of 10th Armoured

Division were to provide a screen to the south of this line of retreat. Positions were to be abandoned as soon as possible, but the retreat needed to be made under cover of darkness, so units were instructed to be ready to move as soon as darkness fell on 30th March.

Rommel now had all four of his armoured Divisions in the area of Alam Halfa; his main problem was lack of fuel and ammunition, as the supply convoys for 3rd SS and 15th Panzer had not reached their units. He redistributed supplies between his tanks, bringing 15th and 21st Panzer to full status, leaving 3rd SS Panzer, in the words of its commander "stranded and left out of the battle", a point that he forcefully made to Berlin. It was also not strictly true, as they had vehicles to head for the captured British supply base, along with the Italians of Ariete. Their orders were to refuel and where possible re-arm and then strike north-east to cut the Cairo to Alexandria road 10 miles south of Alexandria. With 15th Panzer on the left of his line of advance, Rommel moved forward, expecting to meet and defeat the remnants of the British armour during the morning and be astride the coast road by evening. The advance got off to a poor start when it was subjected to heavy air attacks by medium bombers and fighter-bombers, and whilst these did not cause many casualties or vehicle losses, they did disrupt formations and slowed progress. It was also clear that the British knew where they were and that they would be subjected to constant air attack from the nearby British airfields. "Eight Kittyhawks led by Flt Lt Strawson on medium and top cover to 15 Bostons and 3 B-25s bombing 1,000+ MT. On the run in 6+ Me109s were encountered and engaged by four of our aircraft. One of our pilots, W/O Bernier, is missing from this engagement. The remaining aircraft continued with the bombers which on approaching the target divided into two parties. This manoeuvre disturbed the accuracy of the AA which was of heavy calibre and fairly intense. Bombs were released from 8,000ft all falling in the target area and being very well placed." (260 Squadron ORB.) Bombs had been dropped upon stationary badly dispersed MT estimated at 2,000+. The large numbers of MT sound impressive but even when badly dispersed it was not possible to target anything other than an area, and even a near miss had a blast effect that was lessened by the targets being on sand. This was one of the main reasons for using pattern bombing, the idea being that a concentration of bombs was more likely to hit something.

The British tanks were not where Rommel expected them to be, so he sent 15th Panzer in a fan to the north-west and raced on towards the

coast with 21st Panzer. When news of the advance reached Montgomery he ordered Leese to begin an immediate withdrawal and not
to wait for the cover of darkness. The coast road soon became jammed
with men and vehicles, although the convoys were still orderly and
rearguards, supported by artillery, remained in place. Nevertheless,
this retreat in daylight was soon heavily engaged by the Luftwaffe,
with Stukas diving in and 109s strafing the columns. RAF fighters
mounted cover patrols, but it was inevitable that many of the attackers
would get through, and before long the area on either side of the
road was littered with destroyed vehicles that had been pushed out of
the way. In the early afternoon tank shells started to land amongst the
convoy; 21st Panzer had arrived. The orderly retreat now turned into
an "every man for himself" and men and vehicles took any route they
could find to escape to the east. A great many managed to break
through, as the Germans had not yet sealed the route. Slightly further
west, a tank battle had erupted, as 15th Panzer found the remnants
of 10th Armoured Division. In a sharp fight, around 15 tanks were
destroyed on each side before the majority of the remaining British
armour was able to stream away to the east, pursued by the German
tanks. From the air, all looked like chaos as masses of dust-covered
vehicles headed east, enemies and friends mixed up to such an extent
that it was near impossible to decide who to attack. As the day ended,
Rommel was firmly across the coast road, 15th Panzer was regrouping
and awaiting re-supply, and 3rd SS Panzer and Ariete were at the
British supply depot.

The night sky over Alexandria was lit up by explosions; this was not
a bombing raid but the demolitions that had been set some days before
and now had been ordered. The port was already empty of serviceable
shipping with the exception of three fast destroyers, who were waiting
for the last staff units that had been assigned evacuation slots. At the
nearby RAF bases, there was also frantic activity with transport aircraft boarding personnel destined for Palestine, whilst road convoys
prepared to move out in the same direction. Lame aircraft and equipment that could not be moved was being destroyed, but at the same
time fighter and fighter-bomber squadrons were preparing for the next
day of operations and expecting to move to the airfields in the Canal
Zone – or Palestine. Churchill was still calling for a resolute defence of
the Delta area, taking advantage of its natural defensive possibilities
and using the very large forces still available in Egypt to form a new
defence line and hold until reinforcements could arrive. However, the

tens of thousands of military personnel in the Alexandria-Cairo area did not include any effective fighting units, with the exception of 10th Indian Division which had arrived a few weeks before but was not yet fully equipped or trained for desert operations. To have thrown this Division into the battle was considered reckless, and so it was ordered back to the troopships and sent down the Suez Canal. The British armour was shattered and what remained would need time to re-organize and re-equip, and for that it would need time in a rear area. It was clear that neither Alexandria nor Cairo could be held, and the Germans had made it clear that Cairo would be bombed if there was any attempt to defend the city. The Egyptian Government called on Wavell to evacuate Allied forces from the city and declare it an open city and spare it from destruction. This was an easy decision, as the British had no realistic way of holding the city.

The plan to hold a new defence line in the Amiriya area proved impossible, as there were simply not enough troops to create or man any credible defence, and besides, the tanks of SS 3rd Panzer and Ariete were already closing on the area. "We took-off and bombed a group of German tanks that were on the edge of the airfield, and they were already shelling anything that moved. It was clear we could not land back at Gianaclis so after we had strafed them for a bit we headed off to Heliopolis, near Cairo." (112 Squadron.) It was a similar picture across most of the airfields in this area; in some cases units were over-run at their dispersals; at others Luftwaffe fighters took advantage of the confusion and strafed aircraft and vehicles. Those squadrons that could get away headed to the Cairo area, the groundcrew having to make the best of it to destroy equipment and try to escape east. A pilot of 1 Squadron SAAF got airborne in the squadron's "pet 109" and was able to join up with a group of German fighters, shooting down two before making his escape.

The first German troops entered the suburbs of Alexandria in the late afternoon. They expected resistance but found none, although there were still explosions from the port area. Advancing with caution they were soon surveying the remains of the port, where the British had sunk a number of block ships and where smoke and flames still escaped from destroyed buildings. A large number of prisoners were taken and passed back to holding camps in the desert. By evening the city was secured and the Arab population were conducting a lively trade with their new occupiers. Rommel arrived just before midnight and held a conference with his senior commanders and he also met a

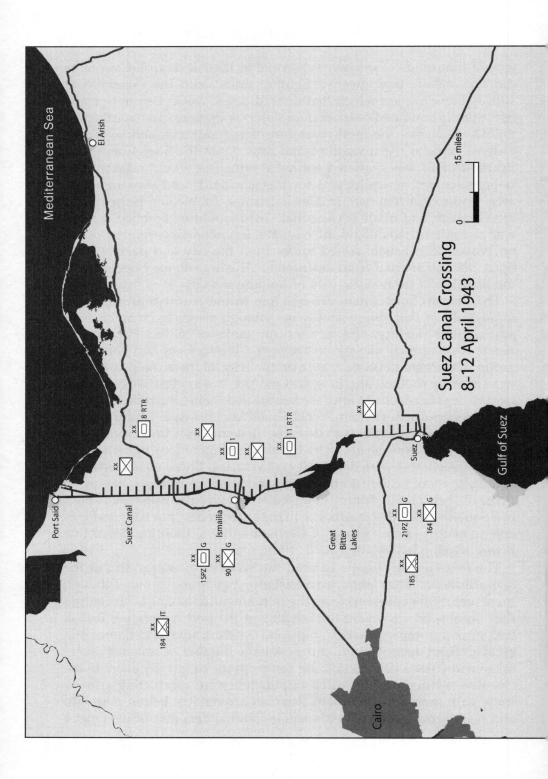

Suez Canal Crossing
8-12 April 1943

Mediterranean Sea

El Arish

Port Said

Suez Canal

8 RTR

1

11 RTR

Ismailia

15PZ G

90 G

184 IT

Great
Bitter
Lakes

21PZ G

164 G

185

Suez

Gulf of Suez

Cairo

0   15 miles

delegation from the Egyptian Government. The latter informed him of their desire to declare Cairo an open city and said that the British had already evacuated the city. He said that he could not accept this unless it included all the airfields in the Cairo area, and gave them 24-hours to agree this. During his commanders' conference it was obvious that time was needed for rest and refit; the armoured Divisions were down to an average of 25% combat strength in tanks, and the troops were exhausted. The supply situation was reasonable, as additional British depots and dumps had been taken, but this did not immediately help the situation in terms of tank strength. There was also the question of the British forces back to the west; the Italians had been slow to move on the positions of 50th and 44th Divisions in the south and it was clear that German troops, with their armour, would be needed to ensure that they could be scooped up. He assigned this task to elements of 3rd SS Panzer, preferring to keep his proven 15th and 21st with him. Ariete was ordered to move towards Cairo but to take no action unless ordered. He had also been told that Mussolini would be arriving to personally take the surrender of Cairo, a triumphal entry like some latter-day Caesar.

As the Allied forces continued to retreat towards Palestine they were largely undisturbed by Rommel, as he needed this pause in operations to prepare his forces for the crossing of the Suez Canal and then the drive through Palestine to the next prize, the oilfields of Iraq. He was confident that the British had little strength left to mount a decisive defence. It was also essential for the Luftwaffe to move into the airfields around Alexandria ready for the new offensive, which he scheduled for 10th April.

The Egyptian Government confirmed the British evacuation from Cairo and its airfields and their delight that the Germans had come to liberate them from the imperialist British. They were less delighted to hear of Mussolini's planned triumphal entry at the head of the Ariete Division. With due pomp, the Italian dictator, accompanied by Kessel-ring but with Rommel noticeably absent, entered Cairo on 2nd April to the somewhat muted cheers of a sullen crowd, although it was not long before the Italians were being parted from their money. As all Arabs knew, conquerors come and go. Rommel was delighted that he did not have to deal with Cairo and that he could focus on his next military objective. Elements of the Allied force had retreated south towards the Sudan and to mask any attempt by this force to return to Egypt he ordered Ariete and the Pavia Infantry Division to move down the line of the Nile to El Minya. By 3rd April the airfields in the Alexandria area were full of Luftwaffe aircraft, including large numbers of Ju52s. A key part of his next offensive was an airborne assault by the German 1st Parachute Division and Italian 184th Airborne Division, neither of which had yet played a part in the campaign.

The British had established themselves on the east bank of the Suez Canal from Port Said to Suez but keeping all the airfields on both sides of the Great Bitter Lake within the defended zone, as the next nearest airfields were back in Palestine. It could have been a strong position if there were enough forces to man it, as the Canal was a major physical obstacle. Montgomery had worked tirelessly to bring together the troops he needed; those that had escaped from Egypt were formed back into their units, where these existed, or used to bring other units up to strength. He had stopped the movement of 10th Indian Division at Ismailia and put it in defensive boxes in that area. He had requested troops from 9th Army in Palestine and had been given the one regiment from the Arab Legion, a battalion of the 11th Sikh Regiment and, more importantly for him, elements of 1 Army Tank Brigade – 8 and 11 RTR. There was a shortage of artillery, an arm on which the British had come to heavily rely and that had proved its worth countless times, and the RAF had a limited number of airfields for its tactical squadrons. The heavy bombers, British and American, were now operating from well-established airfields in Palestine and since the beginning of April had been attacking airfields around Alexandria and the port of Alexandria, although the Germans had not yet made use of the port.

German units had moved into position in the 48-hours leading up to 10th April and had forced the British to abandon their positions on the west side of the Great Bitter Lake. Rommel planned two armoured assaults, with 15th Panzer on the left and 21st Panzer on the right, keeping 3rd SS Panzer Division as a reserve. He had also brought 90th Light and 164th into the line, with one Division supporting each of the armoured units. Combat engineers had been taken from all the units in Egypt and pontoon bridges and inflatable boats and other river craft had been assembled, much of this being captured British equipment. He had also assembled a strong artillery component, although half of this was to be used against the defenders around the Great Bitter Lake, as a deception and to keep British forces looking in multiple places. The assault point for 15th Panzer/90th Light was Ismailia and for 21st Panzer/164th was Suez. Key to the assault was the airborne operation, with the 1st Parachute Division attacking the area in front of 15th Panzer and the Italians dropping behind the defenders in front of 21st Panzer, near Suez. In the expectation that the British line was thin, the paratroops could quickly threaten their rear and prevent reinforcements being sent to vulnerable points. The danger to the airborne troops was that they would be overwhelmed before the assault forces had managed to cross the Canal and push forward to join up. The Canal crossing operation had been rehearsed on tributaries of the Nile that most closely resembled the Canal areas; although water depth, currents and approaches were different this still provided the combat engineers and assault teams with invaluable practice.

On the night of 9th April, the Luftwaffe kept up a steady assault all along the front, intended more to keep the Allied troops awake and on edge. In the early hours of 10th April, the paratroopers were airborne and headed for their short trip to the drop zones; they were preceded by bombers, in part to mask the airborne operation. At the designated drop time the German artillery opened its creeping barrage as the assault parties went across. The first assault party of 90th Light were across before there was any reaction; the second wave was not as fortunate, and the boats were raked by machine-gun and mortar fire from 10th Indian Division. Nevertheless, over 50% of the second wave made it ashore. The infantry slowly moved along the sides of the Canal to suppress the guns that were engaging the crossing point. Once this had been done the Combat engineers began construction of the first pontoon bridge. To the south, the assault at Suez had progressed in a similar way, although the first bridge put in place was quickly destroyed by Allied artillery. Meanwhile the paratroops were in action. The drop zones of 1st Parachute Division were only 4 miles behind the canal and they were dropping from as low as possible to reduce dispersion and using radio beacons that had been dropped by pathfinder aircraft to mark the precise drop zones. Most of the paratroops made it down safely, recovered their weapons from the canisters and formed up to move towards the Canal; one group had the misfortune to land in an area covered by defensive positions held by the Sikhs and those who were not killed were soon rounded up. Having formed their assault teams, they waited for the German barrage to stop and then moved towards the Canal. The hastily constructed defensive positions had not been built for all-round defence and the appearance of the German paratroops from the east caused immediate confusion, with many positions overrun before they had time to react. There were some fierce firefights and with their low firepower – small arms and light MG, light mortar – the paratroops invariably came off worse from these encounters. Where this happened, they flowed around the opposition and moved on towards their objectives.

On the Canal bank, 90th Light had managed to get more infantry across and the pontoon bridge was in place; the first few armoured vehicles crossed without incident but then a concealed British anti-tank position engaged and destroyed three vehicles in quick succession, effectively blocking the bridge. Armour movement was stopped and the blockage cleared whilst the infantry located and engaged the guns. By midday the first panzers were across and had linked up with the paratroops. An attempted counter-attack by what remained of 1st Armoured was brushed aside and this unit effectively ceased to exist. The German combat group moved towards the north coast to cut the main road and encircle the infantry defending the Canal. This led to another sharp tank battle as 8th RTR surprised the lead elements causing them to temporarily recoil; however, additional panzers appeared, and the British withdrew to the north-east. The southern assault had been equally successful, and by midday was well-established on the Allied side of the Canal and heading north to roll-up the defenders and link up with 15th Panzer.

The Allied line had crumbled far quicker than Rommel had expected and as there was no depth to the defences the battle was over almost before it had begun. The road to Palestine and Iraq was open. The Desert War was won, and he sent the following message to his victorious soldiers. "Today you have won a great victory. After years of struggle and hardship you have brought about the final destruction of the enemy in Egypt. During the long hard struggle, you have, through your incomparable courage and tenacity, dealt the enemy blow upon blow. Your spirit of attack has cost him the core of his field army. My special congratulations to officers and men for this superb achievement."

Chapter Seven

Aftermath

Whilst Rommel was winning his battle in Egypt, von Arnim too was pushing against the Allied forces in Algeria and Morocco. He had been provided with two additional Divisions, but of more importance his air and naval strength had been increased, such that he was able to dominate the Western Mediterranean and neutralize Gibraltar. Increased U-boat activity had claimed an ever larger number of Allied ships on the routes from the UK and the US to the ports in Moroccan ports. The Allied COS decided that success was no longer possible and that no further reinforcements should be sent, but rather effort should be focused on the future invasion of Europe, which had been the preferred American option. As the Allies withdrew, von Arnim followed-up but was never strong enough, or, in Rommel's view, bold enough, to take decisive action and destroy the Allies. By the end of April, the Allies had abandoned North Africa. Churchill was furious, but this was increasingly an American-led war in terms of fighting power.

Having chased the Allies out of Egypt, Rommel pushed on through the Levant, facing little opposition and with the strategic aim of linking with a German thrust from Russia. Following the Russian defeat at Stalingrad (see *Disaster at Stalingrad*, Peter Tsouras) the Front there had collapsed, and the Germans had swept south towards the oil fields around the Caspian, and it was a race to see who would reach Baku first.

Chapter Eight

The Reality: The Actual Progress and Outcome of the Campaign

"The first essential condition for an army to be able to stand the strain of battle is an adequate stock of weapons, petrol and ammunition. In fact, the battle is fought and decided by the Quartermasters before the shooting begins. The bravest men can do nothing without guns, the guns nothing without plenty of ammunition, and neither guns nor ammunition are of much use in mobile warfare unless there are vehicles with sufficient petrol to haul them around." This extract from the *Rommel Papers* encapsulates a key element in Rommel's defeat for, unlike the story in this book, Rommel lost the Desert War, El Alamein was a victory for Montgomery and 8th Army, Malta was never taken, and Operation TORCH was, eventually, a success. However, as shown in this book, if certain decisions had been made, if seemingly small changes of circumstance had occurred then the result could have been very different.

What actually happened in those key areas?
The chapter covering the British Operation CRUSADER to the retreat to Gazala (the 'Gazala Gallop') follows the actual history of that part of the desert campaign; its sets the scene for the fluid style of desert war and the role of air power, as well as introducing some characters and units. The only minor changes saw the deployment date of the UAAF's 98th Bomb Group being brought forward by a few weeks. So, by July 1942 the Allies were back in Egypt and Rommel seemed well placed – if he could only get the supplies he needed. And this is where the story of Malta, and our first spin on history takes place.

Malta
The debate whether the assault on Malta, a parachute assault supported by naval landings, or the move in Egypt, should receive support

had not died with the late June meetings. Hitler's view was that the Malta operation would be a costly failure as the Italian Navy would not prove capable of providing the right support – and there were no German naval assets so there had to be total reliance on the Italians. He also stated that Rommel's success to date offered a unique opportunity to finish the war in this theatre. OKW supported the drive to Egypt and the cancellation of the Malta plan; both decisions turned out to be wrong. Kesselring's view was that "the Armed Forces High Command dug the grave of the German-Italian Panzer Army in the North Africa theatre of war. The responsibility for the defeat and all its consequences that made themselves felt in the overall situation rests fully with the Supreme Command of Germany's military forces."

Our spin on the Malta story starts with the loss of the aircraft carrier *Eagle* being earlier than actually happened (it was sunk by the same U-boat but on the PEDESTAL convoy in August), which denied Malta a reinforcement of Spitfires at a crucial moment. From this point on the circumstances change as this reduced Malta's ability to defend itself, which in turn reduced its ability to strike back. Operation PEDESTAL was a vital resupply for Malta and overall our account follows reality, other than bringing the date forward slightly, although in our case the tanker *Ohio* is sunk rather than limping into harbour. The loss of this critical fuel delivery has an impact on operations, just as the sinking of Rommel's tankers had an impact. We also sink one additional supply ship. From early August onwards, our account is all fictitious, as it deals with an invasion that never took place. In reality, Malta's additional Spitfires had been delivered and the island was able to mount a robust air defence; the tanker *Ohio* made it port, badly damaged but with its cargo substantially intact.

There was no invasion of Malta, and with a reduction in German air activity the island went from strength to strength in defending itself but also taking the war to the enemy, with attacks on Sicily and, more importantly an effective anti-shipping contribution.

During October 1942, Allied aircraft and submarines sank some 50,000 tons of enemy shipping on the North African routes. Of the cargo lost, 65% was fuel. One of Rommel's generals later commented: "El Alamein was lost before it was fought. We had not the petrol."

Alam Halfa

With the Allies back inside Egypt and established on the El Alamein line, Montgomery took command of 8th Army and built up its strength and confidence. Our chapter follows the battle of Alam Halfa in its general flow but ends with the Germans in a better position than they were for real primarily because in our version Rommel was receiving the supplies he needed, as his convoys were no longer being sunk.

Rommel's 'six-day' offensive at the end of August 1942, referred to as the Battle of Alam Halfa, was pretty much doomed from the start and Rommel was taking one of his greatest risks. The failure of supply, especially the promised fuel, with all five tankers being sunk rather than four getting through as we have allowed in this account, meant that even where his panzers were successful they could not exploit that success. In the face of overwhelming Allied air power, his static formations were easy targets. Rommel also admitted: ''. . . the first and most serious danger which now threatened us was from the air. This being so, we could no longer rest our defence on the motorised forces used in a mobile role, since these forces were too vulnerable to air attack. We had instead to try to resist the enemy in field positions which had to be constructed for defence against the most modern weapons of war. We had to accept the fact that, by using his air-power, the enemy would be able to delay our operations at will, both in the daytime and – using parachute flares – at night. For no man can be expected to stay in his vehicle and drive on under enemy air attack. Our experience in the 'Six-day Race' had shown us that any sort of time-schedule was now so much waste paper. This meant that our positions had henceforth to be constructed strongly enough to enable them to be held by their local garrisons independently and over a long period, without even the support of operational reserves, until reinforcements – however much delayed by the RAF – could arrive. The fact of British air superiority threw to the winds all the tactical rules which we had hitherto applied with such success. There was no real answer to the enemy's air superiority, except a powerful air force of our own. In every battle to come the strength of the Anglo-American air force was to be the deciding factor.'' (*Rommel Papers*.) Whilst General Stumme commented: ''We are living from hand to mouth; we fill one gap only to see another one open. We cannot build up the basic supply which would enable us to overcome critical situations through our own resources and which allows operational freedom of movement, which is an absolutely vital necessity for the Army.'' Having been repulsed, he expected Montgomery to follow-up and was surprised that he did not do so. Alam Halfa was Rommel's last throw of the dice and he exhausted his meagre supplies and his men. The battle ended with both sides back where they began but with the inevitability that Montgomery would win the race to build-up fighting strength.

TORCH and Tunisia

Our revised account made significant changes to the reality of the North Africa-Tunisia campaign. We brought the date forward a few weeks, but the rest of the account of the Race to Tunis pretty much followed the real events. However, once the Germans had stopped that advance – just short of Tunis – the situation changed. In our account the Axis forces under Rommel build-up more strongly, and Rommel is permitted to make his attack on Tebessa, whereas for real he was ordered to focus the attack on the Thala route. It is with the Kasserine Pass that this alternative history has changed the outcome. The following details are what actually happened from Kasserine onwards.

Rommel, in his usual aggressive style, was not content to wait to be attacked and decided to launch an attack on the vulnerable American sector, his rationale being that these inexperienced troops would be pushed aside and then the whole Allied line could be rolled-up. The offensive spearheaded by the 21st Panzer Division via the Kasserine Pass met with initial success but was blunted and held by a combination of some stout defence and concentrated air power. The pass was a 2-mile-wide gap in the Dorsale mountain chain and Rommel's plan was to concentrate on the inexperienced US II Corps, drive through and capture the major supply bases on the Algerian side and disrupt Allied operations along the coastal corridor. The plan was scaled down by Rome (he still had to seek approval from Comando Supremo) and split his forces as well as giving more limited objectives, although the Americans remained the main target. The German success on the 20th held the promise of a significant victory but the stiffening resistance and the reluctance of Arnim to commit, meant the danger to the Allies was over by the 22nd

Gen Carl Spaatz had placed bombers of XII Bomber Command under Coningham during the Kasserine crisis – not that this did much good for the crucial first few days, as bad weather ground most of the 12th Air Force, although on the 20th P-39s strafed convoys in the Pass; the following day was no better, with muddy conditions at airfields contributing to the problems. It was only on the 22nd, when the land forces, and with much credit to the artillery, had already caused

Rommel to stall, that massive air power came in to play. "Freed from constraints on the ground, British and U.S. aircraft punished the retreating enemy. Although the effect of these missions was not apparent to the Allied commanders at the time, Rommel would later write that his forces 'were subjected to hammer-blow air attacks by the U.S. air force in the Feriana-Kasserine area, of weight and concentration hardly surpassed by those we had suffered at Alamein.' Several days later, Rommel was relieved of command (officially to take 'sick leave') after unsuccessfully arguing with Hitler that North Africa should be abandoned." ("Kasserine Pass and the Proper Application of Airpower", Shawn Rife.)

The operational pace continued into April 1943 as the Germans attempted to regroup and reinforce, and the Allies were determined to disrupt any such attempts; the mass of air power now had total domination of the shrinking operational area, which enabled air attacks on ground forces, prevented (most) enemy air action, and provided near constant, but at times confusing, reconnaissance information. An incident on 1st April once again threw into sharp relief the Patton-Coningham disconnect. Patton signalled: "Forward troops have been continuously bombed all morning. Total lack of air cover for our units has allowed German Air Forces to operate almost at will." Coningham was unimpressed and stated that a limited number of German sorties had been flown – around 30 – a few bombs dropped, and four personnel killed (it just so happened that one was a personal aide to Patton). He also stated that 362 Allied fighters were active, with most of those over Patton's front. The two messages bounced around numerous command levels causing various degrees of upset!

The German attempts to support Tunisia using transport aircraft met frequent disaster, but perhaps the worst day was 18th April, which became known as the Palm Sunday Massacre. A large formation of Ju52s escorted by Bf109s was intercepted in the early evening by 46 P-40s of the 57th Fighter Group, plus 12 RAF Spitfires and a squadron from the 324th FG. The fighters claimed 76 enemy aircraft (61 Ju52s and 15 Bf109s) for the loss of six P-40s and one Spitfire. The day was also memorable in that three pilots claimed five each: 2nd Lt Richard Duffy, 2nd Lt MacArthur Powers, and 2nd Lt Arthur Cleaveland.

The Axis ended up fighting on two fronts in Tunisia as Rommel had retreated and Montgomery advanced; this aspect and the ending of the North African campaign is covered below.

El Alamein

Whilst the Afrika Korps was starved of supplies, the British forces were receiving a veritable plethora of men and equipment, the new British commander, Bernard Montgomery, insisting on overwhelming superiority before he would take the offensive. Montgomery had a superiority of some two to one in men, tanks and guns; and the disparity in fuel and ammunition stocks was even greater. General Alexander, British Commander-in-Chief, regarded the coming battle with confidence. "We had the advantage over the enemy in men, tanks and guns and we had a vigorous and enterprising field commander who knew well how to employ these advantages. The Eighth Army was certainly the finest and best equipped we had put in the field so far ... The RAF had established such complete air superiority that enemy aircraft were unable to interfere with our preparations, and Eighth Army was kept supplied with regular air photographs of the enemy disposition." However, the senior commanders were under no illusions that the fight was going to be easy.

The Allies were now moving ground and air units around in preparation for the offensive; this included some units that had been further back moving to forward locations.

The Battle of EI Alamein was launched on 23rd October 1942 with massive air support provided by the Desert Air Force. Air superiority was immediate and after that the squadrons ranged over the battlefield causing chaos and widespread destruction. In *El Alamein to the River Sangro*, Montgomery stated: "Heavy and sustained air attacks against the Axis air forces and land communications reached a crescendo on 22nd October. The degree of air superiority thus achieved was such that throughout 23rd October our aircraft maintained continuous fighter patrols over enemy landing grounds without interference."

The 24th was also a new record of sorties, with nearly 1,000 being flown during the day. "The whole weight was flung against the battle area, chiefly just west of the two gaps which our infantry held in the minefields. In addition, there were two smaller raids on Daba landing ground, still further to discourage the Luftwaffe ... Compared with the display of Allied air power, the enemy air forces amounted to nothing that day. There were plenty of targets for them, since all our armour lay behind the minefields waiting for the gaps to be enlarged sufficiently for it to pass through. But the Stukas did not come."

October 28th was "probably the day that decided the victory, even though the battle was fought furiously for several days after that. During the morning the airfields were somewhat quiet for lack of good bombing targets. The Kittybombers made several sallies at Daba landing ground. To commemorate the second anniversary of the Italian invasion of Greece, a fighter squadron of the Royal Hellenic Air Force [335 Sqn] strafed what was thought to be an Italian desert HQ. In the early afternoon everything changed. The Afrika Korps was trying to form up for a final full-scale counterattack against the 'fist' [the bulge in the northern sector made by the initial Allied assault]. At once on all the light-bomber airfields field telephones rang, briefing tents were crowded, air crews bundled their flying gear, maps, parachutes into trucks which wallowed off through the dust to the dispersed aircraft. From the neighbouring landing grounds came the Kittyhawks; from yet others the Spitfires. Within the space of the next two and a half hours they carried out seven full-size bombing raids on the Afrika Korps. They dropped 80 tons of bombs. Six times the German tank crews broke hastily and scattered across the desert; six times they reformed. The seventh time they did not re-form. There was no counter-attack by the Afrika Korps. Not again did the enemy try to take the initiative." ("RAF in Middle East".) Whilst there is an element of "air rules" in this RAF account, the essence is true that in the face of air attack the Germans were unable to concentrate a mass of force that could influence the battle.

After an initial defensive battle, and attempted counter-offensive, the German line collapsed, and the retreat began on 3rd November – during which German columns were under almost constant air attack. Rommel recognized the key contribution of the RAF and having ordered the retreat commented that "The British soon spotted our move and attacked the coast road with about 200 fighter-bombers. Their bomber squadrons were also extremely active that day. The Afrika Korps was attacked no less than eleven times during the morning by strong formations of bombers. At midday, I returned to my command post, only just escaping by some frantic driving a carpet of bombs laid by 18 British aircraft." Some German commanders were even more pointed; General Ritter von Thoma, having been captured on the 4th, commented that "Never-ceasing bombing by day and by night had a terrible effect ... ground strafing was at times terrific. I do not know whether more damage was done by cannon or machine-gun. Personally, I should not think it matters much. It all happens so quickly, the planes come down near columns or concentrations and shoot at anything. They are sure to hit something, just by spraying their fire, and then you have added damage caused by panic and confusion."

With the Germans in retreat, the Allied advance was slowed by bad weather, with heavy rain turning the desert to mud and causing difficulties for aircraft and vehicles. Rain and low cloud continued for a few days and reduced air activity, although squadrons continued to move forward to keep as close contact as possible with the battle lines, which in some cases meant almost daily moves, putting a heavy strain on the groundcrew.

On the 12th Montgomery sent a "Personal Message from the Army Commander" to be read out to all troops. "When we began the Battle of Egypt on 23 October, I said that together we would hit the Germans and Italians for six right out of North Africa. We have made a very good start and today, 12 November, there are no Germans or Italians on Egyptian territory except prisoners. In three weeks, we have completely smashed the German and Italian Army, and pushed the fleeing remnants out of Egypt, having advanced ourselves nearly 300 miles up to and beyond the frontier. This is a very fine performance and I want, first, to thank you all for the way you responded to my call and rallied to the task. I feel that our great victory was brought about by the good fighting qualities of the soldier of the Empire rather than by anything I may have been able to do myself. Secondly, I know you will all realise how greatly we were helped in our task by the RAF. We could not have done it without their splendid help and cooperation. I have thanked the RAF warmly on your behalf."

The steady advance of Montgomery's forces continued to irritate Tedder and Coningham and despite outward appearances of harmony, things were being said in the background that revealed their true feelings. The Germans had established a defence line at Agheila and Monty declared that he needed a month to prepare for an assault, a target date being set for 24th December; the air commanders postulated that the 8th Army was waiting for the Western Army (from the TORCH landings) to wrap up the campaign and Monty could stage a drive into Tripoli! At an operational level, Montgomery wanted air support and asked Coningham for concerted bombing to assist the planned offensive. The reply highlighted the lack of Army-controlled supplies and thus the inability to move the bombers forward. Tedder summarized this in a message to Montgomery on 23rd November: "You have,

I know, been pressing for many days for arrangements to be made whereby our Wellingtons and light bombers can operate from Cyrenaica ... I know Army Commander appreciates importance of securing forward landing grounds, but this is useless unless appropriate priority is given to the maintenance of squadrons which could use these landing grounds. A balance must be drawn between land forces and air forces. If our forces are to be properly employed and able to hit where it hurts, they must operate from and be maintained at forward landing grounds. Obviously, there is a price to be paid in terms of corresponding reduction of maintenance commitment of land forces. Surely the Air has paid good enough dividends recently for Army Commander to realize necessity of paying the necessary price."

While Montgomery gathered 100,000 troops and all their supporting equipment around Tobruk for his next push, Tedder and Coningham, continued to fret that the supplies needed for air operations were still not available. "The Army cannot advance without fighters, and the fighters cannot advance without petrol. Only a proportion of the available fighters and practically none of the available bombers can operate in the forward areas." Coningham was concerned that the enemy would slip away and that there would be little he could do to intervene. The long-awaited assault on Agheila commenced on 12th December, with a bombardment of Mersa Brega. The defenders slipped away and as Monty manoeuvred, Rommel ordered a retreat from Agheila on the 14th.

At dawn on 23 January 1943, just three months to the day since the Eighth Army had joined battle at El Alamein, the first British troops entered Tripoli. At the same time RAF advanced parties took over Castel Benito airfield outside the city. Allied land and air forces had now advanced over the desert for 1,400 miles, a distance roughly equal to that from Moscow to Berlin. It was a remarkable achievement and one of which both soldiers and airmen, their clothes and bodies alike stained with the desert dust, could be justly proud. For the capture of Tripoli marked the end of a definite phase in the African campaign.

On 6th March Rommel switched his axis of attack to the 8th Army at Medenine, but met with no success, again thanks to stout defence – and air power. It was Rommel's last shot in the theatre and shortly afterwards (9th March) he went back to Germany. During the first five days of March one RAF Group alone had flown over 1,000 sorties. It was clear that total Allied victory in Tunisia was now just a matter of time, to be counted in weeks, but the trick was to finish off the German resistance, and prevent their escape, in the shortest time and with minimum Allied casualties, and at the same time start the logistics and positioning for the next campaign, the invasion of Sicily.

Montgomery launched his Mareth Line assault on the evening of 20th March with heavy air support. Many squadrons flew intensive rates ahead of the attack, 112 Squadron flew 24 sorties, the morning mission being top cover to Baltimores bombing forward positions, and the afternoon being top cover for 450 Squadron, whose task was to intercept enemy aircraft over the New Zealand troops. No enemy aircraft were seen, but flak was reported as heavy and accurate. US air power was also committed to the battle, with B-25s and B-26s attacking airfields, and B-25s and fighters attacking ground forces. Eighth Army and Desert Air Force were one jaw of an enormous pincer that was closing on Axis forces; the other was provided by the Allied formations under General Eisenhower which had landed in the western Mediterranean and were now moving forward across Algeria

The final Allied offensive was planned for 22nd April, with an air campaign starting on the 19th. Despite the softening up process, and an Allied troop total of 300,000 against the German 60,000 in the area of the push, the offensives, in four thrusts, had all stalled by the 25th. Part of the fault was laid at the feet of Lt-Gen Anderson, GOC 1st Army, for his poor use of the massive air power made available to him – primarily though lack of coordination. In the final days of the campaign the TAF was flying over 1,000 sorties a day. Things were different for the German Air Force, according to a 1947 British study: "In the last days of the North African battle the GAF was an effete force, completely unable to achieve effective intervention: its influence in the last days of the campaign was nil, and Allied aircraft and naval craft were able to patrol with impunity off Cape Bon, preventing evacuation and reducing the defeat of German arms in Africa to a disaster."

Tunis eventually fell on 7th May and German forces in Tunisia surrendered on 12th May 1943; North Africa had been liberated. The Desert Air Force and all the other Allied air arms associated with the Desert and Mediterranean campaigns now looked to the next phase ... taking the war into Italy. "All ranks proceeded to celebrate. Verey cartridges and all kinds of arms were fired during the evening and it was a veritable victory night with a very striking resemblance to November 5th." (112 Squadron.)

The Allies invaded Sicily and from there mainland Italy; in September 1943 the Italians surrendered and changed sides. For the Allies, the Italian campaign was a long struggle, as the Germans established effective defensive lines that took time, effort and cost to breach. The use of airfields in Italy, especially those around Foggia, enabled the Allies to increase the strategic bombing effort against Germany and Austria, all of which contributed to the strangulation of German military capability.

THE TRUE STORY OF
THE
GREAT
ESCAPE

STALAG LUFT III, MARCH 1944

JONATHAN F. VANCE

The prison break from Stalag Luft III in eastern Germany was the largest of its kind in the Second World War. Seventy-six Allied soldiers and airmen made it outside the wire – but only three made it outside Nazi Germany. Fifty were executed by the Gestapo.

Jonathan Vance tells the incredible story that was made famous by the 1963 film *The Great Escape*. The escape is a classic tale of the battle of wits between prisoners and their wardens, in a brilliantly conceived escape plan that is overshadowed only by the colorful, daring (and sometimes very funny) crew who executed it.

From their first days in Stalag Luft III and the forming of bonds key to such exploits, to the tunnel building, amazing escape and eventual capture, Vance's history is a vivid, compelling look at one of the greatest 'exfiltration' missions of all time.

'It shows the variety and depth of the men sent into harm's way during the Second World War, something emphasised by the population of Stalag Luft III. Most of the Allied POWs were flyers, with all the technical, tactical and planning skills that profession requires. Such men are independent thinkers, craving open air and wide-open spaces, which meant that an obsession with escape was almost inevitable.'

John D. Gresham

ESCAPE FROM
Stalag Luft III

THE TRUE STORY OF MY
SUCCESSFUL GREAT ESCAPE

THE MEMOIR OF BOB VANDERSTOK

'Quickly, I climbed up to the surface and immediately found the rope … I felt no signal, so it was not safe yet. Then I felt three distinct tugs and slowly popped my head up … The nearest "Goonbox" was at least two hundred feet away; but, indeed, I was twenty feet from the edge of the woods.'

On the night of 24 March 1944, Bram (Bob) Vanderstok was number eighteen of seventy-six men who crawled beyond the barbed-wire fence of Stalag Luft III. This story details the real Great Escape as depicted in the 1963 cult movie classic, *The Great Escape*.

This memoir sets down the incredible adventures Vanderstok experienced, starting even before he was incarcerated in Stalag Luft III. As a pilot in the Dutch Air Force he witnessed the occupation of the Netherlands and, after several false starts, managed to escape to Britain, where he joined the RAF and became a Spitfire pilot.

Shot down over France in April 1942, he was captured and sent to Stalag Luft III. In extraordinary detail he describes various escape attempts, culminating in the famous March 1944 breakout.

IMAGES OF WAR
STALAG LUFT III
THE GERMAN POW CAMP THAT INSPIRED *THE GREAT ESCAPE*
RARE PHOTOGRAPHS FROM WARTIME ARCHIVES

CHARLES MESSENGER

In early 1942 the Third Reich opened a maximum security Prisoner Of War camp in Lower Silesia for captured Allied airmen. Called Stalag Luft III, the camp soon came to contain some of the most inventive escapers ever known.

The escapers were led by Squadron Leader Roger Bushell, code-named 'Big X'. In March 1944, Bushell masterminded an attempt to smuggle hundreds of POWs down a tunnel build right under the notes of their guards. This remarkable escape would be immortalised in the famous Hollywood film *The Great Escape*, in which the bravery of the men was rightly celebrated.

Charles Messenger served for twenty years in the Royal Tank Regiment before retiring to become a military historian and defence analyst. He is the author of some forty books, mainly on twentieth-century warfare.

Also available in the Greenhill Sniper Library

Lady Death
The Memoirs of Stalin's Sniper
Lyudmila Pavlichenko
ISBN: 978–1–78438–270–4

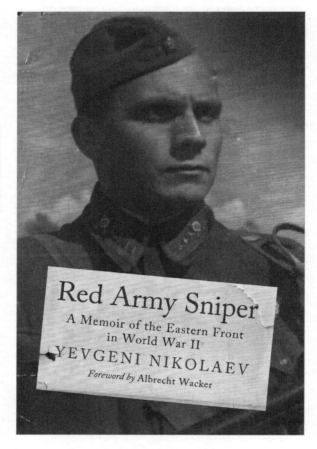

Red Army Sniper
A Memoir of the Eastern Front in World War II
Yevgeni Nikolaev
Foreword by Albrecht Wacker
ISBN: 978–1–78438–236–0